D1146183

FURY

Coming soon:

ENVY

ETERNITY

elizabeth miles

SIMON AND SCHUSTER

First published in the USA in 2011 by Simon Pulse,
an imprint of Simon & Schuster Children's Publishing Division.

First published in Great Britain in 2011 by Simon and Schuster UK Ltd
A CBS COMPANY

Simon & Schuster UK Ltd
1st Floor
222 Gray's Inn Road
London
WC1X 8HB

A CIP catalogue record for this book is available from the British Library.

Hardback ISBN 978-0-85707-199-6
Trade paperback ISBN 978-0-85707-200-9

1 3 5 7 9 10 8 6 4 2

Printed in the UK by CPI Mackays, Chatham ME5 8TD

To my parents

PROLOGUE

High above a freeway, a girl gripped the overpass railing. She almost slipped as she maneuvered onto the tiny ledge, and for one second she felt a sheer moment of panic, clutching and grasping for balance.

The wind was strong. The traffic was a whir below her, a river of cars and headlights streaming together. Her hands were freezing; her fingers numb, cramping. The gold snake pendant at her collarbone glinted even in the dark.

Everything felt hazy—the blackness before her eyes and the blackness of her thoughts. She was breaths away from jumping. She could feel the darkness moving through her.

And then she leaped. She was flying. Falling.

In a flash, she realized she couldn't take it back.

Her lungs were being squeezed to pinpricks. She couldn't

breathe. Icy air swirled around her, terror radiating through her body.

She clawed at the nothingness.

She screamed.

ACT ONE

Ascension, or The Party

CHAPTER ONE

Emily Winters stood in front of her bedroom mirror, a fluffy white towel wrapped around her torso, as she tried to work a tangle from her dark, dripping hair.

The room was quiet, except for the radiator next to her closet—it made its trademark ticking sound, one that had kept her awake as a child. She always imagined an old witch trying to claw her way out of the wall. But she was used to it by now. Just like the tiny mole above her right eyebrow—she'd had it since birth, and the only time she ever noticed it was when someone else commented on it.

Someone like Zach McCord, for example. Last week in earth science, the class no one ever paid attention in, he'd leaned toward her to steal a peek at her quiz. Then he'd looked up into her eyes and touched the edge of her eyebrow. "Beauty mark," he'd said. A shiver had run through her as he turned around, and that was that.

Thump.

Out of the corner of her eye, Em saw something white flash by her window. As she whirled to look, she heard another heavy thump.

She cinched the towel tighter, her heart hammering and her mind immediately churning out visions of robbers and murderers. She waited a second, listening, but heard nothing more. Clutching her plastic comb, she approached the window to peer outside. The front porch light shone on the blanket of winter snow covering the brittle, dark yard and the driveway that sloped down to Em's quiet street.

Of course someone hadn't tried to break in, she told herself, lowering the comb with an embarrassed smile (and seriously, of all the weapons she could have picked—a *comb*?). Nobody got robbed in Ascension, and certainly not in this part of town. It must have been a clump of snow falling from the old oak tree next to the house.

No sooner had her heart stopped pounding when the *bing* of the chat messages began: first one, and then several more, in such rapid succession it sounded like an alarm clock.

Em sighed and went over to her laptop, which was sitting among books and papers on her bed. Em hated working at the desk in the corner of her room—she used it mostly for clothing storage. Currently, the desk chair was completely obscured by a mound of scarves, dresses, and vintage blazers.

Gabs357: *Em? U there?*

Gabs357: *um hello?*

Gabs357: *K well I'm getting ready and I was wondering, hair up or hair down?*

Gabs357: *Emmmmmm! U promised to help! Also I'm torn between the blue sweater dress (w/short slvs) and new jeans w/pink ruffled top . . . what do u think? And where's my black cardigan—do you have it?*

Gabs357: *Are you getting a ride from Chauffeur or should we come get you?*

Gabs357: *I think I'm going to go with the dress. Are you even alive????*

"I'm wearing jeans and a black shirt, in case you're wondering, Gabs," Em muttered. Moving her favorite stuffed animal, a zebra named Cordy, out of the way, she slid onto the bed to type a response.

Zach McCord had won Cordy for her last summer, when Em and her best friend, Gabby, had gone to the county fair. He stopped at one of those freaky machines, the ones where you manipulate a giant claw in order to grab a plush animal from below. Zach, who was ridiculously talented at all things physical, had somehow clawed up two prizes: a pink bear and the zebra.

Zach had casually tossed Em the zebra. "It's cute," he'd said. "Different and cute. Like you." For the rest of the day, his words had filled her with a warm glow, and ever since then, Em kept Cordy on her bed. Sometimes, she found the stuffed zebra offered a better set of ears than any of the humans around her.

Zach had given the pink bear to Gabby, of course, who had squealed and planted an enormous kiss on Zach's cheek.

Which was as it should be. Because Zach was Gabby's boyfriend.

Sorry, was in the shower, she typed to Gabby. *Yeah, JD will give me a ride. I think you left the cardigan in your gym locker, right?* Gabby was known for storing about a thousand spare outfits in there, "for emergencies."

Em smirked and shook her head as she sent off another quick message: *I think the dress is a good choice. And why not hair down. It's a party, after all!* In the time it took to turn away and grab underwear and a bra, Em heard a new volley of *bings*.

Oh phew, hi!!!!! Okay, so hair down, totally. It looks good today anyway.

I was thinking of wearing this new long necklace my mom got me—too much?

With a laugh that sounded a bit like a groan, Em typed, *Gabs, I have to get ready too! Necklace sounds great. See you soon!* Sometimes you had to pick your battles.

Pulling a black tank top from her bureau and skinny jeans

from her closet, Em looked back to the mirror, which was lined with postcards, photos, and notes. Most of the photos were of Em and Gabby.

Short and spunky, with perfectly curled blond hair (thanks to her obsessive morning engagements with the curling iron), Gabby ruled the school with a giggle and a wink. Like her weather-reporter mom, there was something polished, pristine, and optimistic about her at all times. Her football-star brothers had paved the way to popularity with their sports trophies and prom-king crowns—and Em had benefited too. As freshmen, Gabby and Em were quickly and seamlessly woven into Ascension High School's social tapestry, invited to senior parties and allowed to flirt with upperclassmen.

That year Gabby had been voted onto homecoming court, an honor ostensibly open to the whole school but (until two years ago) tacitly reserved for juniors and seniors. And last year, Em had managed to put the yearbook committee back on the map of acceptably cool after-school activities by collecting artifacts—notes, ticket stubs, receipts, candid photos, snippets of class essays—and turning the yearbook into an Ascension scrapbook. Gabby did the layout and Em wrote all the witty captions and pasted in quotes.

Now they were floating through their junior year as they'd always planned to: going to parties without feeling like they needed personal invitations, studying for the SATs, working hard and playing hard (with Em sometimes reminding Gabby about the work, and Gabby sometimes reminding Em to play). They sat at the Gazebo—the good end of the cafeteria, and they parked their cars in the highly coveted front lot.

In this year's yearbook, it was almost certain that Gabby would be voted Cutest in the Junior Class, while Em was a good bet for Most Likely to Succeed. (Succeed at what, Em sometimes wondered.) There were other girls in their circle, like Fiona Marcus and Lauren Hobart, whom they'd known forever, and Jenna Berg, who'd moved to Ascension in eighth grade and somehow fit in perfectly. But everyone knew that the Gab-Em bond was the glue that held everything together. They were kind of like fireworks. They soared as one: Gabby erupting with a loud, colorful *BANG!* and Em creating a different kind of light, the ethereal, sparkling, postexplosion chandelier.

But lately, Em had been feeling more like a sidekick or a personal style assistant than a kindred spirit. Over the past few weeks, Gabby's preferred topics of conversation had not veered from the subjects of her wardrobe, Zach, or the Valentine's Day dance (which was still well over a month away). Just this morning, Gabby had asked Em if she could "please consult with Zach about what he should get me for Christmas" and proceeded to list five acceptable gifts that spanned the spectrum of realism: (1) the delicate blue scarf she'd seen on the website for Maintenance, her absolute favorite store in Boston; (2) an engraved iPod Nano for when she went running; (3) tickets to see Cirque du Soleil when it came to Portland this spring; (4) a puppy; (5) a romantic secret overnight at his stepdad's cabin down the coast.

Gabby didn't always seem to understand that not everyone's life was as perfect as hers.

Of course, there were amazing things about Gabby too. She was the only person Em wanted to be around when she was in a crappy mood. She was the best accomplice to have at every party, every prank, every midnight adventure. And she was a great friend. Like the time in sixth grade when Em had told Adam Dunn that she liked him on the playground and he'd told her to get a life. Gabby had baked frosted brownies with Skittles on top that spelled out D-DAY. They'd laughed and eaten the entire pan of brownies and successfully turned Dunn Day into a holiday. Gabby was just like that. She was like a sunny day, strawberry shortcake, and a snowball fight all rolled into one.

But sometimes it was exhausting, too.

Em stared at her knobby knees and long, almost-black, wavy hair and felt more like Morticia than America's Next Top Model. Some days she was able to appreciate her dancer's build, but tonight she just wished she owned a padded bra.

Bing . . . bing . . . bing. What now?

Emmmm. I made you something—going to share the file now.

Em watched the blue bar stretch as the file loaded, then saw *Em's Getting Ready Music* pop up in her media player.

In case you need some motivation, I put together some songs, Gabby wrote. *But you have to* promise *to leave as soon as the playlist is over.*

Em scanned the song titles. Perfect. Some old-school Britney and Beyoncé, plus some punkish covers of show tunes that Gabby knew Em loved.

As she buttoned her jeans and surveyed her shoe options, singing "Cabaret" quietly under her breath, Em's parents' voices drifted upstairs. That was another feature of the old-school radiators: somehow, they seemed to pipe voices through the house more successfully than they did heat. She couldn't really understand what they were saying, but she could pick out a few words.

Her parents started dating when they were *sixteen*—a fact that made Em cringe. She was the same age now as her parents were when they met. Em couldn't imagine conversing with the same person for twenty years, but her mom and dad never seemed to get sick of each other. They'd met on a ski trip that brought together young people from area schools. That day, Em's mom had been wearing a purple knit hat with two blue pom-poms on top. (Em loved to tease her mom about her apparently awesome teenage fashion sense.) Over the course of the afternoon, one of the pom-poms had gone missing. And though half the guys on the mountain had been searching for the missing fuzzball, only one had found it—stuck to the inside of his hood. Em's dad had taken off his coat inside the lodge and her mom had spied the blue ball.

The sparks flew instantly, they always said, with a wink. *You know what we mean.*

But of course, Em didn't. She had never felt electric passion or the sense of fate unfolding for her. All she had experienced was awkward kissing with boys who didn't know what to do with their hands. She'd certainly never looked into a boy's eyes and "just known."

At least, not with any boy it was actually possible to be with. In fact, that was the reason behind the poem she'd won the regional Blue Pen Award for: "Impossible."

Bang! Em's heart practically stopped for a second before she realized the sound was caused by a snowball hitting her bedroom window. Another one hit and jolted Em back into party-prep mode. That was her ride—lately snowballs were his not-so-charming way of announcing he was waiting outside.

She slammed shut her laptop, wrestled her shirt over her head, and hopped to the window again as she tried to jam her right foot into one tall lace-up boot.

"Five minutes," she mouthed, holding up five fingers to JD Fount, who stood in the yard below her window sporting a goofy grin and moving a tree branch out of his face. JD had always been supertall—so much so that in fourth grade, Mrs. Milliken, the school nurse, had sharply poked his back and barked, "Posture Police!" because he'd been slouching to try to make the other kids feel less short.

Now he stood normally, at six-foot-three, and didn't worry about what anyone thought.

As if to prove exactly that, JD pulled open his peacoat to reveal his latest outfit choice: slacks, a vest, and a purple shirt underneath. Em involuntarily smiled and shook her head, wondering at JD's bold fashion choices, which were a combination of iconoclasm and artistry. He'd been known to get on his soapbox to point out how unfair it was that girls could have fun with fashion while boys were left with jeans and T-shirts. Over the last year, Gabby had taken to referring to him as "Chauffeur"—behind his back, of course—because he was the perfect designated driver. He didn't get invited to most of the parties, but he was always willing to drive Em to them. Em could tell he secretly liked having an excuse to go out on the weekends, and even though he was a huge dork she'd known since they were both in diapers, she had to admit that she didn't mind spending time with him.

When he saw Em's hand signal, JD responded with a wave and a thumbs-up. He was used to waiting. The Fount family had lived next door forever and it was a running joke that the Winters would keep the Founts waiting at their own funeral. Before Em got her license, JD used to take her to school; after they missed first period four days in a row, he'd threatened to make her walk.

JD danced toward his car, knowing Em was watching.

Then he hopped into his beat-up Volvo. Still, Em stood at the window, mesmerized by snowflakes that were just starting to fall. Despite the fact that Em had always lived in Maine, she never got tired of the winter. She loved the way her neighborhood looked during a snowstorm, all the houses capped under white drifts, like meringue crowning a pie. She watched for a moment as one flake faded into another, until faint sirens in the distance jolted her back to reality.

With her boots laced up, Em dabbed on some lip gloss, tucked her hair behind her ears (she rarely did anything more than let it air dry), and grabbed her bag from where she'd last thrown it. She gave herself a final once-over in the mirror, knowing full well she was primping for one person only.

As Em made her way downstairs, her parents' voices grew more distinct. They were debating work stuff again: whether or not caffeine leads to coronaries. For two people who wouldn't know if their own daughter was heartbroken, they sure did care a lot about what happened to other people's hearts.

"I'm going to a party," Em said, popping her head around the kitchen door. The two of them were hunched over the marble kitchen island with glasses of red wine in their hands and a plate of cheese between them, looked vaguely startled to see her there. "It's at Ian Minster's. JD is driving."

"Okay, hon," her mom responded.

"Be careful, sweetie," her dad echoed. He was standing at

the stove with his back to her, his ID from the hospital tossed on the island in the kitchen. Em's mom was leaning next to him, wineglass in hand. Their hips were just touching.

"And then you have to wonder about the viability of all of the red wine research . . . ," Em's mom said abruptly. Just like that, they were back to their conversation.

Rolling her eyes, Em slipped into her winter coat and walked out the door and toward JD's Volvo. She wondered if her parents had actually heard what she'd said. She wondered if anyone would ever look at her and *really* see her.

CHAPTER TWO

Leaving in 15 mins. C u there.

Chase Singer fired off the text to Zach and slipped his new Nokia cell phone, an early Christmas gift from his mom (one they couldn't really afford), carefully into a back pocket of his jeans.

Every year, right before winter break, an Ascension High School senior stepped up to host the party to end all parties. Part holiday gala, part celebration of being halfway done with the school year, the party was the stuff that legends were made of—legends that often took another six months to live down. This year, with Ian Minster's parents away on their second honeymoon, his house was ground zero for reputations to be ruined and reinforced.

Chase's phone buzzed and he fished it out of his pocket.

New text from Lindsay Peters: *Can I crash the Ascension party tonight?* Chase didn't respond. He'd been hooking up with Lindsay, a junior from nearby Trinity High, for a few weeks. They'd met at a football party, and she'd been cool at first. She was willing to drive to see him and not too needy. But now he was bored. She had a nice body—although not as nice when she wasn't wearing a push-up bra—a low voice, and a big smile. But she wore a little too much makeup and laughed too loudly, even when his jokes weren't that funny. Even when he wasn't *trying* to be funny. A couple of weeks ago he'd started telling her about this cool documentary he'd seen about insects, and she'd thought he was telling her the plot of a sci-fi movie. Plus she chewed with her mouth open. No, he definitely did *not* want her to come tonight.

As Chase snapped the phone shut, he saw the time. He had to hurry.

The tiny bathroom at the end of the narrow hall was clouded with steam. Chase grabbed a now wrinkle-free bright red polo shirt from the shower rod. The pipes shuddered and groaned as he turned off the hot water. He wiped the condensation from the mirror and held the shirt up against his dark jeans, evaluating the outfit. Did it look like he was trying too hard? He applied a dab of gel to his short brown hair and pulled at the cowlick that stuck up like an alfalfa sprout on the left side of his head. Dressed in the polo shirt, jeans, and impeccable new sneakers, Chase looked like your average preppy boy—not like someone who lived in a tiny trailer on the outskirts of town with his mom.

Which was, of course, the whole point.

Chase checked his phone; there was another text from Lindsay—*I haven't seen u in a week!*—which he deleted quickly. He was on a schedule: by the time he arrived at Minster's house, the sophomore and junior girls would have drunk just enough to lower their inhibitions, but not so much that they were too wasted to flirt. (At Tina Hathaway's Halloween party that year, he'd no sooner convinced a hot sophomore to ditch the crowd for a private make-out session in the woods than she'd pulled down her pants and started peeing on a tree and giggling. He'd had to half-carry her back to the party, where he off-loaded her onto her friends.)

So tonight was going to be a success. He needed it to be. The Ascension Football Feast was in a little more than a week, on January 2nd. The Feast was an annual postseason celebration of the Ascension Warriors, the town's pride and joy (at least when they were winning), not to mention a major charity event. Most players brought a whole entourage, including parents, siblings, and girlfriends. Last year, he'd arrived alone and felt humiliated when the guys made fun of the fact that he hadn't managed to bag a date.

This year, his best friend Zach was organizing the whole

event, hoping to raise five thousand dollars for a local homeless shelter. There would be a ton of people there, not to mention news cameras. And Chase was the star.

Chase was a damn good quarterback, probably one of the best in the state. College recruiters had already contacted Coach Baldwin to inquire about Chase's post–high school plans. And while it would be cool to get a free ride to a quality school—he'd be the first Singer to attend college, and there was no way his family could afford it otherwise—he wasn't playing for scholarships. On the field was where he felt free, open, smart. He knew what to do, and he had the space to do it. He made the right choices. Sometimes, in the middle of a game, he was surprised to find that he was grinning.

And yet, in the back of his mind, Chase knew that at any moment, everything could come undone. One bad play and it could all close in on you—no holes to run through, blockers and tacklers in every direction. No options.

Smoothing his collar a final time, Chase grabbed his football jacket and closed the trailer door with a satisfied thud, ignoring the fact that it made the whole structure shake ever so slightly.

The night was cold, and the snow that had been forecast was starting to fall. He was trotting toward his car—an old station wagon he shared with his mom—when he remembered that she was working tonight at the convenience store around the corner. He jogged back to the house to flip on the outside light. He didn't like to think of her fumbling for her keys in the dark.

Every time Chase left his trailer on the west side of Ascension, he felt like he was emerging from a claustrophobic cocoon. His part of town was right by the highway, and the buildings—trailers, convenience stores, gas stations, water towers—sat almost on top of one another. First he'd pass the Kwik Mart where his mom worked. Out of habit, he always slowed a little, trying to catch a glimpse of her bottle-blond hair. He liked it when she worked the register. That meant she wasn't doing heavy lifting in the stock room.

A mile past the Kwik Mart, the landscape opened up; the buildings petered out at Williamson Farm, still in operation, with dairy cows and a smell of manure in the air. Here, he'd open his window despite the smell, breathing in the fields, the space, the nothingness. Then several miles of forest, with just a few houses cut into the woods, and then the old part of town, which tried to hold on to historic appeal, with brick buildings, green awnings, and small shops. This was where Ascension's middle school was, a hulking stone prison. Chase loved driving by it. He never got over the thrill of having escaped.

Then he hit the nicer residential neighborhoods. Everything here looked cleaner, and in the summer, greener. The houses were set about an acre apart, each one claiming a small bit of woods for itself. Out even farther past the center of town, toward Minster's neighborhood—where the money really flowed—the lots got bigger, the driveways got longer, the streetlights were fewer. And past Minster's was the high school, out near the lake, with an expansive campus and a newly renovated football field. It took Chase the whole drive sometimes to start loosening up, to shake off the feeling of the thin tin walls around him, the old food smells that lingered in the tiny trailer air, the sense of smallness and dirt.

But tonight, Chase never shook off the claustrophobic feeling: He kept seeing shapes darting at the edge of his vision, but when he looked, there was nothing but snow, whirling out of the darkness.

He hoped the party would snap him out of his bad mood. He was going to choose his date for the Ascension Football Feast tonight. He was going to pick someone quality, too—someone who would make up for last year. A girl who wasn't too loud and smiled at the right times and looked good in a dress. Maybe even someone he could talk to for more than fifteen minutes.

Tonight, Chase planned on finding the perfect girl. He needed it. He deserved it.

When he pulled up to Minster's house, which sat at the end of a cul-de-sac in one of Ascension's newer developments, the party was already raging. Almost every light in the house was on, and a group of smokers stood in the driveway, hopping from one foot to the other to keep warm. He jogged up the lawn and pushed through the front door into a large, marble-tiled entryway. A gold-framed mirror hung on the wall, and below it, a varnished wooden bench.

As he did when he entered most of his friends' homes, Chase felt a moment of unconscious panic. Everything here was so nice, he felt like he shouldn't touch anything.

But no. He was Chase Singer, and Chase Singer *belonged.* He shrugged off his jacket and threw it on the bench with just a little too much force, glanced one last time at his reflection in the mirror, and began his rounds.

A group of underclassmen were overcompensating for their insecurities by being too loud. Jenna and Ashley, two cheerleaders, were standing with Taylor, a field hockey player, and all three of them were flirting with what appeared to be some extremely stoned lacrosse players. Coming out of the kitchen was Minster himself, looking surprisingly relaxed for someone whose enormous house was full of Ascension high schoolers. It appeared that half the crowd was drinking beer from plastic cups, and the other half was drinking a red-orange punch. The lights had been dimmed, so all the rooms were hazy and full of shadows. Pop music—new, dance-y stuff—thumped from a hidden sound system, and even people who weren't dancing seemed to be pulsing with the music. Everyone who came in from the cold took a moment to adjust and to blow on their hands, as though they'd emerged from a long expedition.

He located Zach and Gabby by the keg and the punch bowl and scanned the room for potential hookups. There were some definite possibilities—Jenna or Ashley, of course, and also a throng of sophomores who got giggly as soon as he passed through the living room. This would be fun. He smiled.

He started to tune in to the conversations around him, but then Gabby was calling him over to where she and Zach were standing with Andrea Rubin, Sean Wagner, and Nell White.

"Look who I found," Gabby said. At one point she'd wanted Chase and Andrea to get together, but Andrea had made it clear that she would go out with Chase only if he paid for everything—an impossibility that Chase resented more than he let on. While Chase wasn't the poorest kid in Ascension, he was certainly the poorest *popular* kid in town. And he hated that people knew it.

"Hey, man," Zach said. "Grab a beer—catch up!" He pumped the keg and handed a red cup to Chase, who accepted it and took a big gulp. Something about tonight made him feel like he needed more liquid courage than usual.

"Thanks, dude," Chase said. "What's up? Who's here? Where's Winters?" He addressed the questions to no one in particular; Gabby took it upon herself to answer.

"We were talking about Miller's English final and how

impossible it was," she said. "And everyone's here. Well, almost everyone. Em should be here soon. I don't know what's taking her so long."

Chase nodded and nudged Nell. "You know that tall sophomore?" Nell was a peer adviser and somehow managed to know every single Ascension student's name. She followed his gaze.

"The blond one? Jess Carlsen." Nell paused and Chase waited, expectant. Nell rolled her eyes and went on: "She's into drama or singing or something. I forget which."

Zach laughed. "Homed your radar already, huh, Singer?"

Chase held his hands up in mock innocence. "I'm just trying to get to know new faces," he said.

"You're tracking new blood," Gabby chimed in, and Chase could see her ever so slightly tighten her grip on Zach's arm.

Then, out of nowhere: "Did you guys hear about Sasha Bowlder?" she asked.

At that moment someone must have leaned against the light switch: The overhead lights blazed and suddenly the room and everyone in it was starkly illuminated. For a second Chase had the impression that everyone was frozen. Then the lights were dimmed again.

Chase and Zach exchanged a quick glance.

Zach cleared his throat and asked, "What about her?"

"She tried to commit suicide," Gabby said, her voice low.

Now Chase felt as though the room had gone dark, even though the lights didn't waver.

"By throwing herself off the Piss Pass," Gabby added, referring to the highway overpass around the corner from Fitzroy's, a local dive bar. Fitzroy's regulars often stumbled to the overpass to pee when they were having a smoke; hence the nickname. "Didn't you hear all those sirens earlier? They were, like, earsplitting. I thought there was a terrorist attack or something."

Zach smiled gently. "Ascension, Maine is hardly a terrorist target, babe. Nothing bad happens here."

"Well, what happened to Sasha is *bad*," Gabby said, tossing her hair over her shoulder.

Chase felt something tighten in his chest. Sasha was Ascension's social pariah, but she hadn't always been. Memories came to Chase, fast and thick, like a blizzard: Sasha as a young girl, weaving with him around the mounds of trash and broken furniture stacked up around the trailer park. She lived there then, just a few trailers over in lot 37. They played hide-and-go-seek and flashlight tag. And they shared secrets. Some nights, when his dad was too drunk and really raging, his mom would shuttle Chase over to Sasha's house, just to get him out of the line of fire. And then, when Chase's dad died in the freak factory accident, Chase stayed at Sasha's for a full five days while his mom took care of the funeral, the creditors, and her grief.

He and Sasha would share a bed, toe to head, and tell each

other ghost stories into the night. They preferred the fake scary stuff to the real. At least in stories, when you turn on the lights, the monsters disappear. The first time Chase ever thought about girls as anything other than less athletic versions of boys, it was to wonder what it would be like to kiss Sasha.

But then things had changed. Sasha's mom met a wealthy dentist from York—he swept into Ascension and bought a big house over by the McCords'. Just like that, Sasha wore trendy clothes, could go out for pizza on Friday nights, and could invite people over to watch movies on her big-screen TV. That was sixth grade, and suddenly, Sasha seemed to forget that Chase existed. It was weird—he'd hated her for a while, but in some ways, Sasha ditching him was the best thing that ever could have happened. Because that's when Chase got it—as long as you're wearing the right outfits, saying the right things, impressing the right people, you can blend in. It doesn't matter where you come from, as long as you play the role.

Once Chase saw the matrix, it was easy enough to get in. He talked about girls but not too much. He did well in class but not too well. He excelled on the field, was up for any physical challenge. He became friends with Zach McCord (but never invited him over). Over the course of maybe six months, Chase got in. By seventh grade, Chase Singer was part of the crew. And by the time they got to high school, he was Way In.

Of course, the thing about the matrix is it works the same

way in reverse: Once you're out, you're really, really out. Sasha discovered that too late.

The tides turned against her, easily, almost as if swayed by an invisible force.

She tried desperately to keep a low profile, to avoid the smears. No one could quite pinpoint what her mistake had been. Maybe she had been *too* eager, *too* mean. Or maybe it had all started from some small thing, like freshman year when she wore a fluorescent pink sweater to school and was called "Rainbow Retard" for a few days. Or more likely it was when she made the mistake of letting two boys kiss her at a party in the fall that year. In reality, the kissing thing had probably been a last-ditch effort to be liked. But it was too late. After that the rumors started. Countless rumors—Chase couldn't even remember all of them. Sasha was bi, or she was into porn, or she was just a freak, no further explanation needed.

She began to wear clothes that didn't stand out—and started to slip into invisibility. She skipped a couple of important dances, she began to slouch down in her seat during class, she wasn't involved in any extracurricular activities. And though it had happened seamlessly while most people were looking the other way, Sasha had quickly lost everything she'd once gained. It was the easiest thing in the world to make fun of her. Over time, it became a sport. Eventually, she had just one friend left: Drea Feiffer, whose hair color changed weekly from purple to maroon to jet-black, and whose habit of wearing barrettes, striped socks, and T-shirts featuring Japanese cartoon characters seemed only to highlight the darkness of her general attitude.

Suicide. Chase felt a tingling heaviness in his legs and arms—the same feeling he used to get in church. His mom used to drag him there before she started working Sunday doubles. He'd never liked church—hated it, in fact, but not because he was bored by the priest's lectures about sin. He'd never told anyone this, but he'd actually been scared of the church—the weird smell of burning things, the priest's thunderous voice, and the enormous crucifix over the altar. It had always freaked him out.

Now Chase felt like the room was tunneling around him.

"People don't just—," he started to say, but Zach cut him off.

"Is this a joke, Gabby?" Zach asked.

"Not even," Gabby said, nodding so her blond curls bounced. "It just happened, like, two hours ago! She's going to be paralyzed for life or something." By now more people had quieted down and were gathering around Gabby, which only fueled her on. "What I heard is that she fell into the bed of a *truck*—the guy was totally freaked out—and she's in the hospital. Like in a coma. Someone at my mom's TV station is reporting on it. That's how I found out. My mom asked if I knew her."

Everyone looked shocked, but Chase barely noticed. He

blinked once, twice, and stepped away from the group.

Zach reached out for Chase's arm. "Where you going?"

"I gotta piss," Chase responded, avoiding Zach's eyes. "I'll be right back."

Chase had been to Minster's house a few times before, but all of a sudden he couldn't remember where the bathroom was. He wandered into the TV room, past the huge wall-mounted plasma TV, and into the living room. At a bar in the corner, Chase spied a bottle of whiskey. Perfect—the Minsters' private stash. He moved casually toward the bar, tipping back what was left of his beer, and picked up the whiskey. No one would notice if some was missing off the top, he told himself, pouring a hefty slug into his plastic cup. Then he stood there for a moment, surveying the crowd. The musty, earthy taste of whiskey burned his throat as he took a large swig.

Suddenly all anyone was talking about was Sasha Bowlder. People were as drunk on gruesome details as on the watered-down beer. *Did she leave a note? Was she really paralyzed? Was she at the local hospital, or had she been sped to Portland or airlifted to Boston?*

Chase felt like the room was clenching and unclenching around him, a giant fist. *Suicide.* The word kept replaying in his mind. *Suicide.* And the Sasha he hadn't thought about in years—the normal Sasha, the best-friend Sasha of his childhood, smiling, gap-toothed—kept coasting into his mind.

With one last swig of the whiskey, Chase shifted, moving

away from the bar and the living room, from one conversation to the next. He hated the way the pictures on Minster's walls—Smiling happy grandfather! Smiling happy mom! Smiling happy brothers!—seemed to be following him with their eyes, sneering. He picked up a random beer from a bookshelf in the TV room and chugged it. Man, it was hot in here. He passed the bathroom, finally, and the long line of girls waiting to use it. All their faces seemed to blend together. He was having trouble recognizing them, like everything was happening behind a cloud of smoke. He had to steady himself against a doorframe before shuffling back into the kitchen, where a large group had assembled. Gabby was still holding court, divulging details she'd heard from her mom—and, probably, adding plenty of her own. Even though everyone else was standing, Chase sat down in a kitchen chair with a thud.

"You okay?" Chase looked up to see Zach standing over him, offering a fresh beer and an inquisitive look.

"Yeah, thanks. I just . . ." Chase switched gears. "What do you want to do over the next couple of weeks? You're a free agent!" He quickly looked at Gabby to see if she'd overheard, but she was too deep in conversation with Fiona.

"Free agent—yeah right. I wouldn't be surprised if Gabs plants a video camera in my alarm clock." Zach's breezy tone sounded forced.

"Tough break." Chase leaned forward to punch Zach's

arm. The room swayed as he settled back into his chair. "Is that Guitar Hero tournament at your place really the extent of our vacation ambitions?"

"Well, that and study for the SATs."

"Seriously. If you don't get a perfect score, we're going to have to go on stepfather suicide watch."

A look of embarrassed shock passed between them. The topic of suicide was too relevant to be funny.

And over all this, they could hear Gabby's voice, ringing clear above the dull roar of the party. "We should start a suicide support group, something for all the grieving students," Chase heard her say. Lauren was nodding enthusiastically. It looked like Fiona was tearing up.

He grimaced, pulling his forehead into a mess of little lines. All this mopey bullshit was just too much. He stood up and strode over to Gabby, grabbing her arm and pulling her toward him.

"Since when do you all care about Sasha so much, anyway?" Chase could hear himself slurring his words. "She was a loser. It's not like anyone will miss her."

The group surrounding Gabby got quiet, and she elbowed him sharply, spilling some of her punch on his wrist in the process.

"Why would you say something like that?" she demanded.

Chase's mind felt like it was coated now, thick and white and blank. "You got punch on me," he said. The words sounded distant, as though they came from someone else.

"You're a real asshole," a voice said behind him. He turned, and there was the artsy girl, Jess something-or-other. She was looking at him with disgust. There went that prospect.

He tried to change the subject.

"Five minutes—beer-pong tournament," he shouted, noticing that people were uncomfortably, and subtly, moving away from him. "I challenge any of you to defeat me and Zach." As he headed for the bathroom line, he heard Zach trying to smooth over the moment, urging people to quit gossiping and enjoy the night.

A couple of minutes later, in front of the vanity mirror, washing the sticky punch from his fingers, Chase examined himself. He adjusted the collar on his shirt and turned his face to the left and right, checking for missed shaving spots. Finding no imperfections, he looked himself square in the eyes. *Chase, dude,* he said to himself, *get it together.*

Someone was banging on the bathroom door.

Just then Chase noticed a tiny stain next to the second button on his shirt. Shit. The punch. He clenched his fist. *Get it together,* he repeated. It was only a small spot. Still, Chase knew how easily things could fall apart. And sometimes all it took was one little thing gone wrong: a fumble, a lie, the click of a SEND button. A moment of weakness. Even something as minor as a stain could ruin everything.

CHAPTER THREE

Em was distracted on the drive over to the party. All she wanted was a hint from Zach. Just one hint that he felt what she'd been feeling. That she wasn't insane. That she hadn't imagined all the fizzy, crazy vibes bouncing between them for the past few weeks. Any hint would do. Then she'd let it go. Really.

"Thanks so much for coming with me," she said to JD as they rounded the corner, not realizing that she'd said it just a few minutes earlier.

"Ah, you know. It's always a treat when *eccentrics* like myself are allowed into the presence of populars." JD sighed sarcastically, adjusting his hat. "Perhaps I'll get lucky and some girl will want a piece of the Fountain," he said, invoking his rarely used nickname, the Fountain of Nerdiness.

Em barely noticed. She fumbled with the bag on her

lap, digging for her lip gloss, trying to steal a glimpse of her reflection in the passenger-side mirror. As they got closer to Minster's, she scanned the cars that were already lining the street, looking for a particular blue Jeep Wrangler, one with Ascension High basketball and football bumper stickers lined up neatly side by side.

When they finally arrived at Ian's house, Em's brain was swimming with thoughts of Zach. She felt like she'd already had a few drinks; everything looked just a little off-balance as she walked through the door, like someone had set all the rooms at slightly different angles.

For one thing, the whole mood of the party seemed . . . off. People were drinking and dancing and flirting, as usual, but everyone's voices seemed quieter, and groups of whispering girls kept breaking off, shaking their heads, hugging each other.

On top of that, Gabby was in turbo mode. Her outfit looked great (she'd paired her dress with brown tights and wedge boots), and she'd been right about having a good hair day. As she dragged Em toward the kitchen and the punch, she chattered about her forthcoming family trip to Spain and Majorca.

"Em, you have to promise—pinkie swear—that we'll go to Maintenance when I get back," Gabby said, referring to their favorite Christmastime tradition—one they would have to forego this year. It involved taking the train down to Boston, lunching at a Newbury Street restaurant, and shopping.

"Of course, Gabs," Em said.

"I can't believe I'm going to be away for eight whole days," Gabby said, bouncing from topic to topic. "It feels like a lifetime. Chase is *wasted*, by the way. Watch out. God, Em, you have to promise not to do a single fun thing while I'm gone."

Em grinned. Of course she would miss her best friend, but she was secretly a bit grateful that they would have some time apart. It was just like Gabby to assume that the world would stop when she left and restart the moment she returned.

"Oh, and don't let Zach do anything fun either," Gabby added as they approached the keg and the punch bowl, where Zach was standing with a few other juniors.

Em's stomach flipped. It seemed recently that every time she saw him, she was experiencing him for the first time—his piercing eyes, his adorably shaggy hair, his broad shoulders, the way his nose kind of crinkled when he was paying attention. It was as though a spotlight had been switched on, and in its beam, she saw only Zach.

She knew it was wrong, and she knew it was terrible, but she also knew that this feeling was the one that pop songs were written about. Em threw her shoulders back and prepared for the private heartbreak that had become part of her daily routine.

"Hi, baby!" Gabby bounded toward Zach and gave him a peck on the lips. Em looked away. "Did you miss me?" Without giving him the chance to respond, Gabby barreled ahead. "Not as much as you're going to miss me next week. Look who I found!"

"Is there Red Bull in that punch? You're crazier than usual." Zach laughed and gently detached himself from Gabby, reminding her that the trip was only eight *days* long, not eight years. He motioned to the punch bowl. "Hey, Em." Did she imagine it, or did Zach's eyes brighten when he turned them on her? "Can I pour *you* some of this crazy-making elixir? And watch out for Singer—he's a man on a mission tonight."

Em nodded, trying to ignore the thrill that zipped through her as Zach passed her the cup of punch, accidentally brushing her wrist with his fingertips.

"So I heard. What kind of mission?" she asked.

"I think it's a Football Feast mission," Zach stage-whispered, wiggling his eyebrows ever so slightly. "A date mission, if you know what I mean."

"Oh, Em! Speaking of which, I have to show you the dress I'm going to wear to the Feast," Gabby said, interjecting. "It's kind of a pale purple-blue—like that scarf I love at Maintenance?" She winked and nudged Em for emphasis, but Zach had turned around to talk with Sean. They were probably scheduling ice hoops. Playing basketball on Ascension's frozen ponds was the boys' favorite winter tradition.

"The dress comes up to here," Gabby was saying, hitting

the middle of her thigh. “That’s not too short, right?” She hiccupped and then giggled a little.

For a moment, Em thought about what she would wear if she were going to the Football Feast. Maybe her green dress, the scoop-neck, pencil-skirted one that looked like something from the 1950s? Em knew that she could go if she wanted. Sean or Brian or any of those football guys would be happy to take her. But she could only picture herself walking in on one person’s arm.

There was no way around it: Em had fallen for her best friend’s boyfriend. Over the last few months, Zach had seemed to get her in a way that no one else did. They laughed at the same jokes and rolled their eyes together at Gabby’s antics. Whereas Gabby was usually uninterested in Zach’s college goals or his basketball triumphs, Em paid attention. It wasn’t that she didn’t think Gabby and Zach were a great couple—clearly they were a perfect match on paper, the cute prom queen and the adorable, smart captain of the basketball team—but sometimes she felt like Zach deserved someone a little bit deeper than Gabby.

Someone a little bit more like Em.

Not that she would ever do anything about it. But she had to admit that the prospect of having more than a week to hang out with Zach—without Gabby always around—was exhilarating.

"So the reporter told my mom that Sasha is on life support," Gabby was saying to Abbie Stevens, another yearbook staffer who'd joined the group. "But even if she gets better, she'll probably never come back to Ascension."

Em froze midswallow and grabbed Gabby's arm. "What are you talking about, Gabs?"

"Oh, you just got here. You haven't heard. Sasha Bowlder tried to, you know, commit *suicide*," Gabby said, wide-eyed, lowering her voice again.

Em blinked. "Sasha did *what*?"

"She tried to kill herself by jumping off the Piss Pass," Gabby said, trying to disguise a small hiccup. Maybe it was just because she was drunk, but Gabby seemed to be almost enjoying telling this story, like she was on a stage, performing. "But she didn't die, so . . . she's in the hospital. Paralyzed, or in a coma, or both. It's crazy. I thought it would be nice to send flowers and a card, so I'm starting a collection. We already have, like, fifty bucks. It's great."

Gabby turned back to Abbie, who was now also flanked by Fiona and Lauren, but Em stayed rooted to the spot. She felt strangely shocked and she couldn't figure out why. She and Sasha had not been friends. It's not like she'd done anything to stop the Sasha-bashing. Sure, Em had always made a point of smiling at Sasha in the hallway, but Sasha could easily have misinterpreted that as a popular girl smirking at her.

The conversation had moved on: The girls were done with Sasha ("*so* tragic," Gabby sighed), and they'd started talking about the Behemoth, a new, giant shopping center being erected out near the highway. It was halfway completed and six months behind schedule. This year's Christmas shopping had still taken place at the old mall, which hadn't been renovated since the 1980s.

Em excused herself from the conversation. The room was too hot; and even though she'd taken only a single sip of punch, she felt as though the room was spinning. She wondered if JD had heard the news. She turned and walked out of the kitchen to find him.

As though he'd heard her thoughts, JD suddenly appeared in the hallway, his weird purple-shirt-and-vest combo making him stand out in the crowd, as usual.

"Hey, Em," he said. He was holding a beer, and it looked like he'd barely taken a sip. "I just heard about Sasha."

"Me too. For some reason I just . . . I feel weird," Em said. "I can't explain it." She wanted to talk about how they could have known and how they could have stopped it, but she didn't want to start crying. And she felt guilty caring this much only after the fact.

Em knew she'd laughed at Sasha's expense more than once. By junior year, Bowlder bashing was as much a part of the Ascension curriculum as English or math. But it had reached new levels last week, just before winter break, when someone had plastered mortifying quotes from her email exchanges all over Facebook. In them, Sasha confessed to feeling desperate to be pretty, sexy, smart—which only made her seem more sad and lonely. She wanted to be wanted. The quotes had been up for half the day when Sasha finally noticed that everyone was staring, pointing, and laughing more than usual. Em had seen her holding her bagged lunch in one hand and a soda in the other, staring at an image on someone's phone screen. Quietly, she'd set the lunch down before turning on her heel and walking away. Her only friend, Drea Feiffer, shouted for her to slow down as the cafeteria door slammed.

And now she had tried to kill herself.

"Do you want to leave?" JD pulled at the ends of his perpetually sticking-out hair and looked at Em seriously.

"No one else wants to leave," she said, motioning weakly to no one in particular. "I don't want to make a big deal out of it."

"We don't have to make it into a big deal. Let's just slip out. You look kind of pale."

Em looked gratefully up at JD. "Okay," she said. "Let me just grab my coat. . . . I think Gabby threw it into one of the upstairs bedrooms."

"Sounds good," he said. "I'll wait down here."

Em put down her punch and walked slowly up the grand staircase, which was carpeted but still creaked beneath her feet.

At the top of the stairs was a huge, stained-glass window that looked like something from a Gothic castle. It depicted a sunny landscape but looked eerie with the moon shining through it, casting red and orange shadows on the floor. She turned right and went into the first bedroom, where a heap of coats was piled on top of a queen-sized bed. The room was large and empty-feeling, with almost nothing on the walls. No one else seemed to be upstairs, and the sounds of the party were just a dull throb from below. Outside, Em could see the snow was still falling.

Em shivered. Wasn't heat supposed to rise? Downstairs she'd been too hot; now she was freezing. She bent over the bed to look for her coat in the dim light coming through the windows.

"Looking for something?"

Em whipped around and found herself face to neck with Zach, who at six foot one seemed well proportioned next to her five-foot-eight frame. He seemed to have materialized out of nowhere—she hadn't heard the creaking steps.

"Looking for my coat, actually," she said. "I was thinking about taking off."

"So soon?" Zach pouted.

"Yeah, I'm not . . . feeling that great," she said. But now that Zach was standing next to her, she felt somewhat lighter.

"Aww . . . you should get some rest, then." He gave her a quick hug. He smelled of beer and soap. "Hey, we on for hanging out over break? I could really use another pair of eyes on my essay. Plus, I will destroy you in Guitar Hero to make up for last week's upset."

Hadn't his hands lingered on her shoulders just a minute longer than they should have? Had he noticed how well their bodies fit together?

Em felt a flash of guilt. She shouldn't even be thinking about Zach that way, especially not tonight.

"Yes," she said. "And yes. I promised Gabby I wouldn't let you out of my sight over the next week." She regretted the words as soon as they were out of her mouth.

"Well, that's good." He leaned in, smiling. "Seems like you haven't let me out of your sight at all recently."

All the heat came rushing back to Em's body. "What—what do you mean?" she stuttered.

Zach shrugged, still grinning. "Nothing. Forget it. It's just . . ."

He was being playful, that was all. Right? But then, before she could say another word, he held out his hand, a closed fist.

Em looked at him blankly. "What is—" Before she could finish, he flipped open his hand. In his palm lay one of the silver spiral earrings she was wearing that night. Her hands moved quickly to both ears—sure enough, the right one was missing.

"I saw it on the rug downstairs. I knew it was yours. You were wearing them last week, at Lauren's house."

Then, just as Em was certain that this *was* the sign she'd been looking for—*holy shit, holy shit, it's like Mom and Dad and the stupid pom-poms!*—they heard Gabby's voice.

"I'm fine," Gabby was saying in a decidedly unfine manner. There was a loud crash, as though she had bumped into something, followed by a fit of giggles. She appeared in the doorway, swaying on the arm of Fiona Marcus. Her normally glossy, springy blond hair was a mess and her necklace was turned around backward. "Zachie, Em, I'm totally fine."

"Aw, babe, you're wasted," Zach said, and just like that, all the charged air between him and Em was gone, deflated like a pricked balloon. He slipped an arm around Gabby's shoulders, gently disengaging her from Fiona. "Need to go home?"

Em slipped back into best-friend zone, shaking off—with a bit of self-hatred—the last few moments.

"Where's your coat, sweetie? Zach'll take you home."

Gabby waved a hand in the general direction of the bed, slurring, "Over there. And whatsamatter, Emmie? You look like the Grim Creeper spooked you." She giggled.

"I'll find the coat," Em said to Zach over Gabby's head, ignoring the Grim Creeper comment. It was the name they'd assigned to some guy who used to go to their school. He would walk the halls muttering to himself and staring too long at people. But then he'd dropped out. His name was Colin, or Crow, as some people called him, and Em realized with a fresh pang of guilt that he was also one of Drea Feiffer's friends. Like Sasha. Yet another person they'd all randomly made fun of, just because it was easy. Em shook her head, unable to process it all.

Zach turned to take Gabby back downstairs. Em went through the pile on the bed twice, looking for Gabby's signature BCBG coat, black wool and belted, which Gabby had adorned with an enormous rhinestone heart pin. But after searching for a few minutes (including under the bed and in the strangely empty closet), Em couldn't find it. Gabby must have hidden it somewhere and forgotten about it; she'd probably remember when she sobered up.

So Gabby went teetering off on Zach's arm. He had lent her his coat, which practically engulfed her. Watching them disappear into the night together made Em feel as though she had just inhaled a mouthful of sawdust.

People were shouting drunkenly and trying to catch snowflakes on their tongues as Em and JD made their way to his car a few minutes later. She could see their breath clouding in the air.

"What a weird night," JD said as he opened the car door for Em. She just nodded. Her brain felt like it was on fire, there were so many thoughts whirling around in there. Zach. Gabby. Sasha Bowlder. Jesus—Sasha. There was only so much she could freak out about in one night.

JD made a three-point turn to head back down Ian's street. They sat in heavy silence; it felt as though the events of the evening had a physical shape and were sitting between them. Em stared out the window at the evergreens and bare branches, which tangled and became one as she stared deeper into the woods. They passed Chase, trudging toward his station wagon.

"We should ask him if he wants a ride," Em said, her voice cutting the quiet. "Zach said he was trashed earlier." She hoped JD had not noticed the hitch in her voice when she'd pronounced Zach's name. JD nodded and Em rolled down her window.

"Hey, Chase, you need a ride?" Maybe this—helping Chase—would make up for what had almost happened upstairs with Zach.

Almost happened. The important thing was that it *hadn't* happened. Em hated herself for feeling disappointed.

"No, I'm fine," Chase said. He looked awful; his skin was pasty white. "Really. Go."

"Seriously, Chase," Em persisted. "Just hop in the back. Maybe we'll make a run to Mickey D's?" There was a bit of pleading in her voice.

"I said I'm fine, Winters. Thanks, though, really." Em knew she'd never be able to reason with him. And at least he *sounded* sober. She waved, but Chase was staring at the ground and didn't see her.

Then, as they rounded a curve, JD's headlights illuminated three girls standing by the side of the road. Em yelped; they'd come upon the girls so suddenly, and they were so close, she was sure JD would hit them. But at the last second the car skated past them, with just a few inches of space to spare. For the briefest moment, Em made eye contact with one of the girls: a tall, voluptuous redhead with bright green eyes. Em's heart skipped a beat, and she felt a shock of recognition. It was a combination of déjà vu and that feeling you get when you see a picture of an ancestor who looks exactly like you.

"What?" JD asked, responding to Em's involuntary cry. "What's wrong?"

"Oh, I was just afraid you would hit them," Em said.

"Hit who?" JD scanned his rearview mirror. "I didn't see anyone."

"The girls right—," Em started to say. But by the time Em swiveled around in her seat to look, the three girls had disappeared.

CHAPTER FOUR

Chase had parked way down the road from the party. He didn't like everyone to see the old station wagon if he could help it. Plus, the stinging cold air helped sober him up. He'd appreciated Em's offer of a ride, but he couldn't handle being around other people right now. What he hadn't told her was that he planned to just sit in his car and sober up for a while before he actually went home.

Cars passed—thumping music, hooting cries—then became twin red taillights, winking out. As he walked, he could hear engines in the distance. The same ghostly snow that had been falling all night was still coming down. He felt it on his face, wet and soft.

As Chase stood there, not even feeling the cold wind biting his arms through his coat, he had a sudden jolt of memory.

Being eight years old, and Officer Worelly coming by, so many winters ago, knocking hard on their door. His mom answering in her slippers. His mom crying in the snow. Chase not understanding, as his mother shoved him—too hard—back inside the trailer. That was the day of his father's accident. His first taste of loss.

But with that loss came a kind of relief. He had never liked his father. Chase always believed his father deserved what he got—a fatal blow to the head from a faulty piece of factory equipment. Even at the age of eight, he'd seen his dad hit his mom too many times to feel anything but numb when he found out his father was never coming back.

That numbness surrounded him again now as he walked into the darkness.

Ian's cul-de-sac was way behind him by now, and he'd passed only two or three houses, all of them dark. No wonder no one ever called the cops on Minster. No one could even hear the party. Not like in *his* neighborhood—if you could call it that. There, you could barely flush the toilet without everyone knowing.

His fingers were numb from the cold by the time he got to his car. He was fumbling with the keys—he dropped them once and had to scoop them up, cursing, from the street—when he heard silvery voices nearby. He peered into the darkness.

"Hello?"

Out of the snowy fog emerged one girl, then two more. Chase couldn't help but let his jaw drop a bit; these chicks were amazing. The one in front, a redhead with fair skin, was smiling. The other two—one white-blond and a little curvy, the other petite with wavy, honey-colored hair and a scarlet ribbon tied around her neck like a choker—stood behind her with serious expressions on their gorgeous faces. All three of them seemed to be enveloped in some sort of white light; probably the moon playing tricks with the snow.

Or maybe he was still drunker than he thought.

"Hey, sorry to startle you," the redhead said, stepping toward him. As she did, he noticed a single snow-white streak that stood out from her hair on the left side of her face. "I'm Ty. These are my cousins, Ali and Meg."

Chase stuttered, "Um, hi. Hey. I'm Chase."

"Hi, Chase," all three girls said, practically in unison.

"Our car ran out of gas." Ty motioned up the road a bit, where Chase thought he could just see the outline of a vehicle. "Any chance you could help us?" For a girl stranded in the middle of a snowstorm, she seemed fairly relaxed. All at once, Chase's head cleared.

"Do you want me to, um, drive you to the gas station? Or something?"

"That would be great, thanks," Ty said. "Why don't I go with you, and Ali and Meg can wait in the car?"

Chase wasn't one for new age crap—his mom had been to see a psychic a few times and always came back muttering voodoo bullshit, all about "affirmations" and chakra. Nevertheless, for a split second, he felt like this was *fate*—like a sign from the universe. Sure, the party might have been a bust—the Sasha news was pretty much the definition of a buzzkill, and he'd been in no shape to get numbers or hook up—but now he would get alone time with the hottest girl he had ever seen in his life. It was fate, clearly.

Everything was going to be okay.

"So, was there a party tonight?" Ty asked once they were in the car. He could barely resist the urge to brush the snowflakes from her hair, to lean over and breathe in her musky, floral scent. As he put the car in drive, he felt like he was launching a spaceship into the night, into the snow. He and Ty would explore the dark, winding roads and stark, branch-lined fields.

"Yeah, a Christmas party–type thing," he said, mentally kicking himself for sounding so uncool. She was probably picturing people dancing around in elf costumes. He quickly added, "You know, just a bunch of kids I know."

"Sounds like fun. I *love* parties," Ty said, smiling at him in the dark. "Don't you wish we could go back to having parties like they did centuries ago? With dance cards and formal invitations and choreographed dances? Or masquerade balls? I'd *love* to go to a masked party. Wouldn't you?"

"Totally," he said, thankful she hadn't been there to see him try to set up the beer-pong game. "You, um, study history or something?" He was sure this girl must be in college.

"Or something," Ty said, laughing. Her laugh sounded like clinking coins. Chase couldn't think of anything else to say. He fumbled with the radio dial, trying to tune in to something sophisticated and moody.

"God, the snow is amazing," Ty said, looking out the window. "It reminds me of that old poem. Something about the snow in the air, something something, *the secret of despair.*"

Chase was so entranced that he could barely focus on anything outside the car; the trees blended together outside his window like a movie in fast-forward. This girl was driving him crazy. It was like she was wearing one of those pheromone perfumes.

Then she turned to him, her eyes piercing. "Did you hear all those sirens before? Any idea what that was about?"

His mouth went dry. The sirens were the last thing he wanted to talk about. "Nope. Must be some kind of accident. . . . Lots of people just don't know how to drive in this weather."

"Nothing's ever really an accident," Ty said, once again smiling at him. Her eyes glittered, catlike. "Don't you think?"

Chase didn't really know what she meant, but he nodded anyway. One thing he was sure of: Meeting Ty was no accident.

At the gas station, Ty jumped confidently from the car.

"Want me to go in there with you?" Chase said, nodding his head toward the twenty-four-hour convenience store. Thankfully, *not* the one his mom worked at.

"No thank you, I've got it," she replied, flashing a smile. He watched her go inside and pay for her gas, then saw her brush away—charmingly, still—the smitten cashier's offer to help. Seemingly unfazed by the freezing night air, she stood by the gas pump and filled up the can. Chase got out and jogged over to her, rubbing his hands together.

"Sure you don't need any help?"

"I'm fine," she said. "See? Almost done." Her pale, thin arms glowed in the light of the station as she replaced the nozzle on the gas pump. Chase thought she must be totally freezing, but she wasn't shivering; she was smiling. He'd never seen anyone who seemed so *comfortable*, so effortless.

On the way back, Chase could hardly concentrate on keeping the car on the road. He'd hooked up with plenty of girls before, but Ty seemed older, more sophisticated than any of the girls at school. Ty was just what he needed—a girl like that could more than distract him from all the messed-up stuff in his life right now.

She'd be the perfect date for the Football Feast.

Back at the girls' car, an old-fashioned, boxy, maroon Lincoln Town Car, Ali and Meg filled up the gas tank while Ty took Chase's hand and led him several feet away.

"Thank god we found you," she said, eyes glittering.

"I guess I'm just your knight in shining armor," Chase said, gulping back a nervous laugh. He took a clumsy step forward. "You can repay me, you know." He leaned forward, closing the distance between them, hoping she'd ignore his total lack of game and kiss him.

But Ty dodged him with another musical laugh, shaking her long red hair out of her face.

"Here," she said, "take this." She handed him a bloodred flower with intricate petals. He wondered where it came from, whether she'd had it in her pocket. As she put it in his hand, their fingers touched and Chase felt a spark of electricity.

"I don't think I've ever seen anything like this," he said, turning it in his hand, which felt far too clumsy to be holding something so nice and fragile.

"Well, there are more where that came from," she said, laughing again, as Ali and Meg called to her from the car. She backed away from Chase, maintaining eye contact the whole time.

"Can I get your number?" Chase said at the last moment.

"You'll see me again soon," Ty responded. "I'm sure of it." She smiled. Her teeth were perfect.

She was perfect.

Chase got back into his station wagon, feeling like he was hypnotized. He fumbled with the keys as he watched the Lincoln drive away; by the time his car had sputtered to life, Ty's taillights had faded.

But he hadn't gone more than a hundred feet when he looked in the rearview mirror and slammed on the brakes. He could have sworn he'd seen the girls again, back there. And he could have *sworn* they were pouring gas *onto* the car. Like they were going to burn it.

Chase shook his head and quickly squeezed his eyes closed. When he looked again, the road behind him was empty and dark. *I'm overtired,* he thought. *I need to get my shit together.*

Chase gripped the wheel and pressed on the gas as snowflakes swirled in front of his windshield, faster and faster, until what lay ahead was all a white blur.

ACT TWO

Irreparable, or The After-Party

CHAPTER FIVE

Em woke the next morning with a start, her head filled with the hazy, dark images of a plotless nightmare. She opened and shut her eyes a few times, trying to shake a vague feeling of fear. Rolling over, she came face-to-face with Cordy, half buried beneath the mountain of pillows that Em slept between every night.

When she saw Cordy, her heart leaped as she remembered last night: Zach's knowing smile, his hand on her waist, his desire to hang out over vacation. Vacation, which started today. Gabby was leaving in just a few hours, and tomorrow was Christmas Eve.

Em would be on her own, free to spend time with Zach.

Except, she couldn't. Not after what he'd said last night—did he suspect how she felt? She couldn't let him know. Her head hurt thinking about it.

And then, faintly, from underneath the pillow, she heard

the phone ring. Gabby. Em knew that she had to answer it, but a part of her didn't want to. She let it ring twice more before picking the phone up gingerly and saying hello.

"Hey, babe," Gabby said brightly. "Hope I didn't wake you! We're leaving for the airport soon, and I wanted to say good-bye. Also, do you think I should bring that white bikini I bought last summer, or do you think that's weird for a family trip?"

"Why would it be weird?" Em sat up, trying to get into the conversation.

"Because it's so skimpy."

Em laughed. Gabby did have a truly endearing sense of innocence, of wanting to make people happy. And just like that came the surge of guilt, so strong it turned Em's stomach. Gabby was her best friend. What was she thinking?

"It's not so bad, I don't think. Wear it when you're at the beach without your parents."

"Okay. Totally. I'll only wear it when they go sightseeing or whatever," Gabby said, and then she sighed deeply. Em waited. Was Gabby about to say something about Zach? She wanted so badly to spill her heart, to analyze every move with Gabby the way they would have if this were any other crush. The silence made her chest hurt. She could feel her ears getting red, as they did whenever she lied. "Jeez, I'm hungover," Gabby finally said. "I feel totally brain-dead. Good thing I get to sit on a plane for seven hours tonight."

"Yeah, you were a little drunk last night," Em said, remembering the way Gabby had stumbled down the hall and into Zach's arms. He had morphed so quickly from flirtatious Zach to boyfriend Zach. "Did you throw up?"

"Ugh, yeah." Gabby groaned. "When I got home. Thank god I didn't do it in front of Zach. That's the last time I drink that punch, seriously. I woke up wearing all my clothes. I even had Zach's coat on! You didn't ever find mine last night, did you?"

"I ransacked the bedroom. It wasn't there. Are you sure you didn't put it in the closet?"

Gabby sighed. "No. I definitely threw it on the bed. Oh, well. Maybe someone took it by accident or something."

Em knew this was unlikely; Gabby's coat, with its rhinestone heart pin and hot-pink lining, was one of her trademarks. But she said, "Yeah. Probably. I'm sure it will turn up."

"Ugh. *Promise* me you won't let me drink like that anymore."

"Deal. No punch for you, lady."

"Okay. I gotta go finish getting my stuff together," Gabby said. "I'll miss you so much. If I meet a hot Spaniard, I'll totally send him your way. And seriously, I really can't wait to hang out when I get back," Gabby added out of the blue. "To really spend some quality time together, you know? Boston day and movies and a sleepover."

"Have fun, Gabs," Em said. "I'll miss you." As soon as she

said it, she realized how true it was. She never did anything without Gabby.

"Bye, Em. Remember to keep an eye on Zach while I'm away!"

Em swallowed down the fist in her throat. "Okay," she croaked out. *"À bientôt, escargot!"* Em started saying this after she spent three weeks studying French the summer after freshman year. It meant "see you soon, snail." It was ridiculous but she'd never been able to break the habit and now it had become their ritual for saying good-bye.

Gabby giggled. *"À bientôt, escargot!"*

Em hung up the phone shakily. She had a pit in her stomach the size of a bowling ball and spent the rest of the day watching old episodes of *Sex and the City* on her laptop. Every time the phone beeped, she jumped, but it was only Lauren asking if Em wanted to come bake Christmas cookies with her and Fiona, or JD lamenting about how lame his cousins were. No word from Zach.

With her parents both working overnight shifts to ensure they could have Christmas Eve and Christmas off, Em had the house to herself—a treat she usually enjoyed by making up dance routines in the living room or eating ice cream during marathon phone sessions with Gabby. But tonight the house just felt big and empty. Even bigger and emptier than it felt when her parents were home.

Until, just as she was falling asleep with Cosmopolitans and Manolo Blahniks running through her head, she got a text. From Zach.

What's on your x-mas list this year?

She couldn't help it; she got that tingly feeling all through her body again. She read his text three times quickly. Em was so tempted to write back, *You*, but she also didn't want to seem desperate. *A puppy!* she wrote finally, in a fit of silly squirming.

I'll be sure Santa gets the memo. Sleep tight!

Suddenly the world didn't feel so vast. Em clutched her phone to her beating heart, with the sudden urge to kick off her blankets and dance on the bed.

C u soon I hope, he wrote again, signing off with a smiley face. Em melted. She was right—Zach *did* want her as bad as she wanted him. At least there was one person in the world who thought that she was special. One person who really cared.

It was impossible, all of this. She knew that. Of course she did. But it didn't matter. This moment was all that mattered—that he was thinking about *her.*

She went to sleep that night clutching Cordy to her chest.

"Spring rolls may be the best invention known to man," Em said, taking a delicious, steamy, crunchy bite. "I think I like them more than Twizzlers. Even better than television."

"Big words, my friend." JD grinned at her from between mouthfuls of pork lo mein. "Big words."

A day after the text from Zach, she was still floating. Em's and JD's families had a tradition of getting together on the night before Christmas, ordering in massive amounts of Chinese food, drinking eggnog, and singing carols while decorating the Winters' tree. (The Founts usually decorated theirs weeks earlier—Mrs. Fount was one of those people who had a whole closet devoted solely to holiday decorations.) Sure, spring rolls and eggnog were a strange—and gastronomically dangerous—combination, but it was the only way Em knew how to get into the holiday spirit.

Once the tree was decorated, Em and JD retreated to the den to watch *Emmet Otter's Jug-Band Christmas* while JD's little sister, Melissa, went off to chat with all her new middle school friends, and the parents cleaned up and talked.

Em was settling into food-coma mode on the couch. JD—who'd come to the Winters' this evening dressed in what he kept referring to as a "smoking jacket" (a burgundy-colored velvet blazer that Em could not stop laughing at)—was juggling remotes and trying to turn down the volume on the TV. With his glasses sliding down his nose and his hair spiking up at various angles, he looked like a 1940s mad professor. Just as the opening credits started rolling, Em's phone blinked and buzzed.

"Ugh, who could that possibly be," she moaned, trying to kick the phone toward her hand. "Pass me my phone, Smokey?" But even as the words came out of her mouth, she realized that it could be Zach and she sprang to a sitting position.

"Wow, I didn't know you could move that fast after General Tso's," JD said, pumping his fist as he figured out which remote was connected to the sound system. Twangy banjoes played in the background as Em flipped open her phone. Sure enough, the screen notified her of one new message—from Zach.

What u up to? Wanna come help me hang lights?

Em blushed and her heart sped up to a hum. You don't text a girl on Christmas Eve unless you're *really* into her.

Furtively looking at JD, who was now wrapping an afghan around his legs and digging into the opposite end of the couch, she texted back: *Just chilling at home—be there in a few.* Her hands felt sweaty; her fingers slipped on the keys.

"I gotta go," Em said abruptly. She focused on looking as normal as possible. She felt bad for ditching JD. But it was Christmas Eve, and she was a friend helping a friend, nothing more.

"Whaaaa . . . ? You're that scared of the damn otters?" JD said, obviously thinking she was kidding. He let out a noise of protest as she got up from the couch and walked to the doorway that led into the kitchen. She addressed both her parents and JD at the same time.

"I have to go help Zach with something," she announced vaguely. "You know guys, they can't do a thing without their girlfriends around."

"Oh, is Gabby away?" Em's mom asked, even though Em knew she'd mentioned it at least twice. (And if she hadn't, Gabby certainly had.)

"Yeah—apparently Zach doesn't know how to hang lights." Em couldn't look at JD again; she didn't want to see his disappointment. She knew JD wasn't exactly Zach's biggest fan. In fact, JD didn't really like any of her friends. It was their only legitimate battle: He claimed they ignored him. Em accused him of being standoffish around anyone who regularly actually got invited to, and attended, parties.

"Are Zach's parents at home?" Em's mom asked.

"I don't know. Yes. Maybe. He didn't say. I'll be home in, like, an hour." Em was already bounding up the stairs, two at a time, pushing the guilt from her mind.

In her room she surveyed the clothes on the desk, and on the bed, and then made the conscious decision not to change out of her sweatpants and hoodie. After all, this was an innocent visit, right? But just before she turned out the lights, she went back to her dresser and leaned over to apply a bit of mascara and a touch of lip gloss.

On the drive to Zach's house, Em felt as though she could hardly breathe. She could feel those spring rolls roiling in her stomach. Despite the biting air, Em opened her window a crack, hoping that the fresh air would help clear her mind.

What was she doing?

Oh, nothing much. Just going to my best friend's boyfriend's house, late on Christmas Eve, under a ridiculous pretense.

Em rolled down the window a little more and took a deep breath—in through the nose, out through the mouth, like Gabby had taught her to do after taking a bunch of yoga classes. She pushed the thought of Gabby from her mind.

I'll only stay for a few minutes, she told herself, clenching the steering wheel as if to show the strength of her convictions. *There's nothing wrong with a little harmless flirtation. Everybody flirts. Gabby would flirt with an armchair if she could.* The roads were empty and clouds covered the moon. She had to switch on her brights, and still she could only drive at a crawl.

As soon as she pulled into the McCords' driveway, she saw Zach standing on his front walkway wearing thick Carhartt work trousers and a flannel shirt. He was surrounded by twinkling holiday lights. He turned and smiled as she got out of the car. A blast of snowy air went straight through her. Zach looked like a model.

"Hey, it's Santa's little helper," he called out, tossing her one end of a strand of colored bulbs. "Hook that over that branch by the fence, wouldja?"

Em did, then moved over to a shrub he'd already decorated

with lights. She hoped she looked as good in the holiday glow as Zach did. She'd read once in *Cosmo* that everyone looks good in candlelight, and Christmas decorations were kind of like candles.

"Now I see why you needed me," she said, adjusting the hastily strewn strings. "You're clearly not cut out for holiday house improvements."

"Hey, I think I did okay, considering I did it all myself," Zach replied. He put on a fake pout, and for a moment, the wind blew his hair over one of his eyes.

A shiver ran up Em's neck and she adjusted her peacoat. "Where's your family?" she asked.

"My mom and my stepdad went to some benefit at one of his lawyer friends' houses. Some guy who's helping them get the permits for the new mall or something. Meanwhile, I'm supposed to be staying home and cuddling up with my precalc book."

"I haven't been over there yet—to the new mall," Em said, silently kicking herself for sounding so boring.

"Whatever. My stepdad talks about it like it's the new Empire State Building or something." Zach kicked at the snow in front of him, his chin down but his eyes up, watching Em restring the lights. "I went over there one night to watch them work, and it just looks like a pretty normal mall to me."

"They work at night?"

"Overtime."

"It must be freezing!" The cold made Em's hands thick and numb. She could hardly string the lights; impossible to imagine constructing a whole building.

"Yeah, it's wicked cold." Zach looked up at a darkened window on the second floor of his house. "No wonder my brother went to his girlfriend's house for the holidays. She lives somewhere in California."

Em followed his gaze. "But there's no chance for a white Christmas in California," she said softly.

"Or for awkward, fake, depressing family dinners," Zach mumbled. Em could tell he was trying to keep his tone light, but his face looked pinched, as though the words had taken major effort.

"I know . . . I know the holidays must still be hard for you," Em said, hoping Zach wouldn't think she was overstepping her bounds. Zach's dad died suddenly during a golf game two years ago. Just *bam*, one minute he was teeing off, next minute he was on the ground with a heart that simply didn't want to work anymore. Zach never even got to say good-bye.

Em and Zach had never really talked about his dad's death before. Gabby said he hardly talked about it with her, and Em had never considered, until this very night, how weird it must have been for Zach to have his mother remarry so soon—especially now that Ben, Zach's older brother, was away at college.

Before she could think of anything else to say, he sidled up behind her, taking her hand. For a second, she thought he was only reaching for the lights, but he kept his hand on hers.

"I'm glad you came over, Em," he said, turning her toward him. Thoughts of Gabby flew out of her head. She felt like a girl spinning in a music box. Like she was floating.

"Zach, I . . ." She didn't finish her thought. She'd dreamed about this moment, envisioned it a hundred times. But now that it was here, it felt . . . wrong. Gabby was her best friend and Zach was Gabby's boyfriend and this was not how best friends and boyfriends were supposed to behave.

And then, like a kid, Zach was smiling again. "Hey! I almost forgot your Christmas present!" He dug into his pocket. "It's not wrapped. Sorry. But here."

It was an ornament—one shaped like a puppy. The puppy was wearing a Santa hat, all askew, and emerging paws-out from a half-wrapped box, with a bow around its neck. It was smaller than her palm, but Em could barely keep her fingers around it, she was so happy.

"See?" Zach backed away from her a bit, without breaking eye contact; Em knew she must be grinning like an idiot. "I listened. I'm like Santa Claus."

"Oh my god. A puppy! Just like I asked for. Zach, I—" She looked up to thank him, just as Zach pegged her with a snowball.

"Hey!" She laughed breathlessly.

"I don't want you to think I'm *too* nice," he said, packing another handful of snow as he spoke.

She reached down impulsively and made her own snowball, chucking it at him before taking off across the lawn. She tucked the ornament safely in her coat pocket as she ran. She threw her head back, enjoying the way the air and snow stung her face.

He followed after her. He was laughing too. "You think you're faster than me? I'm a running back, Winters!"

She darted around a pine tree, grabbing some snow off one of its wide branches. Without even bothering to pack it into a sphere, she threw the whole handful over her shoulder. She was laughing so hard her stomach hurt.

"Great aim!" Zach teased her. "I think one of those flakes landed on my shoe." He grabbed at her, and she took off around the side of the house, ducking behind a work shed. She heard Zach come barreling around the corner and skid to a halt, looking for her. She pegged him a few more times before he zeroed in on her location and came racing toward her, shaking his fist. She giggled and zigzagged back over toward the driveway.

And then he wasn't behind her. She slowed, and then came to a stop. The yard was still. She saw no movement anywhere—on the path that had taken them around the house, on the front porch, in the woods all around her.

"Zach?" she called out tentatively. She took a step backward and looked around, but everything was dark and motionless. It was like he had disappeared. "Zach? Okay. Not funny. Come out. You know I'm scared of the dark, right? You win."

Nothing. Except—was that a branch cracking off to her right? She whirled around. "Zach? Stop it! Come out!" She was laughing nervously now. The footsteps they'd made across the snowy lawn seemed to glow in the moonlight, and for a moment she thought she heard laughter from somewhere—not Zach, but a girl's high, silvery trilling. But no. It had to be the wind. "Zach?!"

Bam! He came hurtling out of nowhere—he must have gone around the other side of the house—and tackled her to the ground, making sure to slip a handful of snow down the back of her sweatshirt as he did. She squealed and wriggled as the icy wetness burned into her bare skin. Then they were on the ground, panting. Em was looking straight up at the stars.

"Giving up so soon?" Zach's voice was low. "I expected more from you, Em." She could smell his cologne—something musky and also fresh, like the smell of pine. They were so close that if she only rolled over . . .

"Oh, you ain't seen nothing yet," she said without even thinking about it. She cleared her throat, trying to create some distance between them by getting up and brushing snow from her soaking sweats.

"I bet I haven't." Little points of light were reflected in

Zach's eyes as he stared up at her. Em's stomach made a perfect revolution. Couldn't he tell what he was doing to her?

"Just wait, McCord," she said, punching him halfheartedly on the arm as he too got up. "I'm going home to build a snow catapult that will blow your mind." She started walking fast across the lawn.

And then, just as she was about to get into her car, he called out, "Thanks for coming over, Em. It was great to see you." She turned to respond, which barely gave her time to register the white ball that sailed through the air and hit her square in the ribs. Zach pumped his fist in the air mischievously. "Bull's-eye!"

In an instant, she was running back toward him. She was slamming into him. After another fraction of a second, a pause that felt like a whole, spinning eternity—time enough to choose, time enough to say no, time enough to step back, time enough to do everything she didn't do—she kissed him.

As their bodies pressed together, she could feel his belt buckle through her peacoat, pressing against her stomach. He bit her bottom lip with the slightest pressure. She grabbed at the back of his neck. It was passionate, more so than any kiss she'd ever had.

Too soon, it was over. He pulled away, brushing her hair away from her eyes, then leaned forward and nibbled, once, on her ear. Em's whole body felt like it was on fire.

"Wow," he whispered in her ear, and then took a step

backward, watching her, his arms around her waist. Em laughed nervously, desperate to know what he was thinking.

"Yeah." She gulped. Em looked around, with the sudden conviction that someone was watching them. (Stupid, obviously: Who would be watching, on Zach's secluded property, at 9 p.m. on Christmas Eve?)

His thumbs made figure eights around the small of her back. And now all Em wanted was to curl up on his couch and talk and kiss. She wanted him to run his fingers through her hair. She wanted to tell him that she still kept Cordy on her bed, that she would always remember what he'd said to her that day at the carnival.

But Zach stepped away from her. "You've gotta go home now, little Christmas elf. My mom and Tim will be home any second, and . . ."

The disappointment was physical; a slamming cold wall. But Em tried to sound cheerful. "Yeah, okay. Yeah, of course." She was dying to ask him when they would see each other again, and what their kiss had meant, but she swallowed back the words.

"Hope Santa doesn't find out we've been naughty," he whispered. He took a step away, and Em felt herself, almost involuntarily, reaching out to grab his hand. This was about more than just a kiss. It was so much bigger. He looked at her.

"Have a good night," was all she could say. He squeezed

her hand, before dropping it. For a second she stood there in the soft glow of the holiday lights. Then she turned, and he watched as she got in her car and drove off.

On the way home, Em turned up the radio and sang along, full volume, to the oldies station. The same bowling ball was still sitting in her stomach, but now it felt like it was floating on a sea of whipped cream—still heavy, but surrounded by giddy sweetness. She and Zach had kissed. Zach had kissed her. The memory was looping in her mind.

"I think we're alone now," she sang-shouted.

And then her headlights lit up a figure standing by the side of the road. For a moment Em saw only the person's face in the mist, a gaping mouth, frozen in a scream. . . .

Startled, Em jerked the wheel to the left, then yanked it back in the other direction. She could feel the tires skidding back and forth, quivering uncertainly. Her car went lurching off the road as she desperately braked—too fast, too jerkily. She was on the rumble strip, and then in a shallow drift of snow. She felt the front passenger side collide with and crunch into a low stone guard wall, jolting her entire body forward so her chest nearly hit the steering wheel before her seat belt jerked her backward.

Then everything was silent, except for the radio still blaring: "There doesn't seem to be anyone a-rou-ound."

Shaking, she loosened her hands from the steering wheel, punched the radio dial to turn it off, and unbuckled her seat belt. She didn't think she was actually hurt, but her heart was pounding, and there was a faint trail of smoke rising from the hood of her car. She fumbled with her purse, got out her phone, and dialed Zach's number. She was still only a few miles from his house—he would come pick her up. No answer. She tried again, and it rang and rang. After one last attempt, she called JD.

"Em?"

As soon as she heard JD's voice, Em started crying.

"JD. I went off the road. On Rolling Hill, down by the stone wall? I don't know what to do." Her wailing filled the emptiness of the car, the stifling silence.

"Don't move. I'll come get you," JD said. "I'll be there in a few, okay? Just stay in the car and keep warm."

"Okay . . . okay," she sniveled and hung up, putting her head in her hands. Then she suddenly remembered: The figure. The girl. The one she'd seen in the dark, the vision that had made her swerve. Was there someone out there? Em opened the car door and called out into the darkness: "Hello?"

Carefully, she stepped out onto the road. Snow was starting to fall again, and unlike the flakes the other night, this snow meant business. It *would* be a white Christmas. She looked around, trying to remember just where she'd seen the woman, the figure, whatever it was. Then she saw something—

something dark, crumpled on the other side of the road. *Oh my god.* Her eyes started to water again, and she pulled her hood over her forehead, as though another layer would quiet her racing mind.

"Hello? Are you okay?" She moved closer; her breath caught in her chest. And then all the tension rushed out of her at once. It was a coat, lying there on the asphalt.

"Hello?" she called again as she walked over to pick it up. She looked around, terrified that she might stumble on the girl who owned the coat, lying prone somewhere in the snow. The girl couldn't have just disappeared.

But as she bent down to grab the coat, a curious feeling of dread spread through her. In her hands, the coat felt heavy. Then the hot-pink lining glinted up at her. And there, pinned to the breast of the BCBG coat, was a heart-shaped rhinestone pin.

"What the . . . ?" She breathed out.

She had found Gabby's coat after all.

Em spun in a full circle, as though she might find some explanation in the dark trees, the swirling mist, and the empty road. The coincidence was too much.

She walked back over to her car, holding the coat gingerly in front of her as though it were alive. When she got to the open door, she tossed the coat in first, over toward the passenger side, not caring that it landed on the floor. The last thing she wanted to be staring at was Gabby's favorite coat. And then, as she sat down to wait for JD, she felt something beneath her, stabbing her leg. She pulled back.

Resting on the black leather was a beautiful red orchid, more intricate than any flower she'd seen. Certainly nothing that was in season in Maine right now. Its petals looked like pieces of sugared icing. Its color was the deep, dark red of fresh blood.

Em plucked it from the seat between her thumb and pointer finger, twirling it in her hand. Zach must have left it for her—maybe when he went missing for those few minutes? But why didn't she notice it when she got in the car before?

Em shook the doubts from her mind. Zach had left it for her, as part of her present. He must have. And yet, looking at this . . . thing, she couldn't shake the sensation of being creeped out, and she was careful to zip up her bag tightly when she'd tucked the flower into its depths, as though it might reach out and swallow her.

CHAPTER SIX

Chase knew he had to find Ty, but he had no idea where to look. He'd never seen her or her cousins before, and they'd given no indication of where they'd come from or where they were going. Still, Ty had said she was sure they would run into each other again soon, so she had to be around somewhere. Chase wasn't going to wait for fate to intervene again—he was taking matters into his own hands.

On Saturday, he scoured the old mall, dodging last-minute Christmas shoppers and exploring stores he'd otherwise avoid like the plague, hoping to catch a glimpse of Ty's wild red hair or to hear her tinkling laugh. Later that night, he drove by Fitzroy's and down Ascension's strip of chain restaurants, scanning the parking lots for the maroon Lincoln.

He couldn't let her slip away. He needed to see her. It

was an ache in his muscles, an itch in his skin, a desperate, drumming feeling in his blood. For the first time in years, he thought of one of the last times he'd seen his dad. It was after a two-week-long binge. He was carted home by the cops. Chase watched his father slink inside: skinny, stinking, half dead. When he woke up, the first thing he'd demanded was a drink.

"I need it," he'd said, looking up at Chase with eyes full of desperation. Chase had backed away, revolted.

Weirdly, Chase now understood what his dad meant. What that need felt like.

After driving by the grocery store for the second time, he stopped at Dunkin' Donuts for a coffee and to collect his thoughts. Where would a mysterious, beautiful woman spend the day before Christmas? He drove to the downtown plaza that held a nail salon, a hairdresser, a Reel Time movie theater, and Pete's Pizza. He took a deep breath and walked into the nail salon, craning his neck to see who was sitting at each station. No luck.

A surly woman at the counter sized him up and asked, "You need a manicure, handsome?"

"No, I was just looking for someone," Chase said, turning and walking out of the store. This was ridiculous. There was no way he was going to find Ty. But still the need was there, stronger than ever. A need he couldn't explain. It was stronger than any crush he'd ever had. She was unlike any other girl, and he couldn't shake her from his mind. She haunted him.

"Hey, Singer—getting your nails done for Christmas?" Chase turned to see Andy Barton, Sean Wagner, and Nick Toll, fellow juniors on the football team, walking toward him. Chase noticed the place was called Princess Nails. Perfect.

"No, assholes. Just looking for . . . my mom," Chase said.

"She got a job here now? Upgrade!" Andy laughed. Chase did not.

"Too bad you never upgraded from sitting on the bench, Barton," he said, thrusting out his chest ever so slightly. The others snickered. "I gotta go. See you guys later," Chase said, already walking toward the station wagon.

He could hear the boys still laughing as he got into his car, but just before he closed the door, he heard Sean call out, "Merry Christmas, princess!" He rolled his eyes and gave them the finger as he drove away.

Chase woke late the next day and read a note on the counter from his mom.

Merry Christmas, sweetie! Sorry I had to work today, but you know I can't resist the overtime! Don't touch your presents until tomorrow, like we agreed, okay? We'll have a special Day-After-Christmas celebration. Xoxo, Mom. PS—here's some cash for Chinese food.

Chase stared at the thirty dollars and felt guilty. For as long as he could remember, his mom had worked shitty hours at shitty jobs. He knew it was all for him—so that he could go to school and play football and not worry about getting a part-time job. But thirty dollars was too much for Chinese food—it was like she was trying to prove something to him. It was just depressing.

The afternoon moved slowly. There was nothing on the three channels that came in on the trailer's tiny TV, and Chase didn't want to go out and risk being seen alone on Christmas Day. He avoided the computer.

It was hot in the trailer, so he wore just sweats. He stared at his chest in the mirror for a minute, to see if all the working out he'd been doing this fall was getting him anywhere. Then he did a hundred push-ups on the cluttered living room floor. Finally, he was so desperate for entertainment that he flopped onto his bed with *Macbeth*, which had been assigned as winter break reading.

When shall we three meet again?

Good question, Chase thought.

In thunder, lightning, or in rain?

And then, out of nowhere, there was a knock on the door. Chase jumped a bit, surprised that anyone would be visiting on Christmas. He bet it was their neighbor Mrs. Simpson, who asked for Chase's help every time her pilot light went out.

"Coming," Chase called out, tossing *Macbeth* to the ground.

When he opened the door, Ty was standing on the trailer's sagging stoop, smiling and holding a steaming Styrofoam cup. She was wearing a dress the color of the snow, which made her brilliant hair stand out like blood against the landscape.

"Merry Christmas," she said. "Look! I come bearing gifts. Like one of the wise men." She held out the cup.

Chase was so surprised, he couldn't move or speak. Ty giggled. "Go ahead, take it. It's hot chocolate." She winked at him. "Promise I didn't even spike it."

"Um, hi. I mean, thanks," Chase managed finally. Their fingers touched as he took the cup, and a small electric shock went through him.

"Can I come in?" She didn't wait for him to answer. She breezed past him, into the tiny living room. Chase cringed, seeing it all through her eyes: the lumpy presents underneath the fake tree, the peeling linoleum floor, the tacky "family portrait" of him and his mom hanging over the secondhand couch.

But Ty didn't seem to mind. She wasn't looking around, judging it—she was watching him, waiting for him to say something. She seemed to be radiating light, light that made the cramped space seem bigger, cleaner, and less embarrassing.

"I, uh, wasn't expecting anyone," Chase said, motioning to his sweats and bare chest. He'd been sweating all morning, and now this. . . . Well, at least Ty got to see his pecs. Although, unlike other girls, she didn't seem to notice or care.

"Oh, that's fine," Ty said. "I know it's weird for me to come by on Christmas, but . . . I don't really celebrate it. Doesn't look like you're celebrating too much either." It might have sounded like an insult from someone else; but in that moment, Chase just felt Ty understood him.

"Anyway," she breezed on, "I've been tracking you down ever since you helped me and my cousins with our car. I wanted to properly thank you."

Chase must have been staring at her like a gaping idiot because she added, "I want to take you out."

He couldn't believe it. Ty was doing all the work for him. It was the best Christmas present he could have asked for. All he had to say was *yes*. And he did—practically falling over himself in the process. "Um, sure. I think I'm probably free," he stuttered, looking around the trailer. "I mean, yeah, I'm totally free. So, yeah."

Any game that he'd ever had was gone. In a strange way, he kind of liked it.

Chase darted into his bedroom and changed as quickly as he could, flustered as he struggled with his inside-out jeans, smacking a fist against the wall when he realized he had no freshly steamed shirts. He tried to brainstorm conversational topics that would interest Ty; his gaze fell on *Macbeth*, and he wished he'd read more of it.

As they left the trailer, Chase looked around for Ty's car.

"I walked here, actually," she said as if it was no big deal. No big deal that she'd trekked through the freezing air and six-inch snow to the trailer park on the outskirts of Ascension.

She looked at him sideways. "I hope you don't think I'm stalking you or something."

Chase had to stop himself from saying he wouldn't mind it. "How did you find my house?" he asked.

"I have my ways," she replied coyly, winking at him. His stomach was filled with warmth. "I know my way around here."

"Oh, really? How?"

"My family used to live here . . ." She trailed off vaguely.

"In Ascension? That's cool. What brings you back to the area?"

"I'm taking a year off before I start college," she said, turning to him and offering a wide smile. Her lips were so perfect. "I wanted to come back and see how the place had changed. It's kind of like . . . an extended road trip, for me and my cousins."

"That sounds awesome." Chase tried to play it cool. So she *was* older. "Your cousins—what are they up to tonight?"

"They're coming with us," Ty said with a girlish clap, like it should be obvious. "They're at the Wash-N-Fold down by the drive-in movie theater," Ty told him. "I was hoping we could take your car and pick them up?"

Chase was momentarily disappointed that he wouldn't have Ty all to himself, but two more hot companions wouldn't be too hard to deal with.

When they pulled up at the dingy laundry center a few minutes later, the other girls were sitting on a bench outside: Meg with her wavy, wheat-colored hair, tiny features, and signature scarlet ribbon tied oddly around her neck; Ali with her striking blond hair and Scarlett Johansson body. They were both in tiny dresses, as though they were having an impromptu summer picnic. Maybe they were from Alaska or something, and the Maine winter seemed warm. They slid into the station wagon, greeting Chase as if they were old friends. Chase hoped that meant Ty had been talking about him.

In the backseat, Ali shoved aside a pile of Chase's school books and papers to make room for her giant purse. An English paper fell out of the stack, and Ali picked it up.

"Ooooh, e. e. cummings . . . he's one of your favorites, right, Ty?"

Ty turned halfway around, so that Chase and Ali could both see her face. She seemed electrified by the mention of the poet, who, truth be told, Chase had thought was kind of lame. Why didn't he have to use correct grammar and punctuation like everyone else? If Chase turned in an English paper with no capital letters, he'd get a failing grade.

"I love him. 'Nobody, not even the rain, has such small

hands,'" she recited. "I would die to have a poem written about me."

"That guy from *Bowdoin* gave you a book of his poetry, right?" Meg said in a teasing voice. Chase grimaced. Some other dude was giving Ty poetry.

Ty nodded and shrugged. At least she didn't seem that into this guy, whoever he was.

"That was so romantic," Ali and Meg said, practically in unison. Ty nodded again, but didn't add anything else to the conversation. Chase made a mental note: *Ty loves poetry.*

"So, where are we going, ladies?" Chase silently thanked his mom for having filled up the gas tank.

"Benson's Bar," Ty said as her cousins in the backseat giggled and hooted.

"That place out on Route Twenty-Three?" Chase couldn't believe that a shitty biker bar was where they wanted to spend their evening, but they seemed set on it. Maybe it was the only bar that would be open on Christmas.

"Benson's is our little secret," Ty said, reaching over to squeeze his hand. Chase felt chills up and down his spine.

When they arrived the parking lot was full of Harleys and Suzukis. Chase braced himself to be harassed by the tough bikers. He was practically begging for a fight, a preppy boy walking around with three hot girls. But weirdly, instead of going in the front door, Ty, Ali, and Meg marched around to the back of the bar, where dim lights barely illuminated the snowy back-lot gravel. Chase looked around, but saw no one. The girls, meanwhile, sauntered up to a chalky black door, one that looked rusted shut but that sailed open at the slightest touch of Ty's fingers. A reddish glow fell onto them.

"We're going . . . in there?" Chase hoped he didn't sound as nervous as he felt.

"You're going to love it," Ty said, grabbing his hand and pulling him toward a pale-faced bouncer. This place had a bouncer? Chase could swear this club had never existed before. But the guy waved them by, and then Chase and Ty, with Ali and Meg behind them, were descending down velvet-covered stairs. The carpet felt mossy and spongy under Chase's feet, like he was about to be sucked into it. The last two steps turned around a corner, revealing a dark underground club full of bumping music, flashing lights, and jaw-droppingly beautiful people.

The air smelled sweet and thick, full of a red haze; Chase had the distinct impression of having entered another world. It was hot. Chase didn't know where to look—at that couple who seemed to be performing a circus act in the middle of the dance floor, or at the bare-chested bartender, covered in dark tattoos of snakes and ravens and feathered things. Where had these people come from? And on Christmas! They were definitely *not* from Ascension. He felt completely out of his element, in a good way. Chase wondered briefly if he had wandered into some kind of cult situation. He didn't even care. It was like being around Ty, but multiplied by ten. It was the coolest experience he'd ever had.

"You want a drink?" Ty leaned in close to his ear so that he could hear her above the music. Chase nodded, and she was off, instantly gobbled up by the crowd. Chase stepped forward to follow her into the red haze. *I would follow her anywhere,* he thought as the club's smoke enveloped him.

Knock-knock-knock.

"Chase, are you in there?"

He raised his head groggily from his pillow.

His mom's voice came from the other side of his locked door. "Chase? Good morning, sleepyhead. Come out and open presents. I made pancakes."

Chase looked left, right, down, and up. He was in his own bedroom. His head was pounding. He felt like he was emerging from the deepest dream of all time.

"Chase?" She knocked again.

"Yeah, Mom, I'm up. I'll be out in a few minutes."

"Hurry if you don't want a cold breakfast."

Chase rolled over and stared at the ceiling. What had happened last night? He remembered entering the bar through the hidden door; slowly, more memories came floating back to him. He remembered looking around while Ty got his drink.

He'd seen golden snakes inscribed on the vaulted ceilings; in the bathrooms, the faucets had been snake heads. He remembered dancing so close to Ty that her sweet-rain smell seemed implanted in his nostrils; he remembered getting totally turned on as he watched Ty and her cousins twisting and undulating together on the dance floor, shimmying in their little dresses. Or was that the snakes on the wall, which had been slithering and intertwining? The images got confused in his head.

He didn't remember driving home. He must have been wasted. Chase felt a shot of panic—how would he find Ty again? He swung his feet to the floor and walked to his dresser, hoping to find a scrap of paper with a phone number on it.

Then he saw himself the mirror: a ten-digit number was scrawled in red lipstick on his face. He felt heat creeping up his neck. He was thrilled he had Ty's number, but really, did she have to make him look like such a freak?

And then another memory went tumbling through his mind. How he had tried to kiss her in the smoky light. How Ty had touched his face and smiled, sending a chill down his spine as she whispered, "You'll just have to wait. I have plans for you, you know."

CHAPTER SEVEN

Em wandered through the aisles at Victoria's Secret, touching the lacy underwear and satin bras that hung around her in lilac, turquoise, and hot pink.

It was two days after Christmas, and her car was in the shop with a broken fender, so JD had driven her to the old mall. She was supposed to meet him for a movie in about an hour, but for now they had parted ways to redeem gift cards and shop on their own. She'd been sort of avoiding her other friends, like Fiona and Lauren. It was just too complicated after kissing Zach, and she didn't know how to act normal anymore.

She stopped and stared at a deep purple balconette bra covered in a fine layer of shimmery lace, with a matching thong. She'd never really owned anything like this—cheap cotton stuff from Target had done the job the few times that it had mattered. When she dated Alex Parson freshman year, he'd taken off her shirt, and the turquoise T-shirt bra she'd been wearing underneath hadn't really seemed to faze him one way or the other. Although last year, in a relatively steamy hookup session with Steve Sawyer, she'd stopped him from taking off her jeans, less out of chastity than because she was embarrassed by her plain white bikini briefs.

And it's not like she was planning to do anything more with Zach. . . . It was just that she was ready to finally own some real lingerie.

"Are you sure that's a good idea?" a female voice said.

Em whirled around to face a saleswoman who was looking at her intently—as though she knew Em's secret.

"Um, I don't know," Em said, knitting her brows nervously.

"It just looks a bit big for you, dearie," the woman said, pointing to the purple bra. "Let's get you measured."

Em let out a nervous laugh. Apparently she was even more paranoid than she'd thought. That realization, though, didn't stop her from purchasing the purple bra, matching underwear, and a pair of low-rise black lace boy shorts, then stuffing the whole Victoria's Secret bag into a deeper bag that held a J.Crew sweater and jeans.

JD was waiting patiently with two tickets for the latest apocalyptic natural-disaster film when she came trotting up a few minutes late. His bright yellow and black buffalo-plaid shirt made him look like a lumberjack bumblebee from afar.

"You didn't get anything else?" he asked, surveying her bags.

"Nope," Em said, happy that her hair was covering her ears. "Just window-shopped."

They walked up to the concession stand, where Em was not surprised to see Drea Feiffer looking as morose as usual. The only thing different about her getup today was that it was half covered by the dark-red employee vest she obviously hated. It didn't complement her skinny jeans, which she'd dyed an outrageous shade of purple, or high-top Converse, which were "laced" with enormous safety pins. Not one to bow to the system, however, Drea had adorned her vest with an enormous brooch that she apparently slept in—she was never seen without the silver pin, which was shaped like a giant snake wrapped around an open eye. It wasn't very flattering. Still, Em gave her a small smile. She felt bad for Drea. Rumor was that Drea had been visiting Sasha in the hospital every day. Drea had other friends besides Sasha—other goth types who hung out in the school parking lot—but Sasha had been her closest friend, as far as anyone knew. It must be terrible to see your best friend like that. She couldn't imagine if Gabby . . .

The guilt came, a pulsing shock. She couldn't even *think* about Gabby.

"Hey, Drea," JD said, as friendly with Drea as he was with anyone else. "How was your Christmas?"

Drea's eyes fluttered to Em and back to JD. "Hey. It was pretty rough. I didn't . . ." Drea's voice went up, like she was about to say something important. Em tried not to stare at the circles under her eyes. Drea's best friend had just tried to kill herself, and the poor girl had to sell Junior Mints all day. Em felt a momentary impulse to reach around the counter and hug her. But she'd probably think Em was crazy. Drea cleared her throat, and her dry tone came back. "Didn't have to wear this damn vest for a few days, at least."

"It's not that bad. It brings out the red in that snake eye there," he said, grinning, trying to lighten the mood. "Have you seen this movie?" He fanned the tickets out on the counter.

"Yeah. It's okay. Although, if I see one more disaster movie where the girl still looks hot at the end, I'm going to boycott modern cinema."

"One of those?" JD motioned to Em and said, "She hates that too."

"Yeah? Well, I guess we've got one thing in common, then." Drea reached for the popcorn bags. "What'll it be? Medium popcorn, Sno-Caps, Twizzlers, and two Sprites?"

"You got it," JD said.

As they walked away from Drea, he said in a low voice, "I just feel so bad for her, ya know? She and Sasha were really close."

Waiting for the movie to start, JD bit off both ends of a Twizzler and demonstrated—as he did every single time they saw a movie together—that Twizzlers could be used as straws. They bickered over whether or not to simply pour the Sno-Caps in with the popcorn (Em voted yes, JD voted no, Em won). Em leaned back and breathed in the stale movie-theater smell of old cushions, sticky soda, and buttered popcorn; this was the most relaxed she'd felt in almost a week. Sometimes she forgot how much she loved spending time with JD, who didn't expect anything from her, and who was totally himself. Now he was trying to use the Twizzler as some kind of kazoo. Sure, he could be kind of dorky, but he always made her laugh.

After the movie—which, as Drea had warned, featured totally unflustered and beautiful disaster victims—they walked to JD's car. Em looked toward the coffee shop that JD always referred to as the Crappuccino, a popular hangout, and was surprised to see Zach sauntering out the door. A bolt of electricity rushed through her. She was about to yell his name but stopped herself when she saw him hold the door open for some girl she'd never seen before—an older, pretty girl wearing jeans, heels, and an expensive-looking sweater. They were laughing together as they walked in the opposite direction.

"Were you about to say something?" JD asked.

"No, I . . ." Em trailed off, and JD followed her eyes.

"That guy is such a dirtbag. He's still with Gabby, right?"

"Of course he's still with Gabby." Em was surprised at how forceful she sounded. "That girl could be anyone—friend, cousin, *dentist*. Why do you have to assume it's something shady?"

JD was obviously taken aback by the strength of Em's reaction. He raised both hands defensively. "I don't. I was just guessing, based on how they were walking."

"Well, you have no idea, so maybe you shouldn't go around *hypothesizing*," she said.

"God, Winters. Sorry. Didn't mean to piss you off. Miss Touchy."

"Miss Touchy?"

"Okay." JD grinned. "That sounded less creepy in my head."

Em laughed, but the image of the pretty girl with Zach stuck in her mind as she and JD drove home in silence.

In her room later that evening, Em was organizing her photos and doing her best *not* to think about that girl at the Crappuccino when her phone buzzed, and she caught her breath—maybe it was Zach.

Nope. It was a text from Gabby.

Hey! Txts are expensive but I wanted to say hi and that I miss you! This bungalow is pimped out and I wish u were here to go in the Jacuzzi w/me!

Em felt a brief pang of guilt—but it turned quickly into annoyance. Her devoted best friend was texting her from across the ocean and Zach couldn't get in touch from across town? Impulsively, she dialed Zach's number.

Miracle of miracles, he picked up.

"Hey there," he said in a sexy low voice.

She vowed not to lose her resolve. With her voice shaking the tiniest bit, her thoughts spilled out: "Hi. Listen, I have to say some things. Ask some things. Like, what if this whole thing blows up in our faces? What are we *doing*?" She took a breath and listened, but Zach was silent. She barreled on. "What if Gabby finds out? And seriously, Zach, I don't mean to sound weird, but I saw you today outside the Crappu . . . the Cappuchinery—who the hell was that girl?"

For a second, Em thought Zach had hung up. But then he laughed.

"Someone's a little jealous, huh?" Em didn't respond. "Em, don't worry," Zach said, suddenly serious. "That was just a family friend. Her name's Amanda and her mom and my mom are friends. They're visiting, so I offered to take her out for coffee."

"Oh," Em said dumbly.

"She actually does charity organizing for her sorority, and she was giving me some advice about the Feast. It was really helpful. I'm a little in over my head, you know?" Every word that came out of Zach's mouth made Em feel like more of an idiot. Zach was stressed about the Football Feast—organizing it was a huge responsibility—and here she was, whining about another girl without even knowing the full story. Or really having the right to whine in the first place.

"And about Gabby . . . it's complicated, I know. But we'll figure it out. Why don't I come pick you up," he offered. "We can talk about all this in person. My parents aren't home. We can chill in front of the fire. . . ." He trailed off in a singsong voice.

"Okay," Em said. He was right, it was better to talk these things out in person. But in the back of her mind, she knew they weren't just going to talk. As she waited to hear his horn in the driveway, she changed into her new Victoria's Secret purchases.

Once she was in his car, she felt the same electricity she'd felt the other night. A power that seemed almost out-of-body. It was cold still, and the roads were crunchy with salt from the plows. The moon was big, but the night was cloudy—no stars.

"Get anything good for Christmas?" Zach asked as radio rap offered a staccato background to the drive.

"A few books, yeah," Em said, a bit relieved to be talking about normal stuff. "And a gift certificate to Anthropologie, which is amazing." But after that, they lapsed into charged silence.

Inside Zach's house, Em felt shy. She'd never been here without Gabby—except for one time last year, when Zach had a party but Gabby had strep throat and couldn't come. His stepdad, the real-estate guy, had a taste for modern furniture—black, streamlined stuff that was nice but wasn't very warm. Zach pressed a button to light the fireplace. Em sat on the floor, leaning on a big pillow, watching him move around the room. He poured them each a glass of wine from the bar by the window, then sat down on the plush rug next to her.

Em took a sip, tasting its syrup on her tongue. She wasn't exactly a wine expert, but this one was distinctly sweet.

"What kind of wine is this?"

Zach threw a glance back over to the bar. "The expensive kind."

Em smiled, not sure what to say next.

"So, let's talk. I'm sorry if I seem distracted. It's the Feast, and just the holidays in general. It's tough without my dad around." Zach was avoiding eye contact. Em wanted so badly to see him smile the way he had the other night.

"I understand. I just—I just think we should talk about the whole Gabby thing. How we're going to . . . handle it."

Zach nodded. "Yeah, you're right." He looked at her suddenly. "What do you want me to do?"

"What do *I* want you to do? I mean, what do *you* want to do?"

The corners of his mouth quirked up into a smile. "This." He leaned over and kissed her cheek, brushing his lips against the side of her face. Em shivered.

"Zach," she said, trying to sound sexy and serious at the same time. "I want that, too. But Gabby is my best friend. And she's your girlfriend. We can't just . . . do this. Not if you're still together."

"I'm sorry. You're right. I know what I need to do. Break up with her. But . . ." He rubbed the back of his neck like it ached.

Em took a deep breath and reached for his hand. She gave voice to her biggest fear, hoping that merely saying it aloud wouldn't make it come true. "Do you not want to? Do you think this is a mistake?"

He squeezed her fingers. "No. I . . . I don't know what to do, Em. I feel like I'm being pulled in all these different directions—by you, by Gabby, by my stepdad. . . . Do you know how many times he's reminded me that my future basically hinges on my admission to Yale?"

Em raised her eyebrows. "He said that?"

"Yeah. And he's freaking out about the Feast, too. And my math grade—he keeps threatening to pull me out of Ascension and send me to his old prep school if I don't pass precalculus. He's always saying I need to get whipped into shape, you know? It's just, like, exhausting. Like every single thing I do has to be perfect. You don't get it. Making mistakes is unacceptable."

She knew he was talking about school stuff and his stepdad, but his clipped tone sent a bigger message: Stop pressuring me.

For a moment they sat in silence. She wanted to say more. But at the same time, she didn't want to upset Zach. She tried to choke back all of the doubts and fears rising in her throat.

After a long minute, Zach bit his lip and smiled at her. She was relieved; it was as though some of the awful tension had been released.

"You look pretty," he murmured. And then he was kissing her lower lip, tugging at her hair. They were lying back on the big decorative pillows and she let herself be carried away by the warmth surging through her, by her sudden need. He wanted her so badly. She could feel it. Em forgot about their talk. They grabbed each other's necks and waists and shirts in the flickering light. She couldn't believe how romantic it was. His lips moved down her neck and onto her collarbone; then he raised her shirt and started kissing up from her belly button. In one tangled maneuver, her shirt was off.

"Beautiful," Zach breathed, pulling the straps of the purple bra off her shoulders. And Em *felt* beautiful.

They lay there, knees interlocked. His shirt was off now, her hair was coming undone, and she felt like she was melting into the rug, like she would never be able to move from this spot again. His lips were on her neck, then on her shoulders, on her arms—she was floating, burning.

For a second, Em stared over Zach's broad shoulders into the fire. The flames danced like they were being seduced by a snake charmer. As Zach brought his lips to hers again, she felt even more light-headed. She had never felt so many emotions swirling together before: giddiness and excitement, fear and sadness. She finally understood why people described love as being "swept away," because the old Em had been carried off somewhere. And in her place was this other person, this girl who knew what she wanted and didn't care about anything outside of this one moment.

He started to unbutton her jeans and she arched her back slightly. And then—horribly—she thought of Gabby and how excited her best friend was about V-Squared (her plan to lose her virginity to Zach on Valentine's Day this year). And it was like the bubble she'd been floating in had burst.

"Not yet, Zach," she said, gently moving his hand away.

"But we both want it," he said, touching her face softly. His eyes were lonely. Sad. This was not the Zach McCord Em knew from the basketball court or earth science or late night at Pete's Pizza. This Zach was ten times more intense—and he wanted *her.*

Em's brain swam with images of Gabby, Zach, and the pretty girl she'd seen with Zach earlier that day. And just then, they both heard the front door open and a sharp intake of breath.

When Em scrambled to face the foyer, her world came crashing down. *Oh my god oh my god oh my god. No.*

Chase.

CHAPTER EIGHT

If he'd been in more of a carefree mood, if he hadn't been thinking nonstop about Ty and that night below Benson's, Chase might have laughed. He never would have pegged Emily Winters for a boyfriend stealer.

But he had other things to consider than Emily's out-of-the-blue choices.

He had come to Zach's house to try and unwind. He was thinking they could talk football, maybe shoot some pool on Zach's stepdad's new table—anything to take his mind off his date with Ty. This morning he'd actually used the number that had been scrawled across his face, and she'd asked him to come pick her up on a bench in the middle of downtown after ten o'clock tonight. He'd been so nervous dialing her number that the cell phone had slipped out of his hand twice. He never called girls. He texted; he met them at parties; he stopped by their houses after practice. He hadn't asked a girl out—like for *real*, on a date—since seventh grade. Sasha Bowlder. This was during the phase when she was too cool for him, when he'd tried to get her to speak to him again. And he still cringed when he thought about how that had turned out. He could still remember every detail of the conversation—the blinding sun, the group of Sasha's friends watching from the picnic tables, giggling behind cupped palms—all the words etched into his memory like glass marked up by razor blades.

"Um . . . so, I like you."

"Oh."

"I know we don't talk much anymore, but I'd like to change that." His heart drumming in his chest, mouth dry. "Do you want to go out with me?"

She turns to see if her friends are watching.

"Are you kidding? I would never go out with you. We might kiss, and I do not kiss trailer trash. I hear they all taste like garbage."

The words still made him furious. He was not trailer trash. Ty didn't think he was trash. He wasn't going to mess this one up. He wouldn't let Ty slip through his fingers.

Zach would help him. He'd help Chase relax, and he might offer a few pieces of advice. If nothing else, Zach knew about girls. He knew a lot about girls, in fact.

Zach did a great job of acting like Ascension's faultless hero, but Chase knew a slightly different side of him. Namely, Chase knew about Zach's so-called college tours and the copious sexual knowledge he'd acquired as a result. College girls were a whole other ball game, he'd told Chase.

But Chase could see that now was not the time to be asking Zach for hookup pointers. Emily's face had transformed like a slow-motion replay from confusion to horror as soon as she'd seen him. She was frantic, covering her bare chest with a pillow while she ransacked the couch, looking for her bra, with the other.

"This isn't what you think," she was babbling. "Please don't say anything. Please don't. Gabby—Gabby will kill me. Gabby will die. Please don't—where *is* it?—please don't say anything. Chase, I—Gabby, I don't want to hurt her. I didn't want to—"

"Don't worry, Em. Chase won't say anything." Zach stared at Chase, hard, and Chase didn't like the expression he saw flickering there. It was not a threat, exactly, but something close to it.

Chase immediately regretted coming over. Not only did he have no interest in being involved in this soap opera, but Zach's tone was a reminder of one of the less pleasant features of their friendship: the tallying up of who owed who what.

There was no way Chase would ask for advice now.

Em was still frantically searching the couch cushions.

"Looking for this?" Chase spied the purple bra, which

had somehow landed below the coffee table. He bent over and scooped it up, holding it between two fingers.

"Oh god. Chase—please—I didn't mean—Zach and I just—it wasn't supposed to happen." She stayed where she was, covering herself up, the fireplace creating strange shadows on all their faces.

Chase rolled his eyes. "Maybe you should have thought about all that before taking this off," he said, tossing the bra in her direction. She grabbed for it, and turned to the corner to get dressed. Emily was acting as though Chase had never seen a half-naked girl before. He stood there watching the scene with a combination of amusement and confusion. Zach stood up and pulled on his shirt.

"What's up, dude? Did we have plans?" Zach tried to adopt a casual tone. He might have been speaking a little louder than usual—trying to drown out Em's sniffles.

"No, I, uh . . . I thought you might want to hang out or something. Didn't realize you had company."

"Chase," Emily said, fully dressed and staring at him. She was pale. Chase had never seen her look so shaken. "Please."

She turned and walked out of the room without saying another word to either of them. Chase watched her go—and watched Zach let her go.

"Em, wait!" Zach made to follow her but stopped when he heard the front door slam. He turned to Chase. "Listen, I know

I don't even need to say this, but you've got my back, right? I just, I really don't want . . . you know. For Gabby's sake. This can't get out."

Even though nothing about this whole scenario could surprise Chase, the look on Zach's face right now—halfway to being already over it—made Chase feel sick to his stomach. This kind of thing never used to bother him. But now all he could do was nod in response.

"Hey," Zach said again. "I'd love to hang out, but I've got to take her home. She doesn't have a ride." He pushed past Chase on his way to the door. "We good?"

Suddenly, all Chase wanted was *out*. He was sick of always being the accomplice, the one who kept quiet. He knew he owed Zach everything. He would have nothing at AHS if it weren't for him. And yet, it was starting to feel like a debt he could no longer afford to keep paying.

"I'll take her home," Chase suddenly said, trying to keep the disgust out of his voice. "I'm sure you have more important stuff to do."

The first few minutes of the car ride were silent. Chase heard Emily sniffle some more, but he didn't think she was crying—come to think of it, the only time he'd ever seen Winters cry was in ninth grade English, when they'd been discussing *All Quiet on the Western Front* and she'd started talking about soldiers being resigned to sadness. Chase had to hand it to her—Em really knew what she was talking about, when it came to words at least.

Emily turned her face toward Chase and he could see that her cheeks were wet with tears. Her long hair hung in messy sections around her face, and she was curled into herself with one boot propped up on the dashboard.

"So. You okay and everything?" Chase asked.

Em sniffed and wiped her nose. "I just—I just need some time to figure out what to do about it. About . . . everything."

"I'm sure you will. Figure it out, I mean." Chase fidgeted, his seat belt feeling too tight. He didn't want to just ditch Em and run, but he still had to prepare for his date with Ty.

"So you're not going to tell anyone? About me and Zach and . . ." Em trailed off, staring at him with hope and confusion and embarrassment mingled on her face.

Chase sighed. "Yeah. Whatever. You're fine by me."

Em let out a huge sigh and slumped a little more in her seat. "Thank you, Chase. That's really . . . Thanks. I seriously owe you." Her head bobbed with determination. "Anything you need, I'll do it. Homework help, whatever."

"I don't think you can really give me the kind of help I need," Chase said, staring ahead through the windshield.

"Why? What do you mean?" Em asked. Now she was wiping off her face, trying to pull herself together.

Without intending to, Chase blurted out, "There's this girl."

"Someone I know?" Em was watching him, eyes wide.

He shook his head. Now that he had started talking, he might as well keep talking. Maybe Winters would have a feminine perspective or something. "She doesn't go to Ascension. She's . . . different. And I'm into her. A lot. But she's a little bit impossible. I don't—I can't really tell if she's into me." Chase tapped the wheel with his palm. He couldn't believe he was spilling his guts to Emily Winters, whose bra he'd been holding not twenty minutes ago.

But at least she had stopped crying.

"Do you—do you want me to talk to her for you?"

"No," he said firmly. "Definitely not. I don't know what I want. Just advice, I guess. I want to know how to get through to her."

Em sat up a little straighter. "Well, what does she like? What does she do for fun? Is she girly or a tomboy? What kind of stuff does she wear?"

Chase almost laughed. He was pretty certain, now, that Em Winters was entirely useless to him. "I have no idea what she likes to do for fun. She flits around with these crazy cousins—Ali and Meg, we all went out together one time—and she dates college guys. Like, dudes who read fricking e. e. cummings."

"e. e. cummings is a good poet," Em said reproachfully. "JD and I drove to see his grave in Boston once." She turned away, tracing a pattern on the window with her finger.

e. e. cummings is buried in Boston, Chase thought. He would have to remember that tidbit. He could mention it in front of Ty and impress her.

And then, suddenly, he had an idea.

"You're into poetry, aren't you, Winters? What was that poem you won a prize for? 'Inevitable'?"

"'Impossible,'" Em replied cautiously.

Chase pulled into Em's driveway and shifted toward her impulsively. "Can I have it?" Chase suddenly said.

"Have what?" Em asked, brushing her long, dark hair out of her eyes. "My poem?"

Chase nodded. Maybe this little car ride was going to turn out to be more helpful than he'd thought. "Yeah. That would be perfect. She would love it. It wasn't about a guy, right? It could be about anyone?"

"I—"

He could see Em hesitating.

"Give me the poem and I'll keep my mouth shut, I promise," Chase said. He hadn't meant it to sound so, well, threatening. But it was only fair. An eye for an eye, or whatever. "Deal?"

Em cleared her throat. Finally, she said, "Sure. Yeah. I'll email it to you."

Chase felt a surge of triumph. At last, something might go his way.

"Great. I'll be in touch," he said as she opened the car door. "And, hey—Winters," he said, right before she slammed it shut. "It's okay. Everybody makes mistakes."

Later that night, Chase drove straight to the bench where Ty would be waiting. It was just outside the candy store where Ascension's middle school students congregated after school on Friday afternoons. As he pulled up, Chase shoved aside a memory of himself and Sasha, fourth-grade science lab partners, going to pick out gummy worms and root-beer barrels to see how they would react to being immersed in first vinegar, then soda, and finally milk.

When he arrived, Ty was sitting there smiling, surrounded by the glow of a streetlight, with a book in her lap. The street was otherwise deserted. As he got out of his car, the silence and stillness of the night made him a little uneasy.

"Hey there," she said, not getting up. She looked like a bohemian princess, with her red hair piled high on top of her head and a velvet cloak wrapped around her shoulders. For someone who used to live in Ascension, she didn't seem to have a great grasp of the New England town's climate—beneath the cloak, which was falling off one shoulder, Ty wore a short dress and ankle boots. "Want to sit here for a minute with me?" She tapped the bench next to her. Chase looked up at the starless sky. Snow was predicted and the night was cold. He'd been envisioning a shared cup of hot chocolate at the twenty-four-hour diner one town over, then—finally—a steamy kiss in his car. But he didn't want to disappoint Ty, who looked at him expectantly, as though sitting on a bench at ten o'clock at night in 20-degree weather was just, you know, normal.

"Have a sip of this," she said, pulling an ornate glass bottle from her purse. "It's this crazy Eastern European stuff I got from a friend. It'll keep you warm."

Chase grabbed the bottle as he sat down beside her, and raised it to his mouth. The alcohol tasted like Ty smelled—earthy, sweet, thick, foreign. She watched him take a sip.

"It kind of makes everything glow," she said gleefully. "From the inside out."

He had to agree. He didn't know if it was the booze or Ty's influence or the first symptoms of hypothermia, but everything he looked at—the black fringe of trees by McKeane Park, coated with frost; the snow-spotted street; the dark windowpanes—all seemed to be somehow fluid, boundaries blurring, buildings pouring into one another.

"I've never just *sat* here at this time of night," he said. "It seems so much . . . older. Calmer. Does that make sense?"

Ty smiled. "The buildings, the streets, the town speak for

themselves at night, don't they?" she said. "You can really *feel* the place."

"It's not, like, clogged up with people's bullshit." Chase hoped he didn't sound dumb.

"So true." Ty was looking at him with big eyes and a gentle smile. Then she stood up.

"Let's explore," she said. "It's been *so* long since I've been back!" Chase tried to remember what she'd said about living in Ascension—that she'd moved away ages ago. He wondered what she was doing back here, of all places, but something about her carefree attitude made him keep his questions to himself.

Instead, he tried to take charge. Like he was used to.

"Hey, if you're into exploring, wanna see something cool?" He grabbed her hand and led her down the street, toward the park. The traffic lights were all on late-night, blinking mode. There were no cars on the road.

"It's like a ghost town!" Ty shouted into the night air.

He stopped in front of Ascension Town Hall, where all the windows were darkened.

"Are we getting married?" Ty giggled as she asked the question. "I think it's after business hours."

He didn't answer. Instead, he pushed open a gate at the side of the building. "This way." There was a brick path that led around a corner, opening up into a small courtyard behind

Town Hall. "This is public property," he said, "but no one knows about it. I found it once, just wandering. Sometimes I come here—to think."

"Whoa," she breathed, taking in the silent, snow-covered patio. It wasn't much, but he had to admit that in this light, it looked magical.

"I bet there are even people who work at Town Hall who never hang out in this spot," he scoffed, proud to show her something new.

She twirled around, giving a loud whoop that echoed between the walls. "A secret garden!"

He whooped too, as much for the sound as to release the strange giddiness he felt.

"Where does this path go?" Ty pointed toward another gated walkway backing the far corner of the courtyard.

"Back out toward the middle school," Chase answered. "Over near Rambling Brook."

"Oooh—let's go see if the water's frozen," she said. It was hard to deny her excitement.

She skipped ahead of him, turning around to beckon him every few steps, until they reached the Rambling Brook Bridge, which crossed over the small river that bisected downtown. Ty stopped and peered over the edge. Her hair fell out of its loose bun, and now its long, silky, shock-red strands were blowing all around her face.

"Doesn't the breeze feel amazing?" she shouted. Chase shivered, trying to see what she saw, feel what she felt. But it was a freezing winter night—and the "breeze" had a piercing chill to it.

"Hey, be careful there," he said, trying not to sound tense as he lightly touched her bare, pale arm. As always, when he touched her, a zing of electricity went through his fingers.

"Don't worry," she said, still staring down at the dark, thin stream below them. "The drop isn't bad." It was true. The river was only about fifteen feet below them. But Chase felt a pang in his stomach. It was a different bridge, a different night, a different girl, but he found himself imagining Sasha's fall. Sasha climbing the overpass railing. Sasha looking down below her. Sasha thinking about the drop. Not just the physical fall, but the end of things—how everything you have can disappear in a moment.

Chase felt a spasm in his chest. He had been happy when she was miserable. He had felt vindicated. He had thought, *People get what they deserve.*

Now, thinking of Sasha's last moments, he just felt sick.

"Let's keep going," Chase said, giving Ty a gentle nudge with his hip. In front of them, a streetlight illuminated the first few flakes of snow. They were falling fast.

Instead of moving forward, though, Ty gripped the railing tighter. And then, like a cat, she maneuvered herself from the ground onto the bridge's low, wide railing, her long legs looking graceful as she balanced on the rail, slowly letting go and standing up.

"Hey! Seriously!" Chase shouted, not bothering to control his voice anymore. He didn't want to grab her and cause her to lose her balance, but he couldn't just stand there and watch her get hurt.

She smiled and lifted her arms like a dancer. "I bet I could do a dance up here," she said, pointing her right toe.

"Ty, please get down," Chase said, his urgency increasing. "It's not safe. It's slippery."

Ty twirled to face the river—a quick, tight motion, with her little cape flaring out around her—and then turned to face him again. She looked beautiful, crazy, almost translucent. She pointed her other foot. He blinked snow out of his eyes.

"Ty, please," Chase said again. "You really should get down. A girl almost died like this last week. On a bridge, I mean. Off a bridge."

He couldn't tell if Ty could hear him.

"I'm fine, silly," she said, sticking her right leg out behind her and balancing ballerina-style. "Why don't you get up here with me?"

"Ty, really, please . . ." Chase stretched his hands toward her, as though he could pluck her off the railing.

"Aw. You are such a scaredy-cat," she said, jumping like a

gazelle so that she was just out of his reach but still standing on the railing.

"Okay, you're right, I am. I'm freaking scared. Now will you *please* just get down from there?" Chase could hear the pleading in his voice, on the verge of panic.

"Will you ask me nicely?" She lifted her arms above her head and pirouetted. Her boots clanged against the metal railing, and he felt his heart stutter with terror.

"What—? I *am* asking you nicely. I'm begging you to—"

She cut him off. "Beg me for real," she said. Her smile looked wild.

"Please, Ty." He could barely breathe.

She just shook her head and tossed her hair mischievously. "Uh-uh," she singsonged. "On your knees."

Without thinking about it, he did as she asked, his hands clasped in front of his face. "I'm begging you to get down." *Please don't start crying.* He would *not* cry in front of her. His eyes stung. He saw a flash of light in his peripheral vision, as though a car had passed, but the street behind them was empty.

And then, with a soft leap, she was beside him, pulling him off the ground. His knees were wet from the snow.

Chase let out a huge breath, making a cloud in the frigid air in front of his face. "What the hell was that about?" he demanded.

Ty wrinkled her eyebrows. "Don't be mad! I was just having fun," she said, smiling.

"I'm serious, Ty. I told you a girl practically died that way, and it's like you didn't even hear me or you didn't care." Chase couldn't help it—he was furious still. He didn't want to be out here with her anymore. He was getting a creepy feeling about the whole thing.

"Chase, Chase," she said, more softly now. "Don't you know we all die sometime?"

"What?" He stood there stiffly, staring at her, feeling like the entire evening had been ruined.

"Never mind," she said. Then she grabbed his face with both hands and leaned in close. "I'm so sorry I scared you," she whispered. There was something in her shining eyes that made him believe her. And when she took his hand in her own small palm, he felt a wave of relief wash over him. More than relief, really; it was like he'd had another gulp of that European liquor she carried around—he felt warm and numb. It was all going to be okay.

As they continued their walk, they rounded a corner and found themselves looking at the middle school athletic fields, covered in clean, unbroken snow that unrolled before them like a sheet of blank paper. As they walked into the expanse, they looked behind them to see their footprints, lonely and stark, creating patterns in the crystalline whiteness. Ty's footprints seemed to disappear into the snow much faster, melting away almost entirely.

"Let's make snow angels," Chase said. He hadn't done that since he was a kid.

"Snow what?"

"Snow angels. You know."

Ty shook her head.

"You've never made a snow angel?" Chase laughed. "Maybe there *is* something I can teach you!" He turned and fell into the white fluff, flapping his arms and feet and not caring what he looked like. Not even caring—well, not *too* much—that the new navy peacoat his mother had bought him for Christmas was getting damp from the snow. He gingerly stood up and stepped out of his imprint.

"See? There's the head, and there are the wings," he said, taking Ty's hand and pointing at his creation. She smiled wider than Chase had ever seen, showing off those mind-bendingly perfect teeth, then turned, dropped, and made an angel of her own. She stood up, giggling.

"I did it!" She pointed. Then they peppered the field with angels until they were soaked. As Chase watched Ty run around the field, catching snowflakes and rolling in the snow, he remembered what it was like to be a kid, before things like money and popularity and sports stats and girlfriends mattered. Then he spread his arms wide and let himself sink backward in the snow. The stars winked and flashed above him.

Then she appeared in his vision, standing over his feet, blotting out a piece of the sky. He put out his hands for her to help him up. And as he stood, they were half embracing. He was shivering so badly, he had trouble keeping his teeth from chattering. She had to be freezing. Her cloak was matted with snow.

"Want my coat?" He started to take it off.

"It won't help much," she said, pointing to its dripping collar.

"Let's go to my car." Chase reached for her hand and was surprised to feel it was warm.

They ran back through the streets, breathless and laughing. In the station wagon, the heat took years to sputter to life; they sat huddled close in the front seat, Chase rubbing his hands together with Ty's, though hers felt warmer than his. Chase's heart was thumping in his chest. He was sure that she would hear it.

"Where to?" He prayed she wouldn't ask him to take her home. He wanted to stay with her forever.

"I want to know what it's like to be Chase Singer. Let's go back to your place." She smiled and twirled a piece of damp hair around her pointer finger.

"You got it, beautiful."

As before, having her bright, glowing presence in the tiny space made his home seem less dreary and cramped than usual.

"Want some hot chocolate? I'll make it for you the way my

mom used to make it for me," he said, already assembling the ingredients on the counter. She smiled, then stood behind him at the clunky little stove as he warmed the milk in a small pot, added the cocoa, then mixed in a dash of cinnamon, a dash of cayenne pepper, and a dollop of honey.

"Sweet and spicy, huh?" She leaned into her mug, taking a deep breath.

"That's the secret," Chase said, leaning against the flimsy linoleum counter. Ty stood in front of him, both hands wrapped around her mug (in a tacky pink font, it read: *Over the hill and picking up speed*—a gift for his mom's fortieth birthday). Ty's cheeks were pink and she was looking up at him happily. This was it. She wanted him to kiss her.

Chase put his mug down and cleared his throat. Then, with his hands squeezing the edge of the counter behind him, he bent his head toward her. He could practically feel her soft lips on his.

But like a tape measure snapping back into its coil, Ty whipped away. She looked at him, stricken, and put down her mug.

"I can't—I can't stay," she said softly. In moments, her unfinished hot chocolate was on the table, her cloak was back on, and she was standing in the doorway nervously running her hand through her long, red hair. "I'm sorry. Good night." Then she stepped out the door.

"Wait, Ty!" Chase stepped out after her. "I'm sorry," he

said, shoving his bare feet into his damp, snowy boots. "I didn't mean to ruin everything."

But by the time he got to the trailer's front step, she was gone. He had no idea how she had disappeared so quickly and wondered if maybe she had hitched a ride, or if her cousins had been waiting outside for her.

He looked around. He could see the lights on in the Hendersons' trailer across the park, and the skeletons of trees in the distance. Otherwise, everything was just slushy gray-white. The whole trailer park felt cold, abandoned, like something wonderful had been snuffed out.

As Chase stood there, he felt that itch begin to work in his blood again, that drumming need. He was reminded once again of the night his father died—the silence that seemed to close in around him sometimes when he was alone. But the way he felt now—this emptiness—it was different. Worse, somehow. If he didn't see Ty again . . . well, he didn't know what would happen. He didn't know what he would do.

He *couldn't* lose her.

He stayed there, staring into the dark. He stayed there, thinking about how he hadn't even gotten the chance to ask her about the Ascension Football Feast—he'd wanted to, so badly, but he just hadn't found the right moment, the perfect way to say it. He stayed there, thinking about how beautiful she'd looked under the snowy streetlights, her skin translucent and glowing, even in the yellow-tinged hue of his crappy kitchen. He stood there remembering how close she'd stayed as he'd leaned over the stove.

She dazzled him.

And that's where he was, staring into the night, when he saw the bouncing glow of his mom's reflector vest. That meant it had to be around one in the morning already. Time had slipped away. Chase hadn't even realized his fingers were turning purple.

When his mom saw Chase, her expression clouded.

"Chase? What are you doing outside? Are you okay?" Her hair, graying at the temples, formed a frayed halo around her face.

Chase looked down at his feet.

"I don't know," he muttered, so softly the words seemed to dissolve into the cold.

"Oh, honey. Where's your new coat?"

"Inside." He shook his head, trying to organize his thoughts.

She patted his shoulder, squinting at him, concerned. "Let's go in. I'll make you something hot to eat, okay?"

He followed her numbly into the trailer. He wasn't hungry, but he didn't protest when his mom went to the stove and started making macaroni and cheese. Chase couldn't help but notice how the kitchen had gone back to its normal squalor. The trash smelled, the light flickered. He wondered if that was why Ty had run off so fast. If she'd been disgusted by him.

Restless, Chase grabbed his free weights from the floor underneath the sofa and started lifting. Like he always did when he needed to relieve a little stress, he figured he'd do a hundred reps. But after a hundred, it just wasn't enough. He kept lifting and lifting, feeling his muscles searing but unable to stop.

His mom came over and sat down with her bowl of mac and cheese and dug around the couch cushions for the TV remote. Sweat dripped off Chase's forehead but he kept on lifting.

"Chase, what's going on with you?" she asked, taking a large bite of the noodles.

"Mom! I'm *fine*."

Just then the power went out. As it did, movement at the window caught Chase's eye.

His heart stopped. There, staring at him, was Sasha Bowlder.

She was pressed up against the glass, like she used to do when she would sneak over and make funny faces at him through the window—but now her face was distorted, leering, grotesque.

Bang. The weights slipped from his hands, and without meaning to, he let out a cry.

The lights clicked back on.

The window was dark and empty.

CHAPTER NINE

Em toyed with her soggy cereal, then dropped the spoon onto the marble kitchen counter. She had slept terribly, imagining Gabby's reaction to the news of what had happened between her and Zach. She kept seeing Chase's expression when he'd walked in on them.

She'd gotten a couple of texts from Fiona and Lauren, saying they were planning a girl day (some post-Christmas sale shopping, pedicures, a couple of slices at Pete's), and asking if Em wanted to come. But Em couldn't think of anything more unbearable than spending an entire day with her friends—with *Gabby's* friends—thinking about Zach and unable to talk the whole thing through.

Em was certain that Zach was planning to break up with Gabby. He would do it gently, kindly. It would be hard. And they'd still have to keep their fling a secret for a while. But eventually—maybe next year—when Gabby saw how much she and Zach cared for each other, how undeniable their mutual attraction was, she would forgive Em. She'd have to. Gabby was her best friend, after all. She always understood.

Or was Em completely lying to herself? She tried to eat a bite of her now mushy Lucky Charms but could barely swallow them.

Em hated feeling like her fate was in someone else's hands. She knew she had to wait patiently for Zach to come clean. She knew she had to trust Chase not to say anything.

She sighed, pushed the cereal away, and pulled her laptop toward her. She had to send Chase her poem "Impossible." It had been their agreement.

She mused over the poem, rereading the first two lines:

> You enter my heart like a sudden chill—
> I don't know if it's right, but I know that it's real.

Of course, no one knew who the poem was about. Not Fiona and Lauren, who both came to the awards ceremony last year and cheered for Em. Not even Gabby. Gabby thought Em had made the whole thing up—that she was just *that* good a writer. She had no idea which boy Em truly longed for. Which boy was "impossible."

Just then a new email arrived in her in-box with a little *bing!*

She clicked over to it. There was a new message from an anonymous sender, with the strange subject line *Please, sir, can you spare some change?*

Emily clicked open the email and saw a grainy photo of Chase—snapped from an iPhone, clearly—on his knees on the Rambling Brook Bridge. The photo had been snapped from the side; Chase was shown in profile, in his jeans and peacoat. It almost looked like a picture you'd see in a catalog, of a man proposing to a woman. It could be a diamond ad. Except there was something off about it. Something desperate. Instead of kneeling on one knee, he was on both, right in the snow, clasping his hands together in a way that made it look like he was begging. There didn't seem to be anyone in front of him.

Emily scrolled down. The caption underneath the photo was a continuation of the subject: *Please, sir, can you spare some change? Times get even tougher for the trailer trash of America.* The photo had been sent to Ascension's entire junior class. Chase was going to freak out.

A worming feeling of discomfort began working in Em's stomach. She wasn't exactly in a mood to defend Chase, but still, the photo—and the fact that it had been so widely circulated—really bothered her. Weren't people allowed to have secrets anymore? You know, personal lives?

"People can be so bad," a low voice said suddenly, from behind her.

Em let out a scream, leaping off her stool and knocking it over as she spun around.

"Hey, hey, whoa. It's just me." JD caught her stool just before it clattered to the floor. "Jeez, Winters. Jumpy much?"

"You almost gave me a heart attack!" She swatted at him and took a deep breath, trying to calm her pounding heart.

"Sorry, M&M. I thought you'd hear me come in." He looked soft and crinkly, like he'd just woken up. He wasn't even wearing one of his usual ridiculous outfits—just a pair of old jeans and a dorky T-shirt with a tie drawn on it. "You got that too, huh?" JD pointed to the picture, which was open on Em's computer. She nodded, her heart still thumping fast.

"It's just so . . . screwed up," JD said, plopping onto the bar stool next to Em's. "And lame. I mean, who would do that?"

Emily could tell that JD was really worked up. He kept running his right hand through his hair, as he often did when upset. He looked very mad-professor-ish.

"I mean, I don't even *like* Chase Singer," JD continued. "But I still think it's fucked."

"You *shouldn't* like him," Em said, shifting on her stool to face him. "He made your life hell last year. Remember physics? When every time you answered a question, he'd cough and laugh and call you the Fountain of Nerdiness?"

JD blushed a tiny bit. "First of all, *Emerly*, I *am* kind of a Fountain of Nerdiness. And second of all, even if he'd called me a Fountain of Ugly Fat Smelly Dumb Booger-Eating Eternal Virgins I'd *still* think it was fucked. You know?"

Guilt knifed through Emily. JD was always so damn *good.*

"I agree. It's messed up." Emily closed the photo and tried to change the subject. "So what are you doing here? Aren't you supposed to be babysitting Melissa or something?"

"I'd rather babysit you," he said, leaning forward and moving a strand of tangled hair that was stuck to her cheek. "What are *you* up to? Want to watch a movie?" He beat his palms on the kitchen counter like a drum. His eyes were sparkling too. "What are you writing?"

Now that Chase's picture had been banished to the Internet ether, the poem "Impossible" sat open on Emily's screen.

"A girl has her secrets," she said, and quickly closed the laptop altogether. "So what? You just came over to harass me?" She elbowed JD. "I've got stuff to do."

"Oh, so sorry to interrupt," JD said, throwing his arms up in surrender. "I'm just here for some whole-wheat flour." When Em raised her eyebrows, JD continued, "Your mom told my mom she'd leave it out on the counter. My mom's involved in another classic bread-making experiment. And you *know* how much I love those yeasty, crustless creations."

"About as much as you love eating gravel?"

"Exactly. About as much as I would love to eat that nasty mush I can only assume was once cereal," he said, picking up

Em's bowl and dumping it down the sink. "Next time, just tell me when you're having a nine-one-one breakfast situation. I would have gotten *two* Egg McMuffins if I'd known things had gotten so dire over here."

Em laughed and grabbed the flour canister. As he reached for it, his hands briefly touched hers. He stood there awkwardly for a second, his hair still splayed in every direction.

"Em . . ."

"Yeah?" Unconsciously, she backed up ever so slightly. There was something weird about the way JD was looking at her.

"I—" For a second JD just stood there, staring at her with an expression she couldn't identify. Em's heart caught in her throat. She'd seen this look on television shows. She'd read it described in books. It was the look of someone who was about to confess serious feelings. Then JD's face suddenly snapped back to its normal, playful alertness, and he jerked his chin toward her bag, which she had dumped onto the kitchen table. "What's that?" He motioned to the red orchid, the one she had received from Zach.

"Oh, that?" Em shrugged and fiddled with the hem of her ratty sweatshirt—her dad's old Harvard Med School gear, which she'd been sleeping in since she was about twelve. And for a second, Em wanted to tell JD everything. The earring, the sign, the snowball, the kiss. Maybe he'd have some sage advice. He usually did. But then she looked up into his hazel eyes and knew she couldn't. Not when he was looking down at her like that—like she could never do anything wrong.

He wouldn't get it.

"Just something my mom picked up," she mumbled.

JD squinted at her. "You sure you're okay?"

"Fine," Em said. Her chest ached. "I have a lot of homework to get done before break is over."

"It's just . . . you seem a little on edge."

"I'm fine." Em tucked her hands into the too-long cuffs of the sweatshirt. "A little stressed is all."

"So I guess you don't have time today to hang out with a Fountain of Nerdiness," JD said, heading toward the door. "Or a Booger-Eating Eternal Virgin."

"Aw, JD, that's not true. Don't talk down about yourself," Em teased, following him into the hall as he started to leave. "I know you don't eat your own boogers."

He turned around in the front doorway, letting in a cold gust of wind. "But the Eternal Virgin part?"

Em laughed, twisting her hair into a bun on top of her head. "Well, that part remains to be seen."

Once JD left, Em returned to the kitchen. She fixed herself a cup of Calming Chamomile, just what she needed, and poured it into the mug Gabby had gotten her from Cabo last year. *Caliente!* it said in bright orange letters around the side of the cup. The note

Gabby had included with the gift had said, *For one of the hottest mamacitas I know*. Em still had the note; it was one of the mementos she had taped to the edge of her mirror upstairs.

Gabby would understand. She had to understand.

Em blew on the scalding tea, absentmindedly dunking the teabag up and down, and then reached into the cabinet for some honey.

Suddenly the window over the sink slammed open, and a gust of wind burst into the kitchen. The mug flew to the ground, shattering, and hot tea splashed across Em's sweatshirt. Em gasped and reached over with trembling hands, shutting and locking the window. For a second, it sounded like someone was wailing. She looked outside. Two pine trees swayed at the corner of the yard. Another big gust of wind sent snow spraying off their branches. Otherwise, the yard was still.

Em stood there for a moment, unable to shake the creepy feeling that had washed over her. She whispered the first line of her poem: *"You enter my heart like a sudden chill."* When she'd first written "Impossible," she hadn't realized how scary those words could sound.

CHAPTER TEN

Chase was in a daze. A sleep-deprived, distracted daze. He had tossed and turned all night, obsessively checking his phone to see whether Ty had called or responded to his texts. *U okay?* he'd written. *Can we hang out again this week?* No response. Just a call from Zach, which he'd screened.

And now he was on his way to a football meeting—a post-season wrap-up session at Coach Baldwin's house—where he'd be expected to be *on*. Next year he would be captain of the team, the senior starting quarterback. It was no joke.

He tipped his head to one side, then the other, stretching his neck. He checked his phone again. Nothing. Okay. He vowed to leave his phone in the car and not check it again until after the meeting. He hoped it wouldn't take more than an hour.

As soon as Chase stepped inside Coach Baldwin's house—a

sprawling ranch near Emily's place—he sensed it: The vibe was all wrong.

"It's the local charity case!" Carl Feder, a running back, shouted. Chase looked around to make sure Feder was talking to him. Some of the guys laughed, others averted their eyes.

"Yo, Singer," Andy Barton said. "You need more money for manicures?"

Another voice, from across the room: "You begging for a winning senior season?"

"That'll come naturally," he answered with a smirk.

"Recruiters don't like it when you beg, Singer." This from Barton again, who sat in the corner with a plate of lasagna in his hands.

These barbs felt different from the team's usual banter. "What are you talking about?" Chase asked, addressing no one in particular.

Sean Wagner sauntered over and shoved his phone in Chase's face. On it was a picture of Chase from last night. The night of the snow angels. Chase saw himself kneeling on the ground, fingers clasped, a pleading expression on his face. Ty must have been just outside the frame. Ty. He barely registered the embarrassment of having been caught in that position—Chase, who had built his entire life around *not* being humiliated. All he could think was her name. *Ty. Ty. Ty.* Like a chant, or a spell.

He shrugged, taking a second to collect his thoughts. Then he grinned. "You guys have nothing better to do than follow me around when I'm out with a hot girl?"

"She *is* pretty hot, Chase. Nice work," Zach said, appearing from around the corner holding a plate piled high with salad and pasta. Chase nodded, knowing Zach had no idea who Chase had been out with. It was good to know Zach still had his back.

"Hey, guys—Mrs. Baldwin wants me to tell you that there's more of those breadsticks in the kitchen," Zach announced. He smoothly scooped up a forkful of lasagna and winked at Chase as he walked by. "I tried to warn you," Zach singsonged as he passed. "That'll teach you not to screen my calls."

Chase knew that fending off the barbs was Zach's way of thanking Chase for keeping his mouth shut about what *he'd* seen yesterday. If any of the guys on the team found out about Zach and Em, it could easily get back to Gabby and ruin Zach's game. Zach probably hoped the guys *suspected* something was going on, but was happy to keep them in the dark about the actual details, at least for now. At least until he could tell them on *his* terms. And that's where Chase came in—keeping his secrets once again. This was how Zach worked: You scratch my back, I'll scratch yours.

Chase shook his head, thankful that Coach Baldwin was calling the meeting to order.

As he moved to take a seat on the couch next to his coach, Barton whacked his arm.

"So, Singer, are you bringing this mystery hot chick to the Feast?"

Chase clasped his hands in front of his chest and pumped them in front of Barton's face. "I'm *begging* you to shut the fuck up," he said, much to the others' amusement.

But even still, his hand instinctively went to his right pocket to check his phone; he clenched his fist as he remembered that he'd left it in the car. What if Ty was calling right now, and he missed it? His breath caught in the back of his throat, the same way it did when his shirts weren't steamed correctly, or when he left his playbook in his locker overnight. He needed to fix this.

But Coach Baldwin was asking him something about the South Portland Red Riot defense, and he struggled to focus. The team might think he was pathetic, but they still needed him as a leader. That's how the next forty-five minutes went—Chase would tune out, Coach would ask about this tackle or that passing play, and Chase would snap to, answer as best he could, picture himself on the field, running fast, running past the others.

The teasing stopped. They were talking about the Super Bowl, about the Patriots offense, and, when Coach went into the kitchen to refill his 7UP, about how Amy Cushman had taken off her shirt in Minster's hot tub toward the tail end of the party. It all sounded like background noise to Chase. And then, when he thought he couldn't stand it anymore, the meeting was over. He bolted. He didn't even bother to say good-bye to the others—just threw a nod in Zach's direction as he left. He didn't care that none of them went out of their way to say good-bye to him, either.

He ran to his car, fumbled with the keys to unlock the door. Sitting in the driver's seat, hands shaking, he opened his phone. Nothing but the time blinked back at him. He threw his phone down in disgust.

He turned the key in the ignition and left the phone where it had fallen, on the floor on the passenger side. He didn't care. He had to get his shit together. He was reversing out of Coach Baldwin's driveway, trying to distract himself by picturing York's offensive lineup in his head, when he heard it.

Beep-beep-beep.

Chase practically crashed into the mailbox at the end of the driveway as he leaned down, his foot still on the gas, going backward, trying to grab the phone. He threw the car into park, picked up the phone, and then he couldn't stop smiling. It was her.

He almost didn't want to read the message; he could have stared at her name for the next hour.

Want to come over today? I need you!

Chase's heart pounded. Not only would he get to see Ty

but he'd get to see her house—he knew that was a great sign. But he tried to play it cool. *Yeah, that would be great.*

She responded almost immediately. *Okay. Come to 128 Silver Way.*

Chase pulled into the gravel lot of the new mall, scanning the chicken-scratch directions he'd copied off his laptop, wishing he had a phone with GPS—or Internet at all. *Wait.* This *is Silver Way?* Like many old towns, Ascension had lots of tiny roads—but still, this seemed weird.

The mall, only halfway completed, sat huge and hulking up ahead, monolithic and boxy with a gaping hole at the end where an "atrium" was planned. No wonder people—kids and local reporters alike—called the place the Behemoth. The air was dead quiet except for the distant hum of construction cranes and drills. The place was covered in tarps, so the workers could work in the cold.

He must have missed a turn somewhere. This couldn't be right.

But sure enough, there was Ty, emerging from behind a low concrete barrier, picking her way through the snow and gravel and around orange cones, wearing high heels and a tiny denim skirt. Her hair was tied back with some kind of little scarf, and the thin white streak in her hair glowed in the winter sunset. Chase got out of the car.

"Um, this is where you live?" He swallowed hard. He really didn't know the first thing about this girl. What was she doing climbing around a construction site?

"Yeah, I live in that pipe," she deadpanned, before breaking into her silvery laugh. "Of course I don't live here, silly. Come on."

She grabbed his hand and tugged him away from the car. As usual, Chase felt a shock of electric recognition as soon as they touched. The day-old snow crunched beneath their feet as she led him behind the Behemoth, toward the woods that surrounded it. Chase could see a narrow path cut into the trees. They passed the landscape of gravel and concrete into the shadows of the snow-covered pines. The snow here was untouched, and Chase's boots sank into it as they walked. Night was starting to fall, and the path was barely marked, but Ty blazed confidently forward. Chase stumbled along behind her, trying to keep up. It seemed like she was skimming over the snow.

"So you don't live in that pipe, but you do live in the Haunted Woods, huh?"

"The Haunted Woods?" Ty slowed for a moment, looking at him over her shoulder.

"Yeah—everyone says these woods are haunted by ghosts . . . oooooooohhhhh," Chase said with a shrug, trying to sound dismissive. "It's just this dumb story people tell."

"I've never heard that! Tell me about it—I love ghost stories." Her eyes flashed and she sucked her bottom lip under her teeth. It made her cheekbones even more pronounced.

"It's just some crazy stuff people say to make Ascension seem more interesting. If there are ghosts, they're probably wasted from leftover beer and secondhand pot smoke—there's a clearing to the west of here where kids like to hang out. No neighbors around to call the cops, you know. Some of the parties get pretty nuts."

Ty turned and squinted, like she was trying to remember something. "I heard some story once about these weirdo sisters who used to live out here, like, hundreds of years ago. Do you think they're the ones who stuck around?"

"I haven't seen any ghosts around here yet," Chase said. "But if there are any, I'll protect you."

Ty smiled and kept walking.

"We're almost there," she said, squeezing his hand.

The nearly full moon illuminated a house around the next bend in the path.

"There it is."

In front of the shingled house, which had big, dirty windows and a peaked roof with a stone chimney, there was a small patch of charred-looking grass. There didn't seem to be a driveway, and Chase couldn't see any other structures farther down the path.

Chase's thoughts were like cards being shuffled in his brain. This was Ty's old house? Did Ali and Meg still live here too? Maybe the house was foreclosed. Maybe her family had gone broke or could never sell it. She told him she had moved away. . . .

Suddenly, everything made total sense. No wonder they understood each other so well. Ty *got it*—they were both anomalies among Ascension's population of rich assholes.

"It's not much, but—"

Chase cut her off. "It's cool. Let's go inside." His brain kept up its mad shuffle, considering and reordering different scenarios, different explanations for Ty's mysterious background. Maybe when her family had left Ascension, they'd left in a hurry? Maybe her family was in some kind of trouble. Maybe her parents were in jail and she couldn't go to college because she had to pay off some bills. Maybe her father was in the mob and they were on the run.

Maybe, maybe, maybe . . . The word drilled endlessly in his mind. He wanted to ask her these questions—to know everything about her. But he didn't want to scare her off, either. He knew that just seeing her home was a huge step. He didn't need to push things any further unless she offered. He could sense that, like him, she wasn't a big fan of discussing the past.

Ty went into the house first, walking in the dim light over to a floor lamp that flickered on at her touch. The large, wood-paneled room was nearly empty. A few hard-backed chairs sat in the living room next to a blackened fireplace; a rickety table in the kitchen. The windows didn't have curtains and there wasn't one electronic device to be seen except for an old-school radio. A can of paint sat on the floor in what may have once been a dining room.

Chase took it all in, silently. Out of the corner of his eye, he thought he saw something moving, slithering by, but when he whipped around to look, he saw nothing but a shadow in a bare corner. So they must have sold almost all their furniture. Okay. It was creepy, but he tried to remember how nervous he got whenever anyone saw his pathetic trailer. How much it stung to be judged by what you owned instead of who you were.

"It's creepy down here," Ty said, as if reading his thoughts. "Let's go upstairs."

On the second floor, in her bedroom with slanted ceilings and white wallpaper, the house seemed brighter. Her little room was littered with clothes and shoes and ripped-out pages from magazines, just like so many chicks' rooms he had seen. He loosened up a bit, looked at the perfumes on her dresser and wondered which one, when uncapped, would fill the room with Ty's scent.

Ty sat on her bed, watching him. She looked so calm—not worried at all about what he'd think of her. From beneath the skirt, her long legs stretched out in front of her and she lay back a bit, on her elbows. He'd never noticed how defined her arm muscles were.

Chase reached into his back pocket.

"I wrote something for you," he said, heat flooding his face. "Here."

Ty reached up languidly to take the paper, the paper with Emily's poem on it. While she read it, Chase went to the window, trying to calm his thumping pulse. He could feel his veins throbbing. It was quiet. In the distance, he could see the lights of the highway casting their glow upward, above the trees. The moon shone high and bright. He wondered how often Ty stood here, just staring out into the night, watching the snow.

"You wrote this?" She stood and came up behind him. The hairs on his neck and arms raised in response to her nearness, to her smell. "For me?"

"Yeah. It's not much, you know," he said, suddenly feeling kind of shitty about the fact that he hadn't *actually* written it. At least the sentiment had been there. "But I've been thinking about you."

"It's really beautiful," Ty said. He turned to face her, to make sure she wasn't just humoring him, and he felt her lips graze his cheek, just an inch from his mouth. "Thank you," she whispered.

It was the closest they had ever been. Chase's whole body throbbed. The smell of her skin, the slightest touch of her hair against his arm—it made his head spin. He turned his face fully to hers, hoping for a real kiss on her red, slightly parted lips. But she'd already backed away.

"I was wondering," she said. "Will you help me with something?"

Chase raised his eyebrows. "Of course. What's up?"

"Well . . ." She hesitated—and for a second she almost seemed embarrassed. "This place . . ." She laughed self-consciously and shrugged. "There's no other way to say it. It's pretty much a shit hole right now. I was wondering if you'd help me paint one of the rooms downstairs. I've been trying to fix things up around here."

Instantly, he understood. She was ashamed of the house. "You got it," he said, grinning slowly.

She smiled and grabbed his hand. Once again, he had a creepy feeling as they descended the stairs to one of the dark, empty rooms below. Ty disappeared and came back a moment later with newspapers, which she spread over the floor in the room with the radio and paint can.

She opened the paint—a vivid red color. A bit of a strong choice, but Chase wasn't exactly an interior decorator.

"I've got a roller and a brush," she said, pointing to her supplies. "Which do you want?"

"I'll take the roller," he said. He felt good—helpful. She needed him. As he rolled up his sleeves—he *really* didn't want to get paint all over himself—Ty clicked on the radio, tuning it to a fuzzy oldies station. She hummed as she readied her brush.

The first swath of red spread like blood out of a fresh wound, quick and bright. This was fun. He liked the way the bold color covered over the dingy white. And as he drew the roller back and forth, high and low, he knew his arms looked good. Strong.

"Have these walls always been white?" he asked offhandedly, but he was dying for any speck of information she would give him.

"As far as I know," Ty said. "But red is my favorite color. I always wanted to be surrounded by red. What's yours?"

"My favorite color?"

Ty nodded.

"I guess I'd have to go with maroon and gold," Chase said. "Team colors."

"Close to my colors," Ty said with a smile. "What about your favorite food?" She was over in the corner now, carefully brushing paint next to the window. It seemed like she was digging for more information too.

"Chinese, I guess," Chase said, cursing silently as a few specks of red splattered onto his jeans. "I love crab rangoons."

"Mmmmm," Ty said, and he was so distracted by her licking her lips that he almost didn't notice that she already had red paint all over her shirt. She caught him staring and looked down. "Oops. I'm a slob." She laughed and flicked her brush in his direction. "Now we match," she said, as a few splotches of red landed on his shirt.

He forced a laugh, a guffaw that sounded hollow in the empty room. "Good one," he said dryly.

"Sorry," Ty said, looking concerned. "Are you annoyed? Is that a good shirt?"

"What?" He looked down as though just seeing the spots for the first time. "Oh, whatever. No biggie." He shrugged, and as he did, more paint dripped onto his trouser leg and shoe. He looked down and then at her with a bemused expression. "See? No big deal."

Ty's sudden burst of laughter was almost worth knowing that he'd ruined a pair of trousers—and certainly enough to make him abandon all hope of staying clean this evening. She took her brush, dipped it into the paint can so that it was really dripping, and drew it up her arm, along her neck, and into her hair. The red of the paint clashed with the burnt maroon of her hair.

He laughed, too, this time for real. "Let's finish this wall," Chase said, and they did, flicking paint at each other between brushstrokes. Chase tried to focus on how great it felt to be with Ty, rather than the fact that he'd need to throw away these clothes tomorrow. After a while, Ty stepped back to survey their work. It was dark outside, and the only light came from the bare bulb screwed into the ceiling. Still, the wall was practically pulsing with the vibrant red. She looked at him for his opinion and wrinkled her nose.

"You're so cute. You're covered in paint!" Ty said, coming a bit closer.

"No worries," he said, hoping he sounded nonchalant.

"I have this miracle stain-remover stuff," she said, pointing toward the kitchen. "It cleans everything. I could . . . We could use it to get the paint off?"

"That's okay." He really wanted to play it cool, but she was making it difficult, the way she kept inching closer. And then she was tugging at his collar, her warm fingers brushing against his neck.

"Really . . . Why don't you take this off?" She said it playfully, pulling the little white scarf out of her ponytail as she spoke, so her hair flowed down around her shoulders. She tugged at both arms of his shirt. Then she tried a different tactic, pulling his shirt up from the bottom. His stomach showed and he unconsciously flexed his abs.

Her hands were on his skin now.

Before either of them could have time to think twice, he bent down and kissed her, hard, on the lips. It felt . . . amazing. Like a wave had broken over his head. Like he was swimming in water so cold it pricked his flesh. He could feel her lips turned up in a smile as they kissed.

"So, can I wash your clothes?" She pulled away. "Come on. Don't be shy," she said, motioning for him to take them off.

Chase took a deep breath. He felt pulled by the same otherworldly connection that he'd felt that first night, after Minster's party, and again at the club under Benson's.

"I will if you will," he said.

And then, just like that, she was taking her clothes off, right in front of him. She stepped out of her skirt and pulled her shirt gracefully over her head. Then she stepped first out of her right shoe, then the left, then no bra, then no underwear. Chase had seen girls naked before, but this was new. This was not the fumbling, dim-lit hookups he was used to, full of tangled bra straps and annoying button flies. There was no self-consciousness. There was no strategic posing to cover the things that girls worry about covering. No trying too hard. There was just . . . Ty. Morphing from clothed to unclothed like a swimmer emerging from underwater—smoothly, sleekly, as though it was the most natural thing in the world. Happy. And despite the obvious sexiness of her body, her confidence, her hair falling just so over her shoulders and onto her chest, the action felt somehow not sexy. Ty took her clothes off the same way some people put theirs on. The way Chase put his on, like they were a costume, or a shield against the outside world—the physical representation of the confident, smart, talented man he wanted to be.

Thunderous waves pounded in Chase's skull, cold and salty.

He took his shoes off, and then his socks. His shirt came off next and he stood there, bare-chested, not sure whether to take the next step. Ty came forward and gave him a fleeting kiss. "Now your jeans," she said, running her fingers lightly along his waistband. He felt shivers race along his spine.

"Ty . . ." He trailed off, not knowing what to say. He unzipped his jeans and stepped out of them.

Ty looked him up and down slowly. At least he knew he looked good.

"There's a little bit of paint on your boxers," she said. "Did you know that?"

He really hadn't seen it. "Um, no, it's fine," he stammered.

"I put it there on purpose," Ty said with a wicked smirk. She was standing so close he could feel her breath on his shoulder.

Well, what the hell. He'd gone this far. Chase took off his boxers and stood as defiantly as he could, stark naked, in Ty's red room.

"You are so hot," she breathed into his ear. And with that she was out of the room, holding all his clothes, shouting, "This'll only take a second," from the other room. Chase shifted from one cold foot to the other as he waited. His heart was pounding. He wanted her so badly.

When Ty returned to the room, she had something in her hand, but it wasn't his clothes. "They'll need to soak for a few minutes," she said, "and then we can throw them in the dryer in the basement. In the meantime . . ." She waved her hand in the air. It was holding a digital camera. "I want to remember this forever."

Chase just stared. She wanted to take pictures of him? Like this?

"You . . . you have paint on your arm," he said. It was all he could think of.

"So? It'll look cool," she said.

"I can't even remember the last time I had my picture taken," Chase said, "except for the yearbook, or at some random party."

"Just a few?" She pushed out her lower lip slightly. It was the hottest pout he'd ever seen. He couldn't go much longer without kissing her again.

As if she read his mind, Ty came forward again, nuzzling into his neck, kissing it once. "Okay," he said with conviction.

What they were doing felt hotter, more intimate, than hooking up ever could. She started to snap photos, the lens moving like it had a mind of its own. He stood there shifting on his feet at first.

As she snapped, he felt himself becoming fixated on the flash. It was like she was hypnotizing him. Words started pouring out of him suddenly. "I'm serious. There are almost no pictures of me in the world. There is, like, *one* photo of me and my dad from when I was a kid," he told Ty, finding that the words just flew out of his mouth, almost breathlessly.

Ty listened while she looked through the lens, her milky body glimmering in the moonlight from the window and the dim light from the bare bulb, reflecting off the red walls. "He wasn't around much, you know. Even when he was there—physically present, I mean—he wasn't. And my mom . . . there are pictures of me and her, a few." Chase was swimming; time was water and he was free-floating through it. He sat down on the floor, legs out in front of himself, almost forgetting he was naked. "But sometimes I feel like they're supposed to be proof that she stuck around, you know? Not actual happy pictures but evidence that I even had a childhood." His throat felt hot and sticky all of a sudden, so he stopped talking. Instead, as Ty came closer, he grabbed the camera to take a few shots of her. Her pale white breasts; her stomach, so smooth and soft looking. It was surreal, like he was taking pictures of a perfect statue in a museum. She stayed still while he snapped three pictures, then she leaned forward, taking the camera back from him gently.

"I know what you mean," Ty said, and resumed taking pictures. "But here we are—making new memories. These are *actual* happy pics, right?"

"Yeah." Chase cleared his throat and laid down on the bare floor, staring up at the speckled ceiling. The cold wood cooled his flushed skin. "It's just so hard, you know? I'm all my mom has but—I can't help resenting her sometimes. I just get so focused on my own shitty life, obsessing that I won't be able to make it . . . to make it better. I am so scared of just being what my dad was. Of failing like that . . ." The words were getting tangled in his head, pouring out of him from some unknown place. He couldn't believe he was saying all this stuff, in front of a very naked, insanely gorgeous girl.

"You're too scared, Chase," Ty said, crouching next to him to get a better angle. All of a sudden she wasn't smiling anymore. Her face looked pale, her bright red hair splaying everywhere. "Fear is dangerous."

He watched her as she stood up suddenly and sashayed over to the paint can. She bent over it, and as she did, he scanned the room. At his feet was the tiny white scarf her hair had been wrapped in earlier. He decided he would take it. Later, when his jeans were washed, he'd stuff it in his pockets. He wanted to remember this day, too.

When she stood up again, Ty's hands were dripping with red paint. She'd just stuck them into the can. He looked to her for an explanation but part of him knew better at this point than to try to guess what was about to come out of Ty's mouth. Nothing did. Instead, without saying a word, she walked over and drew a blood-red line across Chase's clavicle, from shoulder to shoulder. Then she laughed. She rubbed her whole hand down his left arm. "Now we match again," she said.

She was out of her mind, there was no doubt about it. But he liked it—he more than liked it. Spontaneously, Chase went over to the can and thrust his own hands into the cold, thick paint. Then he turned her around and drew three parallel lines down her back, from the nape of her neck to the small of her back, just above her perfect round ass. Touching her was even better than photographing her. The slippery paint against her smooth skin was magical. Chase couldn't stop, and he didn't want to.

He grabbed the red paint and with his pinkie traced a tiny heart on her sternum. Then he took her hand, still dripping with the same red paint, and drew it to his own chest. There, he led her thumb in the shape of a heart. He stared into her green eyes and she looked at him, smoldering, too. Whatever Ty was doing to him, it was official: He was hers.

CHAPTER ELEVEN

"There's Michigan!" Em tapped JD wildly on the arm.

"Who the hell would come to Maine—from Michigan—in the middle of winter? Don't they have their own snow?"

"I don't know and I don't care. We didn't *have* Michigan yet." Em pulled a piece of loose-leaf paper from the glove compartment and made a note. "Only thirty-one states to go. . . . God, I can't wait for summer and tourist plates."

They were in JD's car, heading for Dunkin' Donuts. Em's car would be in the shop for the next few days, and JD had become her unofficial driver. They'd developed a great routine: He'd wait for her to wake up, then they'd text, meet in JD's driveway, and head straight for coffee and breakfast sandwiches. Then off to run errands or walk through the mall. Today, Em was supposed to meet up with Chase around three—he wanted her to write him another poem. She didn't really have a choice except to say yes. But first, Em wanted to go to Staples or maybe that stationery store up near Portland to find a new writing notebook. Since she obviously couldn't tell Gabby what she was going through, her journal would have to sub for her best friend.

"So, what kind of notebook are you looking for? A small one, to stick in your bag? Or a big one, like a school notebook?"

"I'm not sure, actually." Em had been contemplating the same question. "I already have my journal-journal. The one I write in before bed. But this one I want to use for writing projects, not just for my own personal thoughts. You know? But I don't want it to be *too* nice—I know I won't use it if it's too pretty."

"Like my hat?" Today, JD was wearing a rust-orange fedora, complete with a blue plaid ribbon around the rim. "It's a little too pretty, huh?" He grinned at her, waiting for her to laugh.

"Yeah, like your hat. Which makes you look like a crazed pimp or a character from a bad detective movie." She laughed as they were pulling into the lot. "Thank god we're here. I *need* that coffee if I'm going to deal with you and your hat all day."

Fortified by hot coffees (lots of milk and one sugar for JD; a little cream and no sugar for Em) and egg-and-cheeses on croissants, they headed to Staples, which sat in a shopping center in the next town over. On the highway, Em sipped her coffee and stared out the window, ostensibly looking for license plates but also thinking about Zach. She'd purposefully put her phone on silent so that she wouldn't be listening for a call from him all day.

Still, she couldn't help thinking of yesterday afternoon. She'd had JD drop her off, claiming that she was tutoring Zach in math—precalc, big test at the end of January. It wasn't too much of a stretch. She and Zach were in the same math class, and she was better than him. She understood how to solve for the unknown.

Actually, Zach had invited her over to watch a movie, but when she'd arrived, he'd been riding his snowplow around in the backyard, making looping figure eights and shouting for her to hop on. She did, grabbing him from behind like she was on the back of a motorcycle, giggling and burying her nose in his scarf because it was so cold.

"You're a good copilot!" he'd yelled over the drone of the engine. She'd squeezed him tighter.

Inside, they'd stripped down to T-shirts, socks, and underwear, sweating in some places and frozen in others, and collapsed on his bed with Netflix. They hadn't watched much of the movie. They'd kissed, laughed, and rolled around in his big bed, in his clean sheets. Everything about him felt so . . . manly. Crisp, plain bedclothes; simple, spare furnishings. The bookshelf in his room held SAT study books and textbooks from the poli-sci course he'd taken last summer at the local community college. He had stopped trying to put his hand down her jeans. They were just waiting until they could tell Gabby, and until then, Emily was so happy just kissing Zach in so many different ways, hard and long or soft and curious, touching his amazing stomach, grabbing his arms. Being underneath him and then crawling on top of him so that her hair formed a cave around their faces.

It felt so real. And so different from every other random hookup she'd ever had—drunk at a party, or in the front seat of a car, hip bones digging into gear shifts, or even the Steve Sawyer "after-school basement special," as Gabby had taken to calling it.

The truth was, Em had never been in love. She knew that. And beyond the fact that she had such strong feelings for Zach, Em had always been jealous of Gabby and Zach's relationship as a separate entity—the idea of long-term partnership, of waking up and going to school every morning and knowing that you would hold the same person's hand between classes. It was what her parents talked about—that feeling of "just knowing."

And for the first time, she thought she did know. Yesterday, on Zach's bed, he'd fallen asleep. Right there, with his head on her shoulder, after kissing for hours. She'd stroked his hair and stared at the ceiling while the credits of some car-chase movie rolled on the laptop at the foot of his bed. This was what it was like to really be with someone. This was what it would be like if she and Zach shared a bed, a room, a life—together. It had made her want to cry, because of how overwhelmed she was. What if they got married? She could picture it. This was love.

"Em, did you hear me? I swear, Georgia just sped by."

"Um. No, sorry, I didn't see." Em shifted in her seat, turning down the heat a notch. She looked at JD, studying his face. The sideburns he'd started growing freshman year. The ridge of his nose, slightly crooked after falling from the highest tree in her yard years ago.

"If we missed Georgia because you were spacing out, I'll kill you."

Em couldn't help it; she leaned over to check her phone. Thank god she did. Her stomach started doing somersaults when she saw there was a message from Zach. *Movie date again?*

She wished she could just teleport over to Zach's house immediately.

"You know what? If I can't find the notebook here, let's just go home," Em said, not caring how sketchy she sounded. "I might need to stop by Zach's again."

"More math tutoring?"

"Yeah, more math. That test is going to be wicked hard." Em could hear her own defensive tone.

"Zach seems awfully preoccupied with his math score of late," JD said just as they pulled into a parking spot. He put the car in park but left it on as he turned to face her. "And you, too. Where is this coming from? You were dying to spend half your winter break reviewing the quadratic equation? With Zach McCord?"

"It's junior year. Every grade counts. We can't all be super-geniuses." She tried to keep her tone light as she moved to get out of the car. JD reached out and touched her shoulder, stopping her.

"Em, I'm just saying. You should be careful. It's starting to seem . . . weird."

"Weird?" Em forced a laugh. "Come on, JD. Chill out. He barely understands the order of operations."

"I'm chill, I'm chill. It's just . . ." JD drew his eyebrows together. "It's like . . . I feel like something's up with you."

"Nothing's *up* with me. Come on. Let's go." Em grabbed her bag from the floor. She could feel JD's eyes burning into her, and even when she'd placed her hand on the door handle, JD still hadn't moved.

"Can I just say one thing?" he blurted out, and then, without waiting for her response, went on, "I think it's weird that you've been spending half your winter vacation servicing the needs of your best friend's boyfriend, while she's off across the ocean."

Em felt her heart stutter. She stared at JD, wide-eyed. It was a blatant accusation. "What. Are. You. Saying?" She tried to keep her face calm, but rising panic was making her feel flushed.

"Remember the other night? When you left on Christmas Eve? That was strange, Em. It wasn't like you."

"JD, stop it. You're being ridiculous—" But as Em talked, fumbling with the lock on the passenger door, she felt her eyes get blurry and she could no longer see what she was doing. Suddenly, the tears came hot and fast. She slumped back against the seat, eyes closed in defeat. Everything she'd been feeling the last few days overwhelmed her. She put her bag down between her feet.

JD cleared his throat and rolled down both their windows just a crack. The glass was fogging. The cold air sliced through the tension between them. "Em?"

For a couple seconds Em couldn't say anything. And then she knew that she was going to tell.

"You're right," she finally spat out. "You're right, okay? The situation *is* weird. It's weird because it's true. I've been spending so much time with him—with Zach—because something is, like, going on between us. We're . . . we've fallen for each other. When I left on Christmas Eve, it was that night . . . I mean, you don't want to hear about all this. But yeah. It's happening." Em didn't know whether to be defiant or apologetic or embarrassed or what. She waited a few seconds, but JD didn't respond. She rubbed her hands on her thighs.

"You know, it's not like this came out of nowhere. It's been building for a long time," she went on. "And it's real. We're just waiting to tell Gabby when she gets home. And, JD, it's been so hard, but I know it's right. I mean, it's wrong, I know that too. But it's one of those things . . . impossible to deny."

He still didn't speak. Was he surprised? Em didn't think she'd ever seen JD's face look the way it did then: ashen, angry.

"Are you serious," he said, finally, slowly; it was more of a statement than a question.

"Yes."

JD was staring straight ahead. His hands were in his lap. "Did you know? Like, when you went over there the other night, did you know that was going to happen?"

"No. I mean, of course not." Em had to keep telling herself that.

"He did."

"What do you mean?" In her panic, Em thought for a moment that Zach might actually have discussed this with JD. "How do you know?"

"Because that's who he is, Em. You really think he would have invited you over on Christmas Eve if he didn't think he could get some?" JD was blinking a lot. Was this what it was going to be like when they told Gabby?

"It's not *getting some*, JD. It's not like that. I know it seems messed up, but I think we're good together. It just feels right. We're going to explain it to Gabby."

"I don't." JD almost spit the words. Em found herself recoiling.

"You don't what?" She tried to keep the tremor from her voice.

"I don't think you're *good together*." Here, JD used exaggerated finger-quotes, mocking her.

Anger flared in Em's stomach. "Fine. You know what? I don't *care* what you think. You don't understand. I didn't expect you to."

"You're right. I don't understand. Zach uses people, Em. Can't you see that? And really? You're going to *explain* it to Gabby? You've said yourself that Zach is her whole world. You think she's going to *understand*?"

Now the anger turned to alarm, ringing inside of her—shrill, hollow. What if JD was right? What had she started? She opened her mouth to defend herself, but JD raised a hand, cutting her off.

"Stop. I don't want to hear any more." He put the car in reverse and started to back out of the spot. He'd apparently decided that the shopping mission was over.

"Oh, so we're done talking?" Em brought her hand down on the dashboard, more forcefully than she'd intended to. "You're always doing this."

"What am I always doing, Em?" JD slammed on the brakes and glared at her.

"Making your high-and-mighty decisions. Like *deciding* to drive off, which *obviously* means that we're done talking. So you can just go home and just—just—look *down* on me without even *understanding* the situation."

"Fine," JD said, pulling back into the parking spot with an angry jerk. "You want to go buy a journal, buy a journal. Maybe your journal won't have any opinions." He waved to the door. "Go."

"What does that even mean? What are you talking about?" She was so angry she could hardly see. But it was more than that. She felt like JD had reached into her stomach and squeezed.

"I have a right to my opinions, Em. You're hurting people." Here, his voice broke a bit, unexpectedly. "You're acting like a spoiled child. And for someone who's not even worth it. Not even remotely worth it."

"Shut up. Just shut up." Em scrunched down in her seat and told herself she wouldn't let JD see how much he had hurt her. "Just take me home."

"Why don't I just take you to Zach's? That's where you want to go, anyway."

"Fine. Why don't you."

The silence in the car was hideous. JD took off the orange hat and threw it forcefully onto the backseat. Em watched him, out of the corner of her eye, running a hand through his hair over and over.

Outside Zach's house—she couldn't believe JD actually brought her there—she took a deep breath and looked at him one more time. He stared stonily ahead. She got out of the car without saying a word, and slammed the door. For a second, as JD peeled out of the driveway and headed home, Em could only stand still, breathing hard. Then, with a firm shake of her shoulders, she walked up the front path to Zach's house.

"Hey, you," Zach said, sweeping her into a hug just inside his front door. Zach's shirt smelled so good that she quickly burrowed into his arms. He held her tight, and she felt the familiar warmth at the bottom of her stomach. She wanted to reach up and kiss him, but JD's words rang in her ears. *Zach is an asshole. You are hurting people. Gabby, Gabby, Gabby.* This wasn't right.

"Zach, I'm nervous," she said, her mouth pressing into the soft cotton.

"Nervous?" He pulled her to arm's length. The front door still stood open. "About what?"

She drew in a shaky breath. "About this," she said, waving her hand between them. "About us. About why you haven't said anything to Gabby yet. Or why I haven't."

"Em, we've hardly spoken to her. She called me once from Barcelona, the day after Christmas, but I barely said hello before she had to go. What am I going to do, throw it in before I say good-bye? We didn't even talk, she just, like, gave me a rundown of the hotel suite."

"Yeah, but we need to say something. Maybe—maybe I should say something."

For a second Zach's eyes turned dark. "I thought we agreed I'd handle it," he said. His tone of voice had an uncomfortable edge to it.

"But I need to know that you're going to. I need to know that we're going to do this the right way."

Just like that, he was all gentle again. "Em, of course I'm going to. I promise. It should wait until she gets back, though. So we can talk in person?" He touched her chin, and she shivered, and he closed the door. "It's going to be okay."

"Okay."

He bent down to kiss her, softly, his hand holding the back of her neck. Then he leaned away.

"You know, I like that about you. You see the big picture." The outside corners of his eyes were slanted down in a concerned way. "Do you wanna come in?"

Em grinned. "Yeah, but I have to be home at three to meet Ch—to meet someone." She felt a little weird telling him about her arrangement with Chase. It was a bit too hard to explain.

Zach gave her a tight-lipped smile—one that said, *Buck up, kiddo*—and kissed her on the forehead, half jokingly, before pulling her toward the TV room.

Zach was right—telling Gabby in person was better. Especially for a situation like this one. Especially for Gabby, who they both cared so much about. See? He'd thought about it. Screw JD and his condescending attitude. She knew what she was doing.

"Sorry about the mess," Zach said, plopping down on the couch in front of several cardboard boxes. Clothes, picture frames, and books were arranged in seemingly haphazard piles around the room.

"What's all this?" Em knelt down by a pile of cloth-bound books. She loved old books—their dusty smell, their thick pages, the random notes and inscriptions that often personalized their pages.

"Just going through some old crap," Zach said.

"These are awesome, Zach." Em had found a pile of old *Life* magazines, crisp and delicate, with huge black-and-white photographs.

"Yeah, those are pretty amazing, huh? They used to be . . . They were my dad's," he said softly.

"Oh, wow." Em didn't really know what to say. She remembered that Claire Lewin had been Zach's date when his mom got remarried—really quickly, it seemed, less than a year after Mr. McCord's death. Em had overheard Claire in the locker room saying that the whole event "felt off, like a really awkward moment on reality TV."

"Yeah, he loved photojournalism. So there are lots of these

books and magazines downstairs. Plus his clothes . . . My stepdad wants to clear things out a little to finish the basement and make room for the new pool table. So I'm just sorting it out into what-to-keep and what-to-dump."

Em nodded and tilted her head a bit, but didn't say anything.

"It's kind of hard." Immediately, he cleared his throat. "But it's cool we finally got a pool table down there. I love pool."

"That's good, then," Em said gently.

"I'll have to teach you to play sometime." He grinned but didn't look at her as he reached for a dark-blue sweater, thickly cable-knit, and held it up in the air in front of him.

"I hope you're putting that in the 'keep' pile," she said. "It would look good on you."

Zach blinked and looked down, folding the sweater on his knees. Em could almost feel him picturing himself in his dad's old sweater. Shit.

"Never mind," she said. "You know what we should do? We should go sweater shopping. Get you something new! Tomorrow. We could go to the old mall, or we could even mini–road trip up to Portland. It'll be fun!"

"Okay," Zach said, putting the sweater aside and smiling at her. She moved to sit next to him on the couch, and he ran a hand through her hair. "I love how your hair feels. It's so smooth and soft. I could touch it all day long."

Em blushed and couldn't help doing a mental comparison of

her stick-straight locks and Gabby's bouncy curls, of which Em had always been jealous. Once, in junior high, Gabby had offered to curl Em's hair for a dance. The results had been horrendous—Em's longer face and big eyes looked cartoonish within the swooping helmet of hair-sprayed dark curls. "Whatever," Gabby had said, turning on her shower. "I'd kill for your hair any day of the week." And she'd waited, humming and dancing and retouching her makeup, while Em had washed out the spirals and the spray.

But Zach obviously liked it, her center-parted, simple cut. She felt a rush of vindication. She practically jumped on him, pressing his shoulders back into the couch and kissing him hard. He kissed her back with just as much ferocity.

Which is why it felt so terrible when, not five minutes later, she heard the trademark bouncy tune of Gabby's ringtone coming from her phone, buried somewhere in her bag.

"Shit, I've gotta get that," she said, disentangling herself from Zach.

"Aw, what's more important than this?" He grabbed her hand, still breathing heavily.

"Zach, that's Gabs's ring. Lemme go." She found the phone and picked up, breathlessly, on the last ring. She signaled for Zach to be quiet. Gabby would kill her if she didn't pick up. Just dialing probably cost a fortune.

"I'll be quiet as a mouse," Zach whispered—too loudly. Em swatted at his shoulder.

"Hey, Gabs," she said brightly.

"What's up? What are you doing?" Gabby sounded far away.

"Oh, I'm just . . . I'm just at home, watching TV. It's freezing outside."

"What are you watching? I can't understand anything on the TVs over here. Times like these, I wish I'd taken Spanish instead of French."

"Just channel surfing." The room seemed oppressively warm, and Zach kept poking her, tickling her, which only made it worse. The tips of her ears were burning. She got up and walked out of his reach.

"Well, I'll be home in less than a week! Three days!"

"That's great, Gabs."

"Are you okay? You sound weird."

"I feel a little weird. Must be something I ate," Em said.

"Poor Emmie! Get JD to bring you some ginger ale or something." And then, to someone in the background: "Okay, okay, I'm coming." She sighed, and groaned to Em, "We have to go to a museum. Can't wait to see you! Tell Zachie I said hi. . . . I haven't spoken to him in two whole days!"

"You're breaking up, Gabs. I can barely hear you. Enjoy the museum."

"'K, love you times seven million!"

"I love you, too." Em hung up. The phone felt like a stone in her hand, and suddenly her whole body felt ice cold.

Zach came up behind her, putting his arms around her waist and his head in the crook of her neck, but she pulled away.

"Zach, that was *Gabby*. We have to be careful. She could have heard you! I mean, do you even understand how crushed she would be if she had any idea what we were doing right now?"

Zach ran his hand through his light brown hair, which flopped right back down into place. "Em, yeah. We talked about this. No need for Gabby to know anything about us."

"Okay, but." Em bit her lip and tried to calm herself. "*Yet*, you mean. She doesn't need to know *yet* but you *are* going to end things with her when she's back. Right? I know I'm probably driving you crazy about this, but it's just really important to me. She doesn't deserve to be lied to."

Zach was back to dumping sweaters into a large trash bag. "I hear you, Em," he said.

Oh god, this was going all wrong. She didn't want him to be mad. "Okay," Em said. "Good. But I just need to know—we should just decide—when. I mean, I thought you said you hadn't talked to Gabby since the day after Christmas," she went on, keeping her tone casual, so she wouldn't sound like she was nagging.

"Or the day after," Zach said casually. "Whatever, it was like a minute-long conversation." He surveyed the piles around the room. "I gotta take some of this stuff to Goodwill. Want me to drop you off on the way?"

Em sighed and grabbed a bag. On the way to the door, he took it from her, then placed both bags on the tile floor in the foyer, so he could grab her and kiss her. She couldn't help but melt into him, his soapy smell, his warm lips.

He grinned at her. "My little worrier," he said. Then he picked up both bags and headed out the door, leaving Em to follow him. And she did.

Chase was sitting on her stoop, waiting for her, when they pulled into her driveway. His expression was unfocused, like he was dreaming with his eyes open. He sat there clenching and unclenching his bare fists. She wondered how long he'd been sitting there.

"What's Singer doing here?" Zach asked.

"I'm helping him with a project," Em said. Now was not the time to get into the whole saga of Chase and the mystery girl.

"'K, babe." He leaned over to kiss her cheek. "I had a great time this afternoon."

"See you tomorrow, right?" she said as she opened the door.

"You got it," Zach answered with a smile.

Sometimes Zach seemed so oblivious. Like, not as affected by how *huge* this situation was.

She and Chase both watched as Zach zoomed away.

"Come on in," Em said. "The next poem is . . . I kind of need to keep working on it for a little while."

Chase wordlessly followed her inside. He hung his coat next to hers, unlaced his shoes, and lined them up neatly next to the bench in the front hall.

"Lots of salt on the roads," he said. "I don't want to trek it through your house."

Em had never seen Chase so pale, or so polite. He sat tentatively on a stool in the kitchen and looked as if he didn't know where to put his hands. His wrinkled, ratty sweatshirt was frayed around the collar and stained at the cuffs. His jeans were ripped at the knees and his eyes had circles under them. Chase Singer, preppiest of the preps, going for hobo chic? It was unheard of. But it was more than his fashion choices. Chase looked haunted, as though he hadn't slept in days. Em kept waiting for his bravado to emerge, to hear a smart-ass comment. It never came.

"You want some hot chocolate? I could make it while you write," Chase said.

"Hot chocolate? Sure. That sounds great." Chase Singer offering to do something nice? This day could not get any more bizarre. "Thanks, Chase."

Once her laptop was open, Em couldn't stop her emotions from surging and flowing onto the page. Her confusion about Zach, about his feelings for her and hers for him, came pouring out of her fingertips. She wrote fast and furious, banging at the keys while Chase banged around by her stove, warming some milk, digging around in her cupboards for cinnamon and cayenne pepper.

It felt almost like her fingers and brain were possessed by something else, the way the words came so freely. And although the poem didn't name names and didn't once say "him" or "he"—so Chase could use it too—it was clearly coming from her own experience, and that made it real. Powerful. Em could feel in her bones that it was a good poem, even better than the first. She was going to call it "Unstoppable."

"Sometimes I feel like Ty could just completely vanish at any second." Chase stood next to her, reading over her shoulder, holding a steaming mug of cocoa. It smelled delicious.

"Who is—oh. Ty?" Em didn't want to pry. He'd tell her, or he wouldn't. She knew what it was like to want to hold the heart's truths as close as possible. To know that once you spoke them aloud, they might evaporate or tangle further.

"Yeah, Ty. She loved the last poem. Thanks." Chase absentmindedly stirred his cocoa as Em printed a copy of the new poem and retrieved it from her father's study. She watched as Chase removed some books from his backpack. He placed the sheet of paper between two of them and repacked the bag. "Don't want to lose it," he said sheepishly.

"You really like her, don't you?" Em blurted.

For a moment Chase looked wary, and Em saw some of his usual bluster and defensiveness. But then his face seemed to collapse, and he just shrugged. "Thanks a lot, Winters. You need me to wash out the mugs?"

She waved away the offer. "I'm a master dishwasher-loader," she joked. Chase gave her a quick smile and raised two fingers to his forehead, an old-fashioned salute. She followed him to the front door and locked it behind him.

Then she returned to the kitchen, sat down, and took a deep breath. Rolled her head around on her neck a few times, stretching. That's when she saw Chase's football playbook on the counter—of all the surprises Chase had pulled that afternoon, this was the biggest one. Em couldn't believe he'd forgotten it. She raced to the front door and opened it to shout after him. But he'd gone; the yard was dim and quiet. She was about to shut the door when the tinkling sound of female laughter caught her ear. It was faint but somehow sounded nearby. She poked her head farther out, looking to see where the sound was coming from. But it was fading already. And all she could see were three dark crows overhead, circling. They looked sooty and ominous against the sky and she slammed the door against them with particular strength.

Dinner was chicken and roasted tomatoes with her parents, who basically spent the whole time discussing, without much input from Em, why she'd be better off taking AP Bio next year instead of AP Environmental Science. Afterward, Em decided to go for a walk. "I just need some air," she told her mom, who was loading the dishwasher and humming.

Things were so confusing. Zach and Gabby. Her fight with JD. How stony and serious Chase had looked today. She wandered down her street, arms wrapped around herself, hat pulled down over her ears. The night was silent and her footsteps echoed around the lawns and woods that lined the street. She thought about Zach's snowplow and Gabby's curling iron and Chase's playbook. . . .

And before she knew it, she was at the tiny playground at the end of her road, the one shared by neighborhood families, with just a slide and a swing set and a wooden seesaw. Em swung open the creaky gate and wandered into the deserted little park, remembering how she and JD used to play here a long time ago. It looked so small now, so underused. She could hardly believe she once thought of it as vast and exciting.

She sat down on one of the swings. Its chain still shrieked with every motion. Some things hadn't changed, at least. She pumped her legs listlessly, letting the cold air chill her even through her coat, hoping it would clear her head, help shake loose the trapped feeling in her chest and throat.

Was this what love was? Complicated, sad, messy? Why

couldn't life just go back to how it used to be, when the biggest problem was who got to go down the slide first? She sighed and looked up at the stars, shoving her hands into her pockets with a quick shiver.

Deep in her peacoat, her hand brushed against a piece of paper. She pulled it out and saw that her name was on the outside fold, but didn't recognize the handwriting. She opened the paper and as she deciphered the words, her breathing got increasingly shallow.

Sometimes sorry isn't enough.

Em leaped off the swing and swiveled around and around in the still, dark playground. For a second she thought she saw a flash of white beyond the seesaw.

Without waiting another second, Em bolted toward the gate, totally shaken. How long had this note been in her pocket? Who put it there? *Sometimes sorry isn't enough.* The words jumbled in her head.

She couldn't shake the feeling that someone was watching her this very second, following her. Her heart hammered heavily as she ran the rest of the way down her block and back to her house, knowing that even inside, she wouldn't feel safe.

Sometimes sorry isn't enough. She didn't know what the note meant. Not really. But she could tell by the cold, black feeling deep in the pit of her stomach that it was true.

CHAPTER TWELVE

Ice hoops were already in full swing when Chase showed up to Galvin's Pond on Friday afternoon. Every year, during winter break, the guys would get together at the pond and set up Zach's portable basketball hoops. Assuming the ice was thick enough, they would half-skate, half-run through unwieldy games of Horse or 21. More than a few nasty bruises had been sustained over the years thanks to these games, but they were worth it. If nothing else, ice hoops was another way to make Ascension's long winters bearable.

The tiny pond was set back from the road, behind a curtain of trees, in the Galvin Nature Preserve. On the far side of the preserve was Ascension's oldest cemetery, one of those historic relics that contained just a handful of crumbling stones. Every Halloween, the land was overrun by a haunted hayride, complete with swamp things emerging from the water and zombies popping out from behind trees. Chase liked the hayride—it was girl bait; they seemed to love snuggling up and being fake scared. Last year, Kelly Van Doran had actually whispered, "You're so brave," into his ear as they'd bounced along the rocky path. During the summer months, Galvin was a cramped swimming hole, crowded with teenagers reveling in Maine's short window of hot weather, too lazy to drive to the beach.

Chase had more somber memories here, too. After Zach's dad's funeral freshman year, the two of them had ended up at Galvin, while folks were still mingling at the McCord house. At home, Zach had been stoic and serious, but by the pond, he'd broken down in tears, throwing rocks angrily into the pond. Chase had sat quietly by, thinking about how different their dads had been. How he almost envied Zach his grief—Zach, who was actually losing a father figure, a mentor. After a while, Chase had pulled a fifth of bourbon from his coat. "Here, have some of this," he'd said. And Zach had drunk gratefully. "Thanks," Zach had said. "I know you get it." Then they'd gone to Zach's car for a Wiffle ball and bat. Chase had fed Zach easy pitches, allowing him the satisfaction of seeing the ball sail through the air, almost to the trees, by the force of his hits.

Today, Galvin was practically deserted. There were only

three cars in the parking lot when Chase pulled up, all of them bearing Ascension stickers.

Winter had come early and strong this year. There was no doubt the pond was frozen solid. As he crunched across the frozen field toward the "court," Chase heard the guys shouting, talking shit, laughing. He could see six or seven of them jumping around on the ice and snow. He rubbed his hands together and pulled his cap down over his ears. No snow was in the forecast today, but the wind was blowing with a particular intensity. His nose wouldn't stop running no matter how many times he dragged his arm across it.

He hadn't really wanted to show up today. Since the painting and picture-taking, he hadn't stopped thinking about Ty: All he wanted to do was see her again. But then Zach had called to remind him about the game, and Chase felt bad. He really hadn't been hanging out much lately.

"Surprised you showed up, Singer." Barton's voice carried crisply over the ice. "Thought you might be busy panhandling."

Great. This again. Chase had almost forgotten about that whole gag over the last few days. "Thought you would have come up with a new insult since then," he tossed over his shoulder as he high-fived Zach in greeting. "Barton, save your shit talk for the court."

He jogged up and down on the ice, trying to get into game mode.

Zach grabbed the ball from Barton's grasp and sailed a jump shot into the basket.

"In the bag, baby." Zach did a small victory dance. "I'm just that good." It was a nice shot, Chase had to admit.

"Speaking of bagging," Carl Feder said with an exaggerated wink. "Which one are you going to bring to the Feast? How can you possibly choose between them?"

"Moving on, Feder. Okay, so we'll have me, Wagner, you, and Nick on one team," Zach was saying, pointing to the players as he spoke. "And Chase, Brian, Barton, Steve, and Will on the other. Sound good?"

Barton scoffed quietly but didn't say anything. The rest of them nodded and assembled themselves into small huddles.

As they split up, Chase heard Steve Sawyer say to Zach, "You know I couldn't even get her trousers off, right, dude?"

So they were talking about Em. Chase remembered the time Steve had come to practice boasting about having made out with Winters. Then the next time he hadn't been boasting so much. He'd brought her down to his basement to watch old episodes of *Saturday Night Live* hoping for a blow job and he'd gotten no further than second base.

"Maybe you just don't have my skills," Zach said, bounding out onto the ice. "So, same rules as last year?"

Chase couldn't help but flash back to the other day, when he'd walked in on Em and Zach. Em had been so embarrassed as she clutched a pillow to her chest and searched frantically for her bra.

"Zach's trying to bone Emily Winters," Barton said, thinking he was filling Chase in on a big secret. Chase nodded and looked away. He didn't want to talk about Em and Zach. It felt shitty. Invasive.

Zach very artfully managed to neither confirm nor deny the allegations. But his confident laugh made Chase feel colder than the wind did.

Chase thought back to the day Zach had told him that he was going to ask Gabby out. It was right at the beginning of last summer. Zach had spent all of their freshman and sophomore years bouncing from girl to girl, including the ridiculously hot UMaine sophomore he'd met when he was out sailing on his stepdad's boat. That was when he'd coined the "college tours" term. But he was getting a bit of a reputation for being a player. So last summer, after a day when a bunch of them had gone to the beach and Zach and Gabby had flirted all afternoon, Zach had told Chase his plan. He was going to ask Gabby out. It was perfect. She was hot. He'd heard she wasn't a prude from Ryan Chandler, a senior on the basketball team who'd taken her to prom and supposedly had inside knowledge. She'd been smiling at him a lot. Her parents would love it. And it's not like they didn't have fun together. She was cute and smart. She giggled a lot. She and Em were always up for sneaking into the

Woods Knoll golf course and drinking rum and Cokes. It was just natural. Easy.

And yeah, he'd cheated on her a few times. Chase had even congratulated Zach. Zach got away with it, and no one got hurt.

But now . . . Chase didn't know if it was because Em had been helping him, or because of how tortured she'd looked when she'd gotten out of Zach's car the other day, but when Zach talked like this, Chase couldn't even fake a smile.

He bounced up and down to get his blood pumping, to show that he was ready to play.

"Okay, so it's our ball first," Zach announced.

Chase's head snapped up. "Why?"

Zach looked quizzical. "My team won last year. Winner's ball."

"Winner's ball does not span a full year, dude."

Throwing his hands up in mock surrender, Zach relented. "Okay. Touchy, touchy. Shoot to see who goes first. Me versus Singer." Zach threw him the ball.

Chase jogged out to the middle of the pond and aimed at one of the hoops. He missed. Zach did the same, shooting for the opposite basket. Another miss. They went back and forth a couple of times, the wind taking the ball in a new direction with every shot. Chase started to zone in on the game, the ball, the feeling of physical exertion.

He swished one right in.

"Our ball," he said, flashing a triumphant grin.

"I still get my shot." Zach toed up to the makeshift line—a thin line carved faintly into the ice. But as the ball sailed from his hands, Chase saw him take a giant step forward. The ball hit the backboard, rolled around the rim, and dropped through the net.

Chase called him on it. "Foul, man! Bullshit. Take it again."

"What are you talking about?" Zach looked at him innocently.

"You stepped way over the line. Take it again."

"No I didn't." Zach looked around at the other guys. "Was I over?"

"Dude, I saw it," Chase insisted. For some reason he didn't want to let this one go. "You can't just make your own rules. Do over."

Zach stood there, not moving. "Jesus, you are really uptight these days, man. First the cock block the other day, now this." He forced a laugh, but his eyes were narrow and hard.

"Shut up, asshole." Chase spoke a little more forcefully. He dug his nails into his palms, feeling his heart beating faster, feeling his vision closing in slightly on both sides. "I'm just saying you can't always bend the rules however you fucking want. You pull this shit all the time. Forget it. Go first. I don't care."

"Okay, guys. Whatever. Zach's team goes first. Let's play."

Barton came up behind Chase. The others spread out, ready to get moving.

But Zach didn't give up.

"What's your problem, Singer? You have something to say to me?"

"Yeah, I said it. Your foot was over the damn line." In the open preserve, their voices echoed. It was getting darker, and Chase's mood was stormy. "You always cheat when you're trying to bag something?" he said with a sneer, turning his back on Zach. He hadn't meant for the words to come out, but he wouldn't take them back.

He scanned the others' faces defiantly, daring them to say something. All of a sudden, there were lots of faces down and feet shuffling.

"Oh, so you're jealous," Zach said, his voice syrupy sweet. "Of my basketball skills or of the fact that Em's into me? I didn't know you had a thing for her. Go ahead—once Gabby's back, Em's off-limits to me. So feel free to take my sloppy seconds. You should be used to hand-me-downs, right?"

That was it: Chase snapped. The anger that had been building for days—no, years—unraveled inside of him. "You're a dick, you know that?" Chase's voice was a low growl.

Zach's mouth curled sinisterly, and Chase could feel his own eyes pulling into mean slits.

"What, you suddenly care about how people *feel* or something?" Zach practically spit out the words. "Chill out. I'm just having a good time." He took a menacing step toward Chase.

"Well, I think you're being a douchebag," Chase responded, not budging a centimeter. "Think about someone else for a change."

"Really? That's what you think? Well, I think you're being a faggot," Zach said.

"What did you just call me?"

"You heard me. Faggot."

The two boys stepped toward each other, and Sean cleared his throat. "Okay, okay. Guys. Come on. Let's play." Barton and Nick moved forward instinctively. But Chase barely heard him. His eyes were locked on Zach's. The anger was a snake, lashing inside him.

Then out of nowhere came the punch. Zach's fist shot out from the right side of his body, making contact with the left side of Chase's face.

"Jesus!" Chase didn't know if he said it or if one of the other guys did, but the word rang out in the open air. His cheek stung and his eyes watered. He felt the rush of adrenaline.

Chase balled up his fist and hit back, making contact with the left side of Zach's mouth. He thought he felt the skin break beneath his knuckles.

Zach charged, head down, into Chase's torso. They fell to the ground, grunting and cursing. Chase hit the ice, hard, with a cracking sound; he rolled over, shoving Zach's head into the snow. Then the others were there, shouting, trying to break it up. Sean and Nick pulled at Zach, while Barton grabbed Chase under the arms and tugged him in the opposite direction.

Zach spit and dark blood spattered to the snowy ground. Chase couldn't tell if the blood was from Zach's oozing lip or nose. He and Zach were both heaving.

Zach looked up at him, squinting. He shook his head ever so slightly, and no one approached him. "You always take things way too far, dude."

Chase tried to shake free of Barton's grip. "What's that supposed to mean?" Even though he knew. He knew exactly what Zach was referring to. The dark secret that had been haunting him ever since the night of Minster's party. The unspeakable thing . . .

Zach looked at him hard. "You know what I'm talking about."

A spasm went through Chase's chest. He shook at Barton again, who was still gripping his arms like he was a freaking animal. "I'm fine, man," he said to Barton. "I'm fine. Lemme go."

Barton finally released him. Chase didn't look at Zach again. He turned on his heel and walked away. As he walked, he touched the skin around his eye gingerly. It was smarting and tender.

He could hear Zach's angry words as he moved. "Fucking psycho. What the hell is wrong with him?"

Back in his car, Chase's reflection leered at him, monstrous, from the rearview mirror. His face was practically maroon with exertion, and a yellow-black bruise was already starting to form around his eye. Just above it, there was a bloody cut. He grabbed his sunglasses from the visor and put them on, even though the winter sun was low and dim. He noticed he was shaking uncontrollably as he pulled the car into gear and sped out of the lot.

Pulling up to the trailer, Chase squinted with confusion at the silver BMW that sat outside. Unless they'd won the lottery (and he'd made his mom promise to stop buying lotto tickets about a year ago—they only got her hopes up), there was absolutely no reason for such a rich ride to be outside the house.

As he got out of the car, though, he saw Em sitting inside the BMW. Must be one of her parents' cars—she usually drove a little dented-up Honda. What the hell was Winters doing out here?

"Hey, Chase," she said with a note of shyness. And then, after a moment of awkward silence: "You left this at my house." She held up his playbook in her mittened hand. Chase didn't know what to say.

"You drove here to give me that?"

"Yeah, well, you're never without it," she said. He watched her pull her nose up at her own stupid joke. "I can't stay, though. I borrowed my dad's car," she added, sheepishly pointing to the gleaming silver.

This day couldn't get any worse. First the fight with Zach, now Emily Winters showing up at the trailer. He didn't even remember what state of shambles he'd left the place in this morning. For all he knew there was still a burnt Pop-Tart on the kitchen counter. There was no way he was inviting her in. He hoped she didn't expect anything from him. He had nothing to give. Especially not to her.

Forgetting all about his black eye, he took off his sunglasses, grimacing when his fingers brushed against the bruised bridge of his nose. Em gasped.

"Chase?! What happened to you?"

His hand instinctively went toward his eye. "I got into a fight," he said sullenly. He couldn't look at her. "I'm fine."

"With who? Oh my god. Are you okay? You need to get some ice on that." He'd seen Emily morph into nurse mode once before—at a Fourth of July party last summer, when Matt Harrison had run straight through a glass door. (It had been so clean that Harrison thought he was running through air.) It was kind of cute when she got like this. But he wanted to be alone.

"I'm fine," he repeated. "It's just a little black-and-blue. Thanks for the playbook." He grabbed the binder and moved toward his door. If he was lucky, maybe she'd just leave.

"Hold on," Em said. "Let me put some ice on it. And some of this cream. I know my dad keeps it in the car—one of the perks of being a doctor's daughter. I'm like a walking first-aid kit."

Before Chase could utter another word, she was rummaging through her glove compartment, tossing questions over her shoulder. "Who did you fight with? Where are you coming from? Does it hurt? Does it feel like you have a concussion?" Apparently she found what she was looking for, and nudged him toward his front door. He didn't answer, but he didn't resist, either. He was too exhausted to bother.

Inside, she took off her hood and shook out her long hair. Then she sat him down on a stool at the kitchen counter, found a dish towel, and gently cleaned off his wound.

"Were you with Zach?" Chase could hear the quiver in her voice. What a little shit Zach was. This girl really liked him. He saw the way her eyes got far away for a moment, and he instantly thought of Ty. He knew his eyes looked like that these days too. He nodded, but Em barely paid attention. She just babbled on.

"Oh, cool. I was just wondering. Because . . . like, because . . . we were maybe going to go sweater shopping today but I never heard from him. I was sure he was just with you or whatever but I was just curious—Wait! Was Zach in this fight too?"

She looked at him, stricken. And he knew he had to tell her. Would she want to know? Probably not. Was he doing her a favor? Maybe. Or maybe he was just trying to hurt her, to hurt Zach, to make everyone else's lives feel as weird and jumbled as his felt right now.

"Yeah, he was in it, Winters. He threw the first punch."

"Oh my god." Em's brown eyes went wide, and she was suddenly, obviously, fascinated. Chase probably could have said Zach picked his nose and Em would have savored the details. "Who were you guys fighting?" she asked, almost under her breath.

"Each other."

Em took a step back. "I don't get it."

"We were playing ice hoops. With the guys. Some stuff came up. Zach punched me. And I punched him back." Chase shifted on his stool, feeling his eye throbbing in pain. Was she going to help him clean this wound up or not?

"So it was all over a game?"

Chase snorted. "Not exactly. I called him out on being an asshole."

"Why—why would you say something like that?" Em squeaked.

"Because he *is* an asshole, Winters. I mean, he's my best friend. Or was. Or whatever. But he treats girls like garbage."

"What are you talking about?" Em's face had gone pale, like the snow outside the trailer.

"He's not going to break up with Gabby, for one thing. He said it, point-blank, in front of a whole bunch of us just this afternoon. And it's not because he, like, loves Gabby or anything. He likes her. But part of that is just because she's easy to deal with. He doesn't have to put in any effort. He can do whatever he wants. And he does." Chase couldn't stop now. He was going to spill it all. "He wants to hook up with both of you, so he does. He wants to meet girls from other schools, so he does. That's the point: He does whatever, whenever he feels like it."

Emily looked sick. Chase had never seen anyone "turn green" before—even during intense preseason practices, when coach had them do sprints in the summer sun and some of the guys threw up. But Emily's skin now had a decidedly puke-green tint to it.

"You're a liar." She said it quietly but furiously. "You don't know what you're talking about."

Chase sighed. Now that he'd spilled everything, he regretted it. Of course she wouldn't believe him. But now he was in too deep to just let it go. "I do, Emily. I'm sorry, but I know *exactly* what I'm talking about." It was, he thought, the only time he'd ever addressed her by her first name.

"Why are you saying this?" She was louder now. Almost hysterical. Chase felt bad, but she needed to know. "It's not true!"

"Look at this," he said, scrolling through his phone. He

found what he was looking for and held it out to her. *From Zach McCord,* it plainly said. It was from three days ago, when Chase had walked in on her and Zach. It read: *Hey man, thanks for the cock block. I only have a few days to make this happen, asshole. Lol.*

And then another one: *Mtg that UMaine chick later. U should come if she has hot friends.*

Em grabbed the phone from his hand. He watched her eyes run over the words. When she looked back up at him, one tear was spilling down onto her cheek. He looked quickly away. He should never have said anything. He didn't want to see this.

"You don't get it," Em said. "This isn't what you think it is."

"Sorry, Winters," he repeated dumbly. There was nothing else to say. He watched her grab her bag and put on her coat in silence. She slammed the door on her way out; the impact made the thin walls reverberate.

For a second Chase just stood there. He listened to Em's car start up and peel away. The trailer was stiflingly hot and smelled nauseating, like damp socks and crusted tomato sauce. He needed out. No. He needed Ty. He picked up his phone, which Em had thrown onto the counter like it was on fire. He dialed Ty's number. It didn't even ring. Straight to voice mail.

He got up, shuffled to the bathroom, and stared in the mirror. His swollen eye looked bad. What if it was still like this for the Football Feast? Did it even matter anymore?

He dialed Ty's number one more time. Again, straight to

voice mail. Christ. He wanted her right now. He wanted *something.*

He suddenly remembered the scarf he'd taken from Ty's the other day. Maybe if he just smelled it, held it in his hands, he would feel better. He stumbled over to where his jeans were draped over the heater.

But when he pulled his hands out of the jeans pocket, there was no delicate white scarf there—just a handful of ashy dust. He let the ash scatter, and brushed his hands off quickly.

Weird. His jeans hadn't burned—they weren't even that hot. Was he losing his mind?

He looked down at his hands.

They were streaked in black.

CHAPTER THIRTEEN

"He's just jealous. . . . It's not true. This isn't true." Emily repeated the words to herself in a low mumble as she drove away from Chase's home, one hand on the wheel, the other holding her head up next to the window. She kept the radio off and her eyes, blurry with tears, staring straight ahead. The words of Zach's text messages looped in her head.

Em shuddered. She wasn't imagining the connection between her and Zach. She couldn't be. They had such a spark—such chemistry—and he was really opening up to her. She couldn't listen to Chase. She had to talk it out with Zach. He would explain everything.

Only a few days to make this happen. No. That wasn't Zach. There had to be some misunderstanding.

But the doubts continued to seep in. She couldn't help

but think about the fact that she and Zach had planned to go sweater shopping today, and he'd never called. Of course she'd popped out of bed at 9 a.m. and gotten dressed in a fake-casual ensemble of her best-fitting jeans and a black cashmere sweater that hung just right. She'd blown out her hair and pulled it back into a "messy" ponytail, choosing carefully which tendrils to pull loose. Then she'd hopped back into bed and stared at the ceiling, dying to call him and willing him to call her first. He hadn't.

And of course that was fine—he was superbusy, she knew that. But Em had to admit that a small part of the reason she'd driven out to Chase's house was to try to find out what Zach was up to. (Okay, maybe it was a big part.) That question had been answered: Zach had been hanging out with his friends, playing basketball. Fine. No big deal. But he'd gotten into a fight with Chase? He'd forgotten to call? Maybe she didn't know Zach as well as she thought she did.

Em was nearing her own street when all of a sudden, without even thinking it through, she slammed on the brakes. Then, with deliberate motions, she pulled into a driveway and made a three-point turn. She was going to Zach's.

His car was in the driveway, so he was definitely home. The light in his room was the only one on in the house. With the same determination she felt before final exams or the first icy ocean plunge of the season, she stormed into Zach's house. No knock. She called out his name.

"Zach?"

She heard his voice, and at first she thought he was talking to her.

"Zach?" She said it again, more quietly this time, advancing toward the staircase. But as she got nearer, Em realized he must be on the phone. She heard him laugh, pause, laugh again, and then say something else. His voice sounded light, friendly, flirtatious—the way it did when he was talking to her. Or Gabby. Who was he talking to? He sure as hell wasn't shooting the shit with a *guy* friend.

Em started walking up the stairs on her tiptoes. As she neared the landing, Zach's words became clearer. "Totally, me too," he was saying. And then: "I miss you too, Gabsy."

Em had never heard him use this pet name, but Gabby had told her about it several times. All of a sudden she felt like she might throw up. She had to steady herself on the staircase banister as he continued talking.

"Let's go out to a nice dinner in Portland when you get back," he said. "I can't wait to see you. And kiss you." Pause. "Bye babe."

He hadn't even put down his iPhone when Em came charging through his bedroom door. She didn't care that she looked insane, that she'd been creeping around in his house, that he looked genuinely shocked and horrified to see her there. She'd heard enough. Chase was right; Zach had zero intention of breaking up with Gabby. This was all a game.

"Em?" Zach stammered. His lip was swollen and his hair was sticking out all over the place. There were bloody tissues all over his room. Even so, he looked hot—wounded and tough. Em took a deep breath, reminding herself why she was there, why she was angry.

"So you and Gabby will go out for a nice dinner when she gets back, huh? Is that where you'll break up with her? Or is that when you'll kiss her? Jesus. Everyone is right about you." Her fingers were clammy and kept sticking to her hair as she repeatedly tucked it behind her ears.

"Em . . ." She could practically see the wheels turning, the lies forming, in his head. But then something happened; his expression changed. He looked calm, or at least resigned. "You're right. I don't know what to say. Except—"

"Did you even like me at all?" She didn't mean to ask. But she had to know. She had to know she wasn't just making it up. "Were you ever going to break up with her?"

He rubbed his forehead. "Look, Em, I do like being with you. You're great. I just . . . I also like being with Gabby. It's kind of like how I play basketball, football, and soccer. I like them all. You know?"

"People are not sports, Zach." Em felt like her heart had

migrated up to the space below her collarbone. "You can only have one girlfriend. Do the math. Oh wait, I forgot. Math isn't exactly your strong suit." The words flew out of her mouth.

Zach nodded. "I probably deserved that."

Em bit back the impulse to say she was sorry. She would *not* apologize. Not to him—not now.

Zach got up off the bed, started pacing around the room, even as Em held on to the cold plaster wall for support. Then, abruptly, he asked, "Do you know how my mom met my stepdad?"

"What?" Em's frustration, and anger, and resentment made her head feel like it would burst. What was he talking about now? She tried to breathe, tried to hear him talk. Part of her still hoped there was some way out of this mess—some way to go back and reclaim that feeling they had the other day, curled up together. Like this was right. She wanted to believe that the texts Chase had shown her were a huge mistake.

"At a florist's. That's where they met," Zach said, his handsome features looking pinched. "He was picking out some bouquet for this *other* woman he was dating at the time. My mom was looking around, and he said that this one particular flower perfectly matched her lips. And she fell for it! She fell for that line." He looked nauseous. "So anyway, this fucking smarmy real-estate guy in some random flower store hits on my mom and *boom!* I got a stepdad. And you want to know why she was there, why *she* was at the florist's?"

Em wasn't sure that she did, or why he was telling her all this in the first place. Zach went on: "She was *picking out flowers for my dad's funeral service.*"

He stared at her as if he wanted applause, or a reaction, or for a lightbulb to go on over Em's head. When she still didn't say anything, he sighed. "I guess I kind of stopped believing in all of it after that—love, commitment, all that bullshit."

But Gabby's face hovered in Em's mind, her big blue eyes and dimples. How trusting she was.

Em struggled to control the trembling of her voice. "Zach, I'm sorry that your mom moved on so quickly. But . . . But . . ." She could feel the tears swelling again.

Zach sighed. He didn't look tortured anymore. He just looked tired. "Em—I don't want to be in this position. I don't want to have to choose."

"You don't want to *choose*? Well, maybe you should have thought of that before you *kissed* me. You kind of *chose* then." In a fit of snapping rage, she felt her palm slap the wall for emphasis. "Don't you get it, Zach? You hurt me. You fucked with my head. And Gabby's. Gabby's even more than mine. And you obviously have *no idea* how much you'll hurt Gabby if she finds out."

He took an unconscious step back and blinked a few times. Then he narrowed his eyes.

"*I'll* hurt Gabby? Just me? You were involved in this, too, you know." He laughed coldly. "You weren't exactly pushing me away."

"You know what? Fuck you, Zach," she said, feeling like the words were sharp edges, shredding her. She was hysterical now, gulping back tears and shame. He was right, she realized as she swung around. He might be the lying asshole, but this mess was as much her fault as his. She slammed his bedroom door behind her. Forever.

She was disgusting. She was a terrible friend. She was totally unworthy of a real relationship. As she walked toward her dad's car, she took a few deep breaths, trying to stall the tears she knew would come. But it worked only until she got into the BMW. Her crying became faster and more out of control as she drove—not toward home, she couldn't face that—but down roads she rarely took and around corners she'd never turned, until she knew she had to pull over. Her sobs were blurring her vision. She needed to collect herself. On the side of the road, Em put her head on the steering wheel and sobbed.

She didn't even bother to conceal her misery when she came home, ignoring her parents' concerned faces and inquisitive murmurs. "Are you hungry?" her mom asked.

"No," Em said. She stomped up the stairs, closed and locked her bedroom door, and threw herself on top of the bed. She thought about what else she could have said to Zach and how bad she felt about blowing up at Chase. And Gabby. Gabby. Should Em tell her? Would Zach? She couldn't believe she'd fallen for it—let him trick her into thinking he really cared. The worst part of it all was that if he asked her to come over now, if he begged for her forgiveness, she wasn't sure what she would do.

No. The worst part was that he wouldn't ask for her forgiveness.

Beep-beep-beep. A text. Em barely wanted to pick it up. Whoever it was, it was someone she didn't want to talk to—Gabby? Ugh, not now. Zach? Even worse. Chase? She couldn't deal with him, either. She picked up a pillow and smothered her face until it felt like she couldn't breathe.

Finally, she flipped open her phone and looked at the screen. It was JD. *Babysitting emergency. Can you bring over some Dr Pepper?*

Somehow the normalcy of that text, the easiness of it, made her cry all over again. Em knew that this was JD's way of breaking the ice after yesterday's argument, and wished the mess her life had become could actually be fixed by something as simple as soda. With a heavy sigh, Em rolled over onto her side and forced herself out of her bed. Maybe hanging out with JD would help. Everything felt so innocent over there.

Em gripped the banister as she headed downstairs, feeling like if she let go, she might just tumble all the way down. She stumbled into the kitchen, grabbed four cans from the fridge, and headed next door. She didn't even put on shoes—just stuffed her feet into woolen slippers while shouting upstairs, "I'm going to JD's!" As she scurried across their snow-covered lawns, feeling the cold bite into her toes, she looked up at the night sky, cloudless and starry. Despite the blackness of her mood, she couldn't help but appreciate its beauty.

"If I'm going to be forced to watch *Sisterhood of the Traveling Pants* for the one millionth time, I need some Dr Pepper," JD said as soon as he opened the door, rolling his eyes. Em almost resented how comfortable—how unmiserable—he looked in a bright red sweatshirt and gray sweatpants that had the word TINY emblazoned down the leg.

But when JD saw Em's puffy red eyes, her dark hair in a huge, ridiculous tangle, he stopped smiling. "You okay?" he asked softly.

Em nodded—she couldn't bring herself to talk about it just yet. Instead, she held up the soda cans.

"You're a savior," he said, taking them from her and letting her into the house. "A savior whose feet must be freezing."

Em came into the familiar Fount home, its faint smell of lemon-scented cleaning products and ginger tea washing over her, making it a little easier to breathe. "Hey, Mel," she said as she walked into the TV room, where caramel popcorn (a shared favorite among the Fount-Winters kids) and Mrs. Fount's mini-cracker-pizzas were arrayed on the coffee table. Em's stomach growled as her appetite came rushing back.

"Hi, Em!" Mel leaped up to give Em a big bear hug. Melissa was freckled and brace-faced, and her hair smelled like berries. She was the closest thing that Em had ever had to a sibling, someone to love and pick on (sometimes simultaneously). Em found that she was smiling into Melissa's hair.

"The movie's halfway over, but you should watch with us," Melissa said, plopping back down onto the couch. She had a tiny pizza-sauce stain around her lips.

"Oh, good. I forget what happens at the end," Em said, gushing while filling a bowl with popcorn. She felt like she could eat the whole bowl. It was amazing how much lighter she felt already, now that she was in the Founts' home. It was like falling into clean sheets in a big bed at the end of a long day.

But then Melissa sat up, suddenly, with an expression of panic on her face. "Oh my god, what time is it?!"

JD looked at his watch—a pocketwatch he kept clipped with a chain to whatever trousers he was wearing. "It's eight thirty-six," he reported.

"Ohmygod I'm supposed to text Jake!" Melissa was halfway out the door before Em could even get the words out:

"Who's Jake?"

"My *boyfriend*," Melissa shouted disdainfully, already halfway up the stairs to her bedroom.

"Her *boyfriend*?" Em gawked at JD, while stuffing a handful of popcorn into her mouth.

"Of course. My eleven-year-old sister has a male companion," JD said dryly. "She gets more action than I do—even if it's just holding hands."

Em laughed a little, slapping his shoulder.

JD coughed, his face softening. "I'm sorry about the other day, Em."

"It's okay." Her throat was too tight for her to say more.

"No, really. I was a jerk," he said, shifting on the couch, "and I'm sorry."

"I . . ." She trailed off. Remembering the fight with Zach made her head pound and kind of erased her memory of the fight with JD. It was all blending together in a huge, blurry, tear-stained mess.

"It's just that I don't know Zach very well, you know? And I just . . . I think you deserve so much more." JD kept crossing and uncrossing his arms, kind of holding one elbow and then grabbing the other. "I know that sounds lame."

It occurred to Em that JD was nervous. For that matter, *she* was nervous. Her pride was more than wounded. It was maimed. "It's really okay, JD. . . . The thing is . . . Okay, can I tell you something?" She sighed deeply again.

"You can tell me anything. Really. I won't . . . I don't need to be so opinionated all the time. Just tell me, whatever it is." His eyes pleaded with her.

Em picked at a hangnail on her right pinkie. "The thing is

that you were right. You were totally, stupidly, right."

"What do you mean?" They were facing each other now, on the couch, each with one leg folded beneath them and one leg hanging over the edge, foot on the floor.

"You were right about Zach, about him being an asshole." She inhaled sharply; the words cost her a huge effort.

"Okay. How so?" He was obviously trying not to push her too hard. She appreciated it, especially since she hated saying the words out loud. It was like as soon as they left her mouth they would be true.

"Like . . . it'soverwithmeandZach." She let the words tumble out. "Whatever it was is over." Tears pooled at the edges of her eyes. "And I can't believe I did this, to Gabby. To myself." Em blushed.

He reached out, grabbed her hand, squeezed it.

"Em . . . I'm—I'm sorry. Even though I'm not sure if that's what I'm supposed to say." He kept squeezing. "Em. You know I wasn't, like, judging you, right? I was just . . . concerned. I think you're amazing, you know?"

Em stared at him, his hair sticking out in every direction, like usual. With him everything felt so natural, so necessary.

"You don't think I'm a terrible person?"

"Of course not." He reached out to touch her arm and left his hand there, his thumb rubbing her elbow.

"I just feel like I don't deserve much of anything," she said, trying to swallow back the tears. "I can't believe I did this. It was so *stupid*." She leaned back and dropped her head onto the back of the couch, willing herself not to cry.

"It's okay, it's okay." JD leaned forward to brush away a tear that managed to leak out despite her efforts. Even after years of shared tents on camping trips and wrestling matches, Em thought this might be the closest they'd ever been. She could feel his pulse through his hand, which was still hovering on her cheek. He opened his mouth like he was going to say more, but he just took a breath instead.

In her gut, Em knew he was about to kiss her. She swallowed. JD was going to kiss her. She was terrified. And yet she didn't flinch or move away.

But in an instant, the moment was over. He reached past her to grab the remote control.

"No more traveling pants," he said, fumbling with the remote. He hit several buttons at once, accidentally switching to a Spanish-language channel before managing to find the guide. "Must start being the one to *wear* the trousers around here and not watch teenage-girl crap anymore. Ooooh, *Real World* reruns! Yes?"

"What season?" Em felt a little dazed.

"Hawaii."

"Is that the one with the crazy girl?"

"They're all the one with the crazy girl," JD said. "Hey,

I have an idea." He got up and disappeared into the kitchen, coming back a few seconds later with two tall glasses and a bottle of his parents' rum. "Just a splash. They won't be back until tomorrow, anyway."

A yummy, sweet, *strong* drink sounded like exactly what she needed. And so they settled in with rum and Dr Peppers.

"Drinking game!" Em proposed, giggling. She was still feeling a little disoriented. *JD almost kissed me.* It was impossible. "Anytime anyone makes out with anyone, take a sip."

"Okay. And anytime anyone does a drunk confessional, take another sip."

"We're going to be wasted." Em laughed, the cathartic, sneezy laugh that comes after a good cry. Despite everything, she felt about a million times better than she had two hours ago.

They watched four episodes, giving up on the drinking game after they realized that their livers couldn't handle it. Em finished the mini-pizzas. ("Jeez, did you not eat for days?" JD asked as she scarfed down the last one.) At some point, Melissa yelled down that she was going to sleep. By eleven, they were horizontal on the L-shaped sofa, heads almost touching, empty glasses in front of them.

"I'm just going to close my eyes for a little bit," Em said between yawns. She grabbed both afghans from behind the couch, throwing one to JD and keeping one for herself. "Then I'll go home."

"Whatever you say, sleeping beauty." He reached over his head to tousle her already tangled hair. And they fell asleep just like that, JD's fingers just skimming the top of Em's head, Em curled into the back of the couch, nose against the soft brown leather. For the first time in days, she fell asleep quickly, dreamlessly.

A few hours later, though, she woke with a start. She had no idea what time it was, and the clock on the DVD player was blinking *12:00*, clearly stuck on reset. She shivered, sat up, and pulled her hair back into a knotty ponytail. Her mouth felt thick with the sweet rum and soda. The moon came in through the sliding door, and she looked over to see JD sleeping silently, his mouth slightly open, his hand still stretched out above him. His cheekbones looked angular in the dark. It was like he was a whole other person—not the boy she'd grown up with, but some guy with a strong jaw and weird hair. Some guy she had just met and wanted to get to know.

Just then she had the strangest feeling, like someone was watching her. But the house was heavy with silence. She scanned the room, her eyes falling on the TV, the lamp, the empty popcorn bowl, the maroon tapestry hanging on the wall. And then she gasped. There, in the sliding-glass door, was a face. A girl. Blond, glowing a little, smiling menacingly.

Em stopped breathing. She blinked and shook her head. And when she opened her eyes, the face was gone. Nothing was there.

Em lay back down, her breath coming fast. Was she going crazy? First the anonymous note left in her winter coat, and now this.

She snuggled a teeny bit closer to where JD was lying, without waking him. She could hear the clock ticking in the hall, the wind blowing branches outside, the refrigerator humming in the kitchen. She lay there like that for the rest of the night, twitching at every sound, unable to fall back to sleep.

CHAPTER FOURTEEN

Tonight was going to be good, Chase could feel it. Ever since Ty had called him early that morning and he'd asked if he could take her out on a real dinner date, his pulse had been racing. She suggested a French place in a beach town about twenty minutes up the highway. He'd briefly panicked—the place, Lumière de la Mer, had a reputation of being one of Southern Maine's most upscale restaurants, with prices to match—but he'd kept his vocal reaction cool. He'd find some way to swing it. He had to. They would kiss again, more than before, and he would ask her to come to the Football Feast. There were only a few days left before the main event, and now that things with Zach and the other guys had gotten so screwed up, he needed Ty more than ever.

He distracted himself for much of the day by reading

back issues of *National Geographic*, pulling out the huge map inserts, smoothing them out on his bedroom floor. Maybe he would see the world with Ty. He took a long, hot shower, partly because it was a special occasion, partly to give his white-and-blue-striped shirt a few extra moments in the steam. He shaved and patted his chin and neck with the same spicy aftershave his dad had long ago kept in a black bag under the sink, and put a sport coat on over his shirt at the last minute. This, too, had been his father's. He'd found it a few years ago in the back of his mom's tiny closet, taking up space. Apparently it was the jacket his dad had worn for his parents' justice-of-the-peace wedding seventeen years ago. With dark jeans, dress shoes, and his shoulders set straight, he could easily pass for a college dude. He felt good, like he did at the start of a game against a school with a good reputation. His muscles flexed instinctively in his excitement.

It had snowed a bit overnight, not so much to accumulate in drifts, but enough to leave a half-inch layer of ice over pretty much everything. Chase worked up a sweat scraping it off the windshield. He considered changing his shirt but realized he didn't have time to steam another one.

Chase picked up a bouquet of flowers from the grocery store, one with lots of bright red flowers, like the one Ty had given him the first night they'd met. The next stop was the one Chase was dreading, but there was no avoiding it. He pulled into the Kwik Mart parking lot, took a deep breath, and strode inside, trying to look natural.

"Chase, honey!" His mom looked up from the magazine rack, where she was restocking the *National Enquirer* and other tabloids. She had been pretty when she was younger, but now she looked kind of faded: too many tanning booths, too many cigarettes. She still tried as hard as she could to look put together—too hard, probably.

"Hi, Mom," Chase said, shoving his hands in his pockets.

"What's up, sweetie? Where are you going all spiffed up? I thought the Football Feast was in few days."

"I'm going out to dinner," he said, aware of how ridiculous the words sounded. "On a date."

"Who are you taking out on a date?" She dropped a *Daily Sun* and bent to grab it off the dirty floor.

"Just a girl I know from around here." He looked around to make sure no one was eavesdropping. "And I was wondering if I could borrow the credit card," he said in a rush. "Just for the night."

His mom frowned. "I don't know, honey. We just finished paying it down. You know it's only for emergencies."

"Well, this is kind of an emergency. I want to . . . impress her." He said the last part shyly. He never talked about this stuff with his mom.

She stopped arranging the magazines and faced him full-on,

her hands on her hips. "Whoever this girl is, she should be impressed with *you*, not the kind of dinner you take her to."

"Mom, please. Can I have it, or what?" He hated asking. But he had to. In his mind, there was no other option. He would do anything to make it work with Ty.

"Okay," she said, letting out a breath. "Yes." She even smiled. "Just promise me you won't do anything you'll regret. Just think with that smart head you have up here," she said, swatting him lightly with a rolled up *Us Weekly*.

"I promise, I promise," he answered, hopping ever so slightly from one foot to the other. He didn't want to be late to the restaurant—Ty had asked if they could meet there because she had some family stuff to do first.

Chase's mom walked slowly to the register, pulled her bag from behind the counter, and took out the hardly used card. They'd both learned the dangers of debt when creditors formal and informal had started calling in the weeks after Chase's dad's death.

"Just be careful, Chase. I love you." She leaned over the counter to squeeze his cheek. He jerked away a bit, and then felt guilty.

"I love you, too, Mom. Thanks." He gave her a quick smile, so she would know that he meant it.

He walked quickly back to the car. Across the street, the lights were still on in a crappy little pet store that somehow stayed open in a practically abandoned shopping center. One of the empty store windows next door was boarded up, and the board rattled in the wind, a rhythmic thumping.

He could make out a figure standing right in the front display window of the pet store. The person's face was illuminated by the flickering sign: Man and Beast, the store was called. Chase squinted—was that a girl? Moving closer, he saw that it was. It was Drea Feiffer—and she was holding a giant snake. She was standing with a friend of hers, some guy with bleached-blond hair who had dropped out of school last year and who, as far as Chase knew, went only by the name Crow.

Chase was too far away to tell for sure, but it seemed like Drea was staring right at him through the glass. Chase shook his head and looked away quickly, jogging the rest of the way to his car. What freaks.

Lumière de la Mer was right off Route 1, and easy to find. Chase was early; Ty had not yet arrived. The place was crowded with holiday revelers, including several other people from Ascension—a few with their families, plus a group of senior girls.

"Hi, Chaaaaaase," two of them (Becky something and Jamie St. Louis) drawled. Becky had a lopsided birthday party hat on her head. A few weeks ago, Chase would have been plotting how to hit that, but tonight he just waved and smiled as the hostess sat him at a table for two. Wait until they saw who he was meeting here.

"Our Eve of the Eve tasting menu is quite popular tonight," the waiter—dressed in a stuffy, gold-buttoned uniform—told him as he settled in. He remembered to unfold his napkin and put it on his lap. "Would you care for something to drink? A glass of wine while you wait?"

This guy wasn't going to card him? No wonder this place was so popular.

"Yeah, I'd love a whiskey on the rocks," he said with as much cool as he could muster.

"What type of whiskey, sir?"

"Uh . . ." He didn't think "whatever's cheapest" would cut it here. "Maker's Mark, if you have it," he said, saying a silent thank-you to Ascension's parents and their well-stocked bars.

The drink came, and he sipped it as he waited. Every time the door opened, letting in a blast of cold air, Chase craned his neck to see if it was her. Ty was late, but not too late. Ten minutes. Whatever. Fashionably late was still a thing, right? When fifteen minutes rolled around, he ordered another drink, this time a bit sheepishly. "My friend is running late," he told the waiter, speaking loudly in the hopes that others would hear. Chase pulled out his phone and tried, discreetly, dialing Ty's number. Straight to voice mail.

The waiter came back when Chase had been waiting for

twenty-five minutes. Chase debated getting one more drink. On one hand, he couldn't afford three top-shelf whiskeys plus a fancy "tasting dinner" for two. On the other, this was getting a little embarrassing. The senior girls were definitely whispering about him; he wouldn't be surprised if they'd already posted it on Facebook: *Chase Singer has been sitting alone for half an hour at Lumiere de la Mer. Who's standing him up?* Yeah, he'd get the drink. Just one more.

The first sip of his third whiskey in less than an hour put him over the edge. He hadn't eaten very much all day and he was feeling warm and woozy. The breadsticks at the next table were looking extremely appealing. Maybe he could ask for some, just to tide himself over. Instead, he caught the waiter's attention and signaled for the check.

But shit, wait, who was that coming through the door? Chase's chair made a terrible sound as he stood, shoving it back violently. Sasha Bowlder had just walked into the restaurant.

She was walking toward him. And there was blood flowing from her head, around her face.

What. The. Fuck.

Chase lurched forward, steadying himself on the table, swiping the tablecloth in the process so all the glasses tipped precariously. She was coming toward him. And there was all that blood. He let out a mangled half cry. He was going to be sick. He tried to move away from the table, pushing the chair back farther, and then there was a loud, thunderous crash.

Every head in Lumière de la Mer swiveled toward him. Or, more accurately, toward the fancy dessert cart he'd just overturned. Chocolate mousse smeared the floor; pink-red plums oozed from a shattered tart. Delicate, lacy cookies were shattered next to actual shards of china plates.

"Oh my god, are you okay?" Sasha ran toward him, but all of a sudden she looked nothing like Sasha and there was no blood. It was just some random girl.

Chase wanted to crawl under the table and stay there for good. He couldn't believe how badly this evening had gone.

Under a veil of repeated, mortified apologies, Chase scrawled his signature on the credit card slip. Thirty dollars *plus* tax, just to humiliate himself, to sit in a bullshit restaurant for forty-five minutes waiting for someone who never came, and then to have a hallucination and ruin a lot of fucking pastries.

This was it. He was done with Ty.

Chase drove fast to the mall with the radio blaring, trying to drown out his anger, pounding his hands against the steering wheel in time with the beats. He was buzzing from the whiskeys and from anger, embarrassment. He didn't care how hot Ty was, how amazing she made him feel. She was going to get a piece of his mind. No one pulled this on Chase Singer.

But when he arrived at the Behemoth parking lot, he

realized it was dark except for a few construction lights, and he didn't remember exactly how to get through the woods to Ty's house. He got out and walked a couple of paces, and as the cold air knocked away some of his confidence, he realized that this mission was hopeless. He was never going to find that path, and even if he did, how would he stay on it without a flashlight? He wasn't about to go traipsing through the woods alone at night . . . especially not the Haunted Woods, even if he didn't believe those stories were true. Damn. This was getting worse by the minute.

But then he thought he noticed a tiny opening in the brush, snow that looked like it was tamped down by crusty footprints. He took a few steps, trying to let his eyes adjust to the dark. Yes, this was a path. It had to be the same one. He grew more confident as the narrow clearing widened, revealing what was certainly the same winding trail they'd walked down the other day. He followed it to where he was sure the clearing, and Ty's house, had been. The moonlight shone brighter here—there weren't as many trees around. He was positive he'd arrived at the spot where he'd caught the first glimpse of Ty's rickety home. But nothing was there, only some trees licked with black, as though there'd been a bonfire here recently.

Chase stumbled back the way he came, cursing Ty and his poor sense of direction. As he emerged into the parking area and started striding back toward his car, he recoiled. There, lying in the gravel lot between him and his car, was some nasty dead animal. Roadkill. Possibly something that had gotten in the way of one of those giant construction cranes. A possum, maybe? Surrounding it were three feral cats, playing with it, poking it, picking at it. They'd approached silently, in seconds.

"Beat it!" he shouted at the cats, picking up a rock and tossing it in their general direction. Their eyes shone bright and green and glassy under the moon. They looked at him calmly, then resumed their task. "I said get out of here!" Chase yelled again even louder, his fury with Ty mixing with repulsion at the skinny creatures in front of him.

Instead of leaving, one of the cats tugged at a piece of the corpse until it separated from the rest of the body. It slinked toward him, the bloody meat dangling from its mouth like an offering.

"Get the fuck away from me," Chase said, kicking at it, walking a wide semicircle around the nauseating spectacle and getting back into his car. His hands were shaking.

Everything good ends in shit. He knew this. He *knew* this. He should never have gotten in this deep.

And then he got her texts, several in a row, like a deluge breaking through cracks in a dam. The first: *Chase? Are you there? I'm so so so so sorry*. And the second: *Please answer, Chase? I'm so sorry I'm so late. A family thing came up. I couldn't get away*. And then: *Please let me explain. I couldn't get out of it. I really wanted to. Please, I really care about you. I'm sorry.*

He tried to stay mad, but he could feel himself softening immediately. As soon as her name popped up on the screen, he felt the familiar driving need to see her, to be around her, to inhale the smell of her skin and float away on the sound of her laugh. The force of it made his head spin. He pulled over, and then typed: *Don't be silly. It's okay. Things happen. Let's just reschedule.*

He began driving again. The car's defroster was pumping like a workhorse and still the window was gray and spotty. He looked up and realized that he hadn't been paying much attention to where he was going; he was nearing the Piss Pass, about to head onto the bridge that straddled the highway below. He'd made an effort not to drive this way since Sasha's suicide attempt. It was too creepy. But here he was. He heard his phone chime with a new text.

He reached over to grab it, taking his eyes off the road for a split second. And just then he felt his tires hit the ice. They seized and slid, and his car careened wildly to the right. Chase was certain, in the panicked way that people become certain, that he and his car were about to sail through the guardrail.

He weaved in a fishtail motion, with the front of his car pushing forward and the back of it trailing from side to side. The wheel jerked under his fingers, unresponsive. He would go flying to the highway below, just as Sasha must have.

But then his motion was no longer out of control, he was back in the right lane, and the ground below him was solid.

"Holy shit." Chase pulled over as soon as he crossed the Piss Pass. He said it again: "Holy shit." His pulse was throbbing, his head felt disconnected from his body. His knuckles, gripping the steering wheel as though it were the only thing keeping him in the car, were white, and he was having trouble breathing.

He almost died. He definitely just missed death.

He was *way* too drunk to be driving. What the hell was he thinking? He drew in a few long, gasping breaths, felt his pulse start to slow a little. He massaged his chest hard with his knuckles; the seizing tension there made him feel like he was having some kind of heart attack.

He looked down to see that his phone was still blinking on his lap, showing one message from Ty.

Careful. The roads are icy tonight.

CHAPTER FIFTEEN

The snowy trees rushed by the train window, a blurred palette of grays and whites and browns. Gazing at the blue sky behind the trees, and the ocean hidden beyond them, Em was mesmerized, silent. She willed away thoughts of Zach and Gabby and love and jealousy and focused only on the landscape. Her journal was sitting open on her lap, resting against her thighs and her new dark jeans—a Christmas present from her mom. The pen had slipped from her fingers into the crevice of the binding. She'd tried to write, but no words came.

It was Saturday morning, New Year's Eve. Tonight Em's and JD's parents were going to some kind of lefty political party in York—mostly doctors and lawyers—and Em and JD had decided to go to Boston and celebrate First Night. She'd ignored calls from some other friends, just like she'd been ignoring them all break—they *had* to know something was up by now—and had pointedly deleted the one text she'd received from Zach: a plaintive, pathetic *Hi?*

JD pawned Melissa off on a freshman babysitter, told his filmmaking friends he was headed for Beantown, and had taken the morning train down to have brunch with his aunt Sophie. Em had met her a few times. Sophie Downs had never married, was as smart as a whip, and had an antique writing desk that looked out over the sardine-packed brownstones of Beacon Hill. Sometimes Em thought she had more in common with Aunt Sophie than with her own relatives.

She and JD had agreed to meet at five o'clock in Harvard Square; the train ride was about two hours long and scheduled to get into North Station around two thirty. That would give her just enough time to stop at Maintenance and pick out a really nice gift for Gabs.

Em shifted in her seat, closing the journal and depositing it in her bag. She'd write later, once she had a chance to gather her thoughts. Out of the corner of her eye, she thought she saw someone staring at her, and when she turned to look, she sharply drew in her breath.

Sitting diagonally across the aisle was a blond-haired girl that looked remarkably—freakishly—similar to the one she'd been dreaming about or hallucinating or whatever. The one she'd seen in JD's window last night. Em realized she was gaping, smiled perfunctorily at the girl, and whipped back around. It had to be a coincidence.

"I like your bag." All of a sudden the girl was standing over her. "And the flower."

Em had pinned the red orchid to her bag a few days ago—after the sleepy afternoon in Zach's bed. And even after their blowout, Em had not been able to bring herself to get rid of it. Even though she knew Zach had played her, she almost *had* to keep it. It was a gift from him, and one of the only symbols that he had liked her, at least. It was the one small token reminding her that she hadn't imagined the whole thing.

"Um, thanks," Em said, wishing she were holding a book that she could pretend to be reading. The girl was model pretty, but Em couldn't shake the feeling that there was something off about her.

"I'm Ali." The girl was holding out her hand for Em to shake. Em hesitated before reaching out and quickly clasping the girl's hand, which was freezing.

"Hi. I'm Em." Em noted with relief that the train was pulling into North Station. She made a show of gathering her things, looking down to rearrange the items in her purse.

"Have a great evening, Em," the girl said with a laugh, as though she'd just told a joke. She floated toward the doors. Em didn't even leave her seat until she saw the girl step off the train and get swallowed by the crowd.

It was nothing, she told herself, over and over. Just a strange interaction.

But she couldn't get rid of the coldness that snaked into her from Ali's icy grip.

As soon as Em was out in the street, she felt better. In fact, she'd changed her mind completely about the orchid now. The fresh air made her realize that it really didn't matter anymore what had happened versus what had simply been in her head. The point was that, either way, it was *over.*

She ripped the flower off her bag and threw it on the train tracks.

Purse under one arm, hot Dunkin' Donuts coffee in the other (procured the moment she got off the Amtrak), Em proudly navigated the T from North Station to Newbury Street without once consulting the subway map. She made a mental note to tell JD, who constantly teased her for having no sense of direction. Aboveground, the sidewalks were flecked with slush and salt, and holiday lights twinkled in the trees. There was an electricity in the air: Girls wrapped in thick scarves ran by with their cell phones pressed to their ears; parents tugged at bundled-up children who were hypnotized by lights and sounds and window displays. Em smiled, looked up at the big buildings, the library, the sun setting over the brownstones. She couldn't wait for the fireworks.

By the time Em arrived, the salesgirls in Maintenance were dying to get out for the night, Em could tell. And who wouldn't be? But she took her time going through the store, touching scarves and holding sweaters up to her chest. She needed to find the perfect present, one that would make up for everything she'd done over the past week. One that proved that she knew Gabby, that she cared about her, that she wanted things to go back to normal.

She saw it on a mannequin before she saw it on a rack—a cornflower-blue silk scarf with silvery lace woven into the fabric. The scarf Gabby wanted. In the display, the scarf was paired with a soft, thin sweater of the dustiest pink—like something from a Civil War–era attic. It was a beautiful combination, and it was one Em knew Gabby would love.

The scarf was fifty dollars; the sweater was missing a price tag.

"How much is this sweater?" Em asked, holding out a sleeve.

"It's one twenty-five," a sullen clerk told her.

So almost two hundred dollars, all together. That was exactly how much money Em had in her purse, and her parents would slaughter her if she used her credit card for something other than an emergency. She hesitated, but only for a moment.

"I'll take them both," she said. "Extra small." She watched as they wrapped Gabby's gifts in lacy tissue paper and gold ribbon.

The clock on her phone told Em that she was going to be late to meet JD. She had to take the Red Line from Park Street outbound through Cambridge. She repeated the directions like a mantra; the last thing she needed was to get lost. Juggling her bags and the T pass, she hurried down to the Park Street platform. She pulled out her phone to text JD and tell him she was running a little late, but stopped short when she saw the girl again—the blond one, Ali. She was standing on the opposite platform and staring at Em. The girl had the strangest smile on her face, like she knew a really good secret. As a train rushed by on Em's side of the tracks, the girl's hair blew all around her face like a lion's mane.

Em's stomach did a little flip. Was this girl stalking her?

She entered the train and sat down with a sigh of relief as it started moving. The car was full but not cramped, and the air smelled like wet wool. The train went past one stop, then another, and Em sat quietly, watching everyone around her, wondering what it would be like to live in a big city, where everyone had their own lives and not the ones prescribed by parents or best friends.

She was in the middle of transferring Gabby's present to her shoulder bag when she heard someone cough.

"Excuse me. Does this train stop at Kendall Square?"

Em looked up, about to point to the T map above their heads, when her heart stopped beating for at least five seconds.

Standing there, in front of her, on this train—despite the fact that just moments earlier, Em had seen her on the other platform, headed in the *opposite* direction—was the girl. Ali. It was impossible.

"You—you're following me," Em gasped out.

The girl shrugged, not offering any explanation, just cocking her head with that same psycho smile.

Em felt her throat go dry. She tried to swallow, or cough, and her saliva seemed to choke her right below her tonsils. She jumped up just as the train started to slow down for the next station. Then she bolted toward the train's sliding doors.

"Excuse me, I need to get by," Em croaked at the passengers, aware of how frantic she sounded. "Excuse me!"

By the time she reached the doors, the announcer was ringing the bell. *Please stand clear of the closing doors.* She slipped through just as the doors started to clamp shut.

But she wasn't all the way out. Her huge shoulder bag got cinched in the closing doors—and her arm was still entangled in its strap.

As the train chugged to a start, Em had to walk faster and faster, panic building inside of her, struggling to extricate her arm.

"*Stop! Stop!*" she shouted, and the people inside motioned to her as though trying to convey some crucial information, but the train did not slow down. She tripped as the train started moving faster than she could run. She fell to her knees, and in doing so, wrenched her arm free of the bag's strap. She watched as her bag, and the train, and the girl, disappeared into the blackened tunnel.

Em climbed to her feet, trembling. She began to whimper. She was stuck now, with no bag, no phone, no wallet . . . and no idea what to do. At least she was at Central Square—only one stop away from Harvard Square, where she was supposed to be meeting JD. She didn't want to risk getting back on the T, so she made her way up to the street. She'd walk westward along Massachusetts Avenue. Luckily it was a straight shot between Central and Harvard. But judging from how many people were below-ground, it would be mayhem once she emerged on the street.

It did seem that everyone in Boston was taking advantage of the weather. Mass Ave was a madhouse, and once she got closer, she could see that Harvard Square was clotted with students, jugglers, tourists, shoppers, singing drunkards, and couples making out in public. Street vendors lined the Pit, where performers danced with fire. She nervously looked around. JD hadn't given her an exact meet-up spot. They'd agreed to text when she arrived at the square.

Em had to find a pay phone—did pay phones even exist anymore? She made several full circles before heading down a street lined with bars. If worse came to worst, she would just ask a stranger to borrow their phone. Em couldn't help but think of her parents and how worried she knew they would be if they knew what was going on.

And then her eyes fell on one of the craft tables, where a woman was selling chunky cable-knit sweaters—Irish and thick—like the one Zach held up the other day. Em felt like her heart would break.

"You forgot something," she heard from behind her. Em whirled around, and there she was. The girl. Still smiling that grotesque smile. Holding her bag, with a red orchid pinned to it. It made no sense—Em specifically remembered taking off the flower, throwing it onto the tracks. Her whole body went to ice.

"What do you want from me?" Em choked out.

The girl's smile grew even wider, until it seemed to stretch across her whole face. "Just doing my job as a Good Samaritan," she said, still holding out the bag.

"Leave me alone." Em wrenched her bag from the girl's hands. Her voice was high-pitched, hysterical. "Okay? Are you listening? Leave. Me. Alone." Then she turned and sprinted through the crowd.

It was like a maze, or a sick fun house. Loud, colorful, distorted, scary. Em darted this way and that, rummaging around in her bag as she ran, digging for her cell phone. When she found it, she read the text from JD: *Meet me in front of Au Bon Pain.* Okay. She knew how to get there. With a deep breath,

Em consciously tried to slow her steps, but she was still walking like her heels were on fire. Crossing the street between the Pit and Au Bon Pain, she felt a swish of air around her calves as a cab screeched to a halt just inches from her body.

"Watch it, girlie!" the cabbie yelled.

Em couldn't even scream back. She just ducked her head and scurried forward, furiously fighting back tears.

Hands clamped down on her shoulders, and then Em did scream.

"Hey, hey, Em! It's okay. It's just me!"

Em turned to see JD, forehead crinkled, concerned. He smoothed her hair back from her eyes. His long, navy-blue sailor's coat and chartreuse scarf made her want to sob; she wanted to wrap herself up in the familiar garments.

"You okay?" JD had to bend his knees to peer searchingly into her eyes. "You looked like you were being chased."

For a moment she considered telling him about the girl, the dreams, the visions. But it was New Year's Eve—she didn't want him to think she was crazy. She would deal with her own psycho ghost hallucinations without dragging JD into it. She shook her head. What the hell was wrong with her?

"I'm okay. Just a little jumpy today, I guess."

"Yeah. It's wild out here tonight." JD slung his arm around her shoulders, and Em leaned into him without thinking about it. "Sophie told me that the best place to watch the fireworks is from this bridge down here—come on. I'll show you."

Em gratefully let him grab her hand and lead her through the crowd. She snuck one glance behind her.

"You sure you're not on the run, James Bond?" JD squeezed her hand, watching her eyes as they scanned the people behind them.

"I thought I saw someone I knew," Em said vaguely.

"Don't worry. If we run into someone from Ascension, I'll drop your hand like it's diseased."

"That's not what I meant, and you know it." Em whacked him with her purse, watching with satisfaction as one of the new orchid's petals fell to the salt-pocked sidewalk. Slowly, her heartbeat was returning to normal.

The view from the John W. Weeks Bridge was lovely and expansive, and JD wrangled them into a spot right up against the railing, with nothing between them and the water but a few inches of carved concrete. As the fireworks began—slowly at first, then expanding in color and magnitude—Em forgot all about the events of the past week and the creepy girl with her weirdo smile. For the first time in a long time, she felt totally safe and secure. Like nothing could go wrong. She let herself lean back into JD, let her ear touch his cheek. The fireworks boomed and exploded and wrote themselves across the sky, while music and laughter drifted through the crowd, across the water.

Even through several layers of thick winter clothing, Em thought she could feel JD's heartbeat. It was solid and steady, like it was creating a rhythm with her own. For one crazy moment, she felt the wild urge to run her fingers through his hair, to kiss him. She was acutely aware of every place on their bodies that was touching. She wanted to grab him, right there, on the bridge, in front of everyone. She wondered what his mouth felt like, how his lips would move if they touched hers. A sense of rightness washed through her.

And then it was the fireworks finale—a great spectacle of blues and reds and whites, right as the clock struck twelve. Em wondered how many times they'd had to practice to get the timing just right. JD squeezed her shoulders, bent down to shout "Happy New Year!" in her ear. They hugged—a lingering hug. But the moment passed, and he ruffled her hair as they pulled away.

"Pretty awesome, right?" She didn't even need to look at him to know that he'd be looking at her like he always did—like an old, old friend.

"Yeah, it was. It was beautiful," Em said, gazing toward the city skyline as though it contained an answer to a question she had yet to ask.

By the time they reached North Station, Em was exhausted. Her fingers were frozen even beneath her mittens, and she was sick of lugging around her bag—every time she looked at it, a shiver went through her as she remembered the girl on the train.

"I'm gonna get some hot chocolate," she told JD, motioning toward a cart in the corner.

"I'll buy our tickets," he responded. "Meet me by the kiosk over there."

She nodded and went off into the crowd, bumping into people and being bumped, secretly praying that she wouldn't see that girl's vacant eyes and wan smile staring out of the mass of people. Since she'd used all her cash, she paid for the drinks on her mom's credit card: The whole *day* had been one big emergency, as far as she was concerned. The hot chocolate was thick and steamy, and she took a big gulp, not caring that it scalded the back of her throat as it went down.

She fought her way back over to the platform, holding the hot chocolates carefully and craning her neck to see JD's bright scarf.

There he was, over by the ticket window. Was he talking to someone? Em squinted to see. Yes, he was talking to a girl.

Her heart dropped all the way to her toes. JD was talking to *the* girl, who was twirling a piece of her pale blond hair around her pointer finger.

No. No no no no no.

Em started moving faster, as fast as she could in the packed mass of people. The hot chocolate sloshed on her hands and wrists, burning at first and then becoming ice-cold. She tried to keep them in her view, but it was impossible, and by the time she got to JD, the girl was gone.

"Who were you just talking to?" Em asked, breathless and wide-eyed. "Who was that?"

"That girl?" JD looked at her quizzically and grabbed a cup of the cocoa. "Nice job keeping it all in the cup, dude."

"Do you know her?"

"Hey, hey, hey," JD said with mock defiance. "You're the one who didn't want to be seen with me in public. She was just asking for directions."

"JD, I'm serious. You've never seen her before?"

"Only in my dreams, babe. . . . Kidding! Kidding!" JD backpedaled and Em knew her face had gone white. "I've never seen her, and she was just asking if this train goes to Providence. I told her it didn't. That was that."

"Okay. Okay." Em exhaled. "I'm sorry about the hot chocolate."

"It's fine. I didn't want all of it anyway. Jeez. I'll have to remember—no talking to other females, or risk the wrath of the Emerly."

"Very funny."

As they boarded the train, JD handed Em her return ticket and she slid it into her bag, next to the petals of tissue paper and the stuff she'd bought for Gabby. She'd blown her Christmas savings, but it was worth it. Gabby was coming home tomorrow, and Em vowed to come clean as soon as possible. It would be painful, she knew that. More than painful. It was going to be ugly. But they'd get through it. They had to—they'd been friends forever. Right? Friends understood that other friends made mistakes.

JD had given Em the window seat, but rather than lean on the cold glass, she bent toward him. Right now, the comforting, familiar smell of that weird sailor's coat—like a woodstove, old and piney—was the only thing keeping her from totally collapsing. As she started to drift off on his shoulder, a whisper ran through her dreams: *You forgot something . . . You forgot something . . . You forgot something.*

CHAPTER SIXTEEN

There were snakes, golden, glowing snakes, and they were writhing, morphing from beast to human and back again. The snake faces started to look like Ty and her cousins. They were laughing, the way the girls did—high, silvery, with abandon. Ty was moving closer, holding out a white feather. "Fly away," she whispered. Chase took the feather, turning it and spinning it between his fingers. And then it was in his mouth, scratching against his tongue and lips. It was in his throat. It was choking him. He gasped for breath; the plumes stuck together, blocking the air, catching his saliva. He coughed and coughed and . . .

Chase woke thrashing and hacking. He struggled to make his breath come naturally. He shuddered, recalling with vivid postdream clarity how Ty had seemed to step from the snake's skin, the same way she'd stepped out of her clothes that day at her house. He lay there for a moment, stretching his feet, yawning, and scratching his stomach.

Bang. As usual, he stubbed his toe on the bedframe. For once, it came as a relief. But even away from his dreams, he felt strangled—today was the Football Feast, and he had no one to go with. He cleared his throat. He couldn't get rid of the little tickle at the back of it.

It was six fifteen a.m., and he had half an hour to get to school. Their first day back. Zach had called an early-morning meeting to take care of last-minute Football Feast preparations. Coach wanted to go over some talking points, in case the media or any college scouts were in attendance. Chase didn't even want to go to the damn dinner anymore, but skipping it was not really an option. As he threw his legs over the side of the bed, Chase vowed to make the best of the day and night. He and Zach might be fighting, and his life might be in shambles, but he was the star quarterback of Ascension, and this was his night to shine.

Chase knew no matter how screwed up stuff was between them, Zach would never let it interfere with tonight's event. There was some small comfort in that, in Zach's public-relations finesse. None of the invited guests, no one outside the small circle of witnesses at the pond, would have the slightest inkling that the best friends were fighting. He wouldn't have to worry about watching his back, at least not while there were TV cameras around.

He looked in the mirror to see if his eye looked any better. That cream Emily had rubbed on helped a little: The stormy blue it had been the day before had morphed into a still visible but less sprawling bruise, tinged in yellow and black. He touched it delicately. Still hurt like hell, though. He'd have to steal a little of his mother's makeup later to try to cover it. He couldn't have reporters asking questions about this. For now he'd wear sunglasses.

In the car, he cranked up the music—loud. He drummed along on the steering wheel as he drove through the dim morning streets. He took some deep, rib-filling breaths and talked to himself a little. *It's a new year. Fresh start. Here we go.*

But when he pulled into the Ascension parking lot—past the banners heralding the team and tonight's event, past the pep squadders already wearing their uniforms—he immediately felt that something was off. And it was more than the fact that Coach Baldwin had foregone his gleaming silver whistle for a classy red and blue tie. Yeah, he was a few minutes late to the meeting, but not enough to warrant the complete lack of eye contact, the palpable discomfort when he entered the room. None of the guys even looked at him as they began discussing who would sit where and who would give what speech. Had Zach talked shit about him after all?

"The thing to emphasize is teamwork," Coach was saying. "We work as a team, supporting Singer—" Here, he was cut off by random snickers from around the room. "Something funny, gentlemen? Brewer?" Coach glared at Tom Brewer, who was sitting in the front of the room, trying in vain to keep a straight face.

"No, sir. We're all here to support Singer, that's for sure." More muffled laughter.

Chase shifted uncomfortably in his seat. What was going on? He stared at Zach, willing him to look up, but Zach was studying the floor with undistracted focus, his hair hanging in front of his eyes. Chase could see that his top lip was still a bit swollen.

When the meeting let out, the halls were full of students hugging, loading up lockers, eating bagels, and checking their second-semester schedules. As he walked toward the cafeteria—he *really* needed coffee, and luckily the AHS caf starting serving it a couple of years ago, though it tasted worse than the stuff from the Kwik Mart—Chase felt the strange sensation of eyes following him, and not in a good way. He waved to a group of girls but they only smiled awkwardly back at him before pretending to be deep in conversation. *What the . . . ?*

Chase felt cold all over. This was literally his worst nightmare—one he used to have as a child, all the way through middle school: In the dream, he would show up at school and suddenly realize that his clothes were ripped, tattered, and covered in stains, and his friends would make fun of him. But this was worse—his clothes were clean. The dirt was invisible.

And then he walked into the cafeteria. That's when he saw them, and it all became clear. Pictures of him were everywhere: naked, exposed, blown up to life-size and plastered above the cash register. Words from Emily's poems in a speech bubble coming from his mouth, like a cartoon.

There in the Gazebo was one of him standing awkwardly below the dim lightbulb in Ty's living room. And another of him lying down on the floor, the red wall pulsing behind him even on film, his pale thighs like they had a spotlight on them. So close you could almost see the goose pimples.

The room got hushed as he walked in. Everyone looked at him expectantly, waiting to see his reaction. He stood there shaking. His mind was full of flashes of light and sound, miniature explosions. He couldn't hold on to a single thought. He was going to have a stroke or something. A janitor was circulating too slowly—removing the pictures one by one.

"They've been up all morning," he heard Drea Feiffer say with a hint of sympathy in her voice as she brushed by him. "The janitor's cleared most of them from the hall already." He turned to watch her walk down the hall, her Doc Martens and black jeans like a life raft floating away after a shipwreck. And then she was gone, and he was alone again.

He took a couple of unsteady steps backward. He felt like the biggest freak Ascension had ever seen.

Then, racing down the hall, he thought only of where he

could go, where he could hide. He ducked into the boys' bathroom by the science wing, only to run into Wagner and Barton. They were laughing hysterically as he walked in, examining a different picture of him that hung above the sink.

"Wow, you're a real queer, huh, Singer?"

Chase was speechless. It felt, now, as though the feather from his dream had expanded in his throat; he really was choking.

Wagner banged into him as he walked by. "When did you turn into such a freak, dude?"

"Maybe we should show these to the TV cameras tonight, huh? Then everyone will know that Ascension's star quarterback is a faggot."

"You guys don't know what you're talking about," he said weakly.

"We know exactly what we're talking about. Who do you think you are, some Calvin Klein model?" Wagner looked pleased with himself.

"Nice poems," Barton muttered. "What is it that you're 'so scared to tell'? That you're totally gay?"

With the line from Emily's poem echoing in his head—*Some truths you just can't tell*—Chase wheeled around and stumbled out, back into the hallway, which felt hot and narrow and crowded. Like a scene from a horror movie, where he could see everything that was going wrong but wasn't able to do anything about it.

There was only one place to go—the old gym, a sweaty-smelling building down by the teacher parking lot. It had been replaced three years ago and was only used these days if it was raining and more than one team needed a place to practice. Sometimes smokers hid in the old locker rooms when it was too cold to hunch down by the tennis courts' broken fence. It was bound to be demolished or renovated sooner or later, but right now it was the empty refuge Chase was seeking.

He burst through the doors, dizzy and confused. This was not supposed to happen. Not to him. He was too careful to let shit like this happen. . . . But he hadn't been careful enough, not with Ty.

He took a few deep breaths in the chalky air and coughed out the smell of smoke and rubber mats and varnished floors. His cough echoed in the empty room, but there was another sound, too. A sniffle, a sob.

Chase looked around. At the top corner of the bleachers, her shoulders skimming an old felt champion banner, was Em. She was staring at him, wiping her nose and smoothing a hand through her long, tangled hair. She was wearing only jeans and a tank top that showed her bra straps.

"What are you doing here?" Em called out from across the room, her voice sounding small in the big space.

"I could ask you the same question," he responded, still standing in the doorway.

Like a crab, Em moved down a few rows in the bleachers, but didn't get up. Chase took a few steps toward her.

"God, it's freezing in here," he said, rubbing his arms. She didn't answer immediately, and he felt the silence yawn between them. He felt the urge to talk, to fill the space, to write over everything that had gone so wrong for him. He came a little closer to her. She flicked her eyes to him once, then dropped them again. "Remember how hot it used to get during assemblies?"

Em nodded. Her face was all red.

"There was that one, during freshman year, when Gabby was running for social vice president—" He didn't even get to finish his thought before Em hunched over and started shaking.

Jesus. Now he'd made her cry. Chase held still for a moment, squinting into the light filtering through the dusty windows along the top of the gym. He hoped the moment would pass.

"She won," she said with a gasp. He inched closer, barely able to make out what she was saying. "She won because she's so great. And I'm so terrible." She was doing this sad little thing, picking at tiny threads in her jeans, not looking at him.

"What's up with you, Winters?" He slid into a seat next to her. He didn't really want to deal with Emily's drama—he didn't have the energy for it—but he had nowhere else to go, anyway.

"Gabby. *Gabby.*" She wailed it the second time. And then

she started talking and she wouldn't stop, except to cough and sniff and swallow. "We were going to meet this morning, before school, like usual. We meet at Dunkin' Donuts and we get half coffee, half hot chocolate."

Chase nodded. At least hearing about someone else's problems was better than thinking about his own.

"And so I walk up to her this morning and I'm all smiling and holding out this gift I got her, this great present—I really wanted to make things right, Chase, really—" Here, Em held out her hands to him, gripping his knee, like she was begging him to believe her. "And she . . . she . . . she *threw her drink in my face*!" Em recoiled as if she were feeling the hot liquid for a second time.

"She threw coffee at you?"

"*Yes!* You don't even get it. She's usually the one who offers *me* clothes if I stain mine—she has a whole extra wardrobe of outfits in her gym locker!" Em wailed, pointing at her ruined sweater, tucked haphazardly into her bag. "And . . . and it hurt, Chase," she said now, quieter. "It hurt so much. She . . . she called me a slut. A liar, a slut, a traitor." Em took a deep, haggard breath. She kept tugging at her hair and picking the cuticles around her nails, which were already shredded and chewed bloody. She was a mess.

"She was saying that I hit on Zach and that it was all my fault," she went on, not even letting Chase respond, "and that I was a deceitful slut who tried to steal people's boyfriends. Like, as if Zach had no part in it. As if I had just been lying in wait, you know?"

"Were you?" Chase blurted out bluntly.

"No! And then she said she was going to tell everyone at Ascension about what a terrible person I am. She said she had some kind of text message that proved it. She drove off and I was just standing there. With coffee all over me."

Chase rubbed his forehead. A monster headache was brewing just behind his eyes. "How did she find out already? Didn't she only get home last night?"

Em shrugged and laid her head across her knees. "When she got home from the airport last night she realized she'd left her contact stuff at the hotel, so she went to buy some more. Apparently some pixie girl walked up to her at CVS, right in the aisle, and told her. I didn't even have time to ask *what*, exactly, she was told, but it seems that Zach got clean off the hook. And the worst part is that she'd believe some 'red-ribbon-wearing fashion victim'"—here, Em used air quotes—"over me, her best friend."

"Red-ribbon-wearing fashion victim?" Chase repeated. Weirdly, the description rang a bell, though he couldn't place it. Em shrugged again.

"Gabby's words," she said, able this time to crack at least a small smile. "I have no idea how some random stranger even *knew* about it. Or what Zach said. He was clearly not going to incriminate himself. . . . I guess everyone must know. But that's not the worst part. The worst part is that this happened at all. That I let this happen. That I deserve this." She was crying again, but more softly now. More desperately.

"Emily . . ." Chase threw his hands up. He wasn't very good at comforting anyone, much less a crying girl. But after a moment's hesitation, he put his hand on her back. She stiffened for a moment, then relaxed into his touch. He knew how she felt—to plummet from safety and security to nothingness, social-outcast status, overnight. "It's okay. I know you didn't mean to hurt Gabby. You just . . . got in over your head."

She turned her head a little, and he could see a drop of snot running down her lip. "Really?"

"Yeah. I mean, sometimes you think you know what you want, and then shit just spins out of your control and you can't do anything about it. It's beyond you. Unstoppable." His voice caught a little at his own words. At the things in his own life that he couldn't take back.

They sat in silence for a few minutes, Chase rubbing Emily's back, surprised at its boniness. Surprised to be touching her. Surprised to give a shit about her at all, really. They heard the bell for second period ring, but neither of them moved.

"I saw those pictures," she said quietly. "I'm sorry."

Chase got hot all over and removed his hand from her

back. He thought about the photos and how he'd never be able to live them down. He shuddered involuntarily, remembering the way his face looked in one of them, thrown back, laughing, totally out of control. Not one person at Ascension had ever seen him like that. For a moment they sat in silence. And suddenly Chase had the desperate urge to tell Emily, to confess everything, to figure out how and why his life had gotten so screwed.

Without intending to, he blurted out: "You ever think about karma?"

"Karma?" Em wrinkled her nose.

Chase could feel heat spreading through him. "Yeah . . . like, what goes around comes around. You ever think that could be true?"

"What do you mean?" Em asked.

Chase hesitated. It was all on the tip of his tongue.

"Well, like how my dad was such a dick to me and my mom, like he would get drunk and just wail on her, and then one day he got bashed in the head by a machine and that's what killed him. It just seems like . . . everything comes full circle. Like maybe that asshole deserved to die. Ya know?"

He could see his story had only upset Em more, and he wished he could take it back. Everyone already knew about his dad—it was old history. Chase didn't usually like to bring it up.

Em looked at him with pity.

Chase elbowed her. "Don't listen to me. I'm just the naked guy who writes poems."

Em smiled a little then. "Good poems," Em said, elbowing him back.

"Yeah, you know, I got a friend who can really write."

"Oh, so we're friends now?" Em said it sarcastically, but her eyes were wide and hopeful.

He thought about Zach. What their friendship had been. How it had soured so easily. "I'm not sure I have many other options," he said, smirking. "I don't think I even had many friends to begin with." And then, as if saying that had flipped a light switch in his head, Chase smacked his forehead.

"Oh, shit. Shit shit shit."

"What? What's wrong?"

"The freaking Football Feast is tonight." Chase fidgeted with the cords that hung from his sweatshirt hood, then shook his head determinedly. "There is no way in hell that I am stepping foot in that room with those people. No chance."

"No, you can't not go, Chase. You're going to be captain of the team."

Chase thought about his teammates, about how everyone had looked at him in the cafeteria. "I'm not sure I even have a team anymore."

"You can't just not go," Em repeated. "It's too important. It would be total defeat."

The idea came to Chase in an instant: "Why don't you come with me?"

Em stared at him, incredulous. "Me?"

"Yeah." The more he thought about it, the more perfect it seemed. "We'll make a great couple, the freak and the slut." He smiled at her with closed lips, not sure if he'd gone too far. But she looked like she was really thinking about it.

"Gabby will be there. With Zach . . ." Em bit her lip.

Chase shrugged. "Maybe you'll get another chance to talk to her. Either way, you don't have to worry—they don't serve coffee at the Feast."

Em cracked a small smile, nodding slowly, thinking about it. She took a deep breath. "You're sure?"

"Why not? Things couldn't get worse."

"Fine. Yes. Okay." Em smiled gingerly. Chase smiled back. They were two pariahs, sitting on a bleacher, going to the Feast together. It felt good. Like a big ol' Fuck You to the rest of Ascension.

Beep-beep-beep. That was his phone. It sounded like it was far away, but it was right by his feet, in his backpack. He knew who it was going to be from, and he didn't want to look. Em nodded toward his bag.

"You gonna get that?"

With a sigh, Chase leaned over and grabbed his cell. Sure enough: one new message from Ty. *Plz plz plz,* it said. *I need to explain. I must see you. ASAP. All a mistake.* In a second, Chase was on his feet. All the confusion, sadness, and anger came rushing back to him, rattling his whole body.

"I gotta go," he said abruptly, his heart racing.

"So I'll see you later, right?" She was looking up at him, concerned. The same way she'd looked at him the other night, when he'd come home bloody and bruised.

"Yeah." He was distracted now. "Um, I'll pick you . . . I'll meet you there. I'll wait for you right inside the doors, okay?"

He didn't wait for her answer. He shoved his hands in his pockets and squared his shoulders like he was gearing up for a tackle. He was going to meet Ty, and he had a feeling this would be their last play.

CHAPTER SEVENTEEN

Em couldn't get through to Gabby. She'd tried chat messaging. She'd tried texting. She'd tried calling—her cell *and* her house. Nothing. Well, nothing except a thinly veiled lie from Gabby's mom, who seemed more confused than anything else by Gabby's obvious refusal to come to the phone. Gabby and Em never fought.

She was desperate to get in touch with Gabby, to explain herself. To make things better. To assure her that it had all been a big mistake, and to vow to do whatever it took to make Gabby trust her again. Maybe she would even tell Gabby about the other stuff—there were other girls, it wasn't just her—if she thought Gabby would believe her. But every mode of communication was failing her.

So she'd made a decision: She was going to pull Gabby

aside tonight, at the Feast, when Gabby couldn't avoid her. She would make her see that their friendship was more important than any boy. Even a boy like Zach McCord. Even that boy, who had just broken her heart . . .

It wasn't going to be easy.

To steel herself for the task at hand, there was one last thing she had to do: burn Cordy.

Em was ready. She had the charcoal, check. The lighter fluid, the matches, the barbecue tongs, her warmest winter hat and gloves. And of course, she had Cordy. She held him up, this lump of fluff and fake zebra fur. She hugged him, breathing in his stuffed-animal smell, part like carnival, part like Em's bedroom, and part something else. Her heart hurt looking at his stupid black plastic eyes and the unraveling threads around his tufted mane.

This was it. Her feelings for Zach, and this whole mess, would go up in smoke with the stuffed zebra. They had to. Em had never believed much in talismans, but one thing was for sure: She didn't want Cordy anywhere near her pillows. She knew that somewhere in Cordy's ashes, she'd be able to resurrect her friendship with Gabby, her old self, her life before she ever kissed Zach.

Her parents would be home around dinnertime, and she needed time to get ready before the Feast, so she had to get started. Em sighed. All she wanted to do was camp out in the basement with JD, some rum-and-Pepper floats, and Scattergories. But no, she had to put on a dress—she was going for simple, black, classic—for a fake date with Chase, of all people. Em had to admit she was a little worried about him. After he'd gotten that text message this morning—he'd looked so spooked, Em was sure it was from the girl, Ty—she hadn't seen him for the rest of the day. Not that she'd been looking hard. Em's day was spent avoiding eye contact with pretty much everyone. She had no idea what, or how much, Gabby had told.

A cold wind picked up as Em stood there shivering in her alpaca mittens on the Winters' back porch, cuddling Cordy to her chest and fiddling with her fire-making supplies. It was scary not knowing what people were saying about you. Em realized how many times she and Gabby had whispered about other people behind their backs. Nothing really malicious, but outfit appraisals and mean nicknames and I-can't-believe-he's-with-her's all the same. She'd never stopped to think about how terrible it felt to be on the other side of the whisper-shielding hand.

With determination, Em prepared her dad's grill for the offering. She poured out the charcoal, spritzed it with lighter fluid, and set the grill screen back on top of the black stones. She lit a match, dropped it in, and watched as the blue-orange flame whooshed from stone to stone. It was nice to feel warm even in her frigid backyard—maybe, once all this was sorted out, she and Gabby could host a winter bonfire, complete with roasted marshmallows and campfire songs. *If* it ever got sorted out.

Then, slowly, staring into the flames, Em leaned closer, holding Cordy over the grill. At the count of three, she would let him go. *One. Two . . . three.* It was easier than she expected.

The acrid smell of burnt synthetic fibers quickly replaced the familiar smell of the grill, and she backed away with a wrinkled nose, watching as Cordy's extremities shriveled in the heat.

There was a noise, something off in the back of the yard. Em's heart skipped. An animal? JD? She peered over the grill, trying to see beyond the flames and smoke.

All of a sudden, her scarf, too, was ablaze. Em shrieked, grabbing at it. She could feel the heat gobbling up the wool, closer and closer to her chin. She screamed, unraveling the scarf as quickly as she could, flames lashing at her hands. With a final twist, it came loose; she threw it to the ground, watching as it fizzled in the snow, releasing a plume of black smoke.

She doubled over, catching her breath and checking her neck for burns. Holy crap.

When her heart had returned to its normal rhythm, she took Cordy's charred remains from the grill and used the tongs to shove the sizzling mess into a snowbank. Steam drew upward as the snow softened around it. Once again, the eerie note she'd read at the playground rushed into her head—*Sometimes sorry isn't enough*—as she kicked more snow over the ashes, completely burying them in a blanket of pure, clean white.

As Em drove to the community center downtown, she pulled at the hem of her dress, hoping it screamed *Not a Slut* as loudly as a dress could. Her hair was pulled back in a neat bun and she was wearing flats. She wanted to look as saintly as possible. And she went a few minutes late, hoping Chase would be waiting just inside the double doors of the lobby, as they'd arranged.

But Chase's car wasn't in the lot when she pulled up. *Maybe his mom dropped him off?* No. She got out and jogged to the lobby, the cold air driving straight through her nylons. He wasn't in the doorway, either. And just as she was debating whether to go inside and look for him or stay put and pretend to be deeply involved in checking her text messages, she heard Gabby's voice.

Em must have looked like a deer in headlights as Gabby sailed through the door on Zach's arm. Em wondered which of them looked more stricken. She knew her face was horrified; Gabby looked enraged; Zach seemed to want to melt into the woodwork.

"What. Are you. Doing here." Gabby's words were like daggers, and Em could tell she was truly shocked to see her here.

"I'm . . . I'm . . . I'm meeting Chase." Now was her chance.

Em struggled to find the words to speak to Gabby. This was what she'd come for and all of a sudden she was mute.

"No one wants you here," Gabby said coldly, leaning into Zach's arm, which was slung around her shoulders. He didn't remove it. Em bit the insides of her cheeks.

People passed by them, coming now in twos and threes, and every time the door opened, a cold gust of air washed over them.

A surge of strength and power came through Em all of a sudden. Gabby was *hers*, not Zach's. And Gabby deserved better. They both did. "I need to talk to you, Gabs." Em looked at Zach, wondering if he would say something. Her skin was burning. She had never been so humiliated in her life. "I need to explain."

"I don't want to talk to you," Gabby said icily. "I don't want to talk to you ever again, in fact. I thought you were my friend. I thought you were my *best friend*." Gabby's voice broke then—and it made Em's heart hurt.

"Zach?" Em finally addressed him directly. She didn't know what she wanted. Anything but the vacant stare he'd been wearing for the last three minutes.

That's when Gabby reached out and pushed Em's shoulder, hard. Em stumbled back into a coatrack. A hanger jabbed her in the shoulder. "Don't you *dare* speak to him," Gabby said too loudly, her voice getting shrill. "Why won't you stop, Em?

Leave me alone. I don't trust you. I don't want you around me and Zach anymore. Period. Now please move." She swept past Em, and Em could see that tears were spilling out of her eyes. Zach trailed like a puppet in a daze.

Gabby *pushed* her. Her oldest friend; her best friend. Her almost-sister. For a second Em swayed, thinking she might faint.

Part of her wanted to flee the building, flee Ascension forever. Another part of her wanted to storm right back in and tell Zach to admit exactly what had happened over the break—every last detail. Make him writhe. Make him say it. Make him admit he'd done as much wrong as her.

Her phone beeped—she had missed a call from Chase. Probably explaining where he was.

"Hi, it's me." Chase's voice sounded tinny and high in his message. "It's Chase, I mean. Listen, I'm not going to go tonight. I'm sorry. I just can't. Something's come up. I've got to do this. I have to know, one way or the other, you know? So . . . don't go to the Feast. Or if you're there already, leave. Sorry, Em." *Click.*

Em listened to the message a second time, a feeling of anxiety starting to gnaw at her. Chase sounded wild—almost feverish. And scared.

Should she call him back? Go to his house and figure out what the hell was going on? Even through her own mortification—more football players were arriving now, with families and dates, everyone staring at her as she stood in her stupid dress outside the center—she couldn't stop thinking about Chase. He sounded like he was losing his mind.

She had to make sure he was all right.

More snow was beginning to fall; a storm was in the forecast.

Em followed Main Street toward Route 4 and the highway. She crept along, windshield wipers moving at their fastest speed, feeling the slick ice beneath her tires. She couldn't get Gabby's wrathful voice out of her head. Or Zach's detached stare. She tried to focus on Chase, on his stuttering, fractured message. She was heading toward Chase's house first, and if she didn't find him there, she'd . . . well, she didn't know where she'd go. She'd figure something out.

And then, just before the highway overpass, she thought she saw something out of the corner of her eye. Her car squealed to a stop and she peered out the windshield. All seemed still. Her headlights illuminated nothing more than five feet in front of the car and the steady drive of white flakes to the ground. She looked to the left and to the right.

"Help" she heard faintly through the glass. She still didn't see anything. She turned off the wipers and rolled down the window, straining to hear more, but all she heard were rustling branches and snowy wind. She wished with all her might that another car would come down the road, but there were no lights in either direction. Nor from above, for that matter. Em finally understood why her dad always griped about Ascension's lack of attention to "basic public-works maintenance"—she could really use a working streetlight right about now.

"Hello?" Em said into the night. And as she did, the streetlight above her suddenly sputtered to life with an electrical snap. Right below it, just ten feet from her car, lay a petite girl, around her age, wearing only a willowy gray dress with a tiny high-collared jacket over it. She was on the ground, one leg bent crookedly underneath her.

"Oh thank god," the girl said, offering up a weak, elfish smile. "I thought no one would ever come."

Em opened her car door and looked around. The girl was right—it was deserted. Just blankets of fresh, untouched snow in either direction. Not even a set of footprints.

Where had this girl come from?

"Are you okay?" Em got out and took a few steps forward.

"I think my leg is hurt," the girl said, pointing to her left knee. "I was walking along and got hit by a car. It just drove off. I don't know what to do. My phone fell into the snow and it's not working."

Something about this girl, her leg, the lights, the snow, was creepy. Em couldn't shake the feeling of having met the girl before—not at Ascension High, but maybe around town, or in Portland? The girl's grayish eyes felt familiar. Every fiber of Em's being was urging her to *run! Leave!*

But what was Em supposed to do? Abandon a stranger by the side of the road? That would be great for karma. First she hooks up with her best friend's boyfriend, then she leaves a hit-and-run victim alone on a snowy night. That would look perfect on her ethical résumé.

"I'm going to call nine-one-one," Em said, squatting beside her.

"Please," the girl sat up, grimacing slightly. "I think I can get up. Can you—can you maybe just drop me at the hospital?"

Em hesitated for just a second. "Of course," she said.

"Great." The girl smiled at her. Her delicate features were calm and she seemed unfazed, despite the rather dramatic situation. She was acting as though Em were offering to do her laundry or let her cut in line at the grocery store.

"Do you want me to call someone for you? Your parents or a friend?"

A *friend*. She thought of Chase. But maybe she was being overdramatic. He'd had a rough few weeks—no wonder he sounded weird. Just because they'd been friendly recently didn't make them besties, and Chase might not appreciate that she was trying to barge into his personal business. And though she was heading toward his house, she had no idea whether he would even be home. She would call him later, after she stopped at the hospital.

"That's all right," the girl said, reaching up to take the hand

Em offered her. "I'll call someone from the hospital." Her hands were freezing. She must have been waiting outside for a long time. Em was surprised she was the only one who had stopped to help. Maybe she wasn't such a terrible person after all.

Em helped the girl—whose name, she announced, was Meg—to the car. The girl seemed light, almost weightless.

Just before Em started the car, she sent Chase a quick text: *worried about u. call me, ok?*

"I hope I'm not keeping you from anything," Meg said politely as they started driving toward the urgent-care center downtown. Em's mom worked there sometimes.

"No, it's fine. I was just on my way to meet a friend. . . . He can wait."

"I'm sure he'll understand," Meg said, smiling at Em in the dark. Em didn't say anything else. She wasn't feeling particularly chatty.

When they pulled up at the hospital, Em looked at Meg. "Do you mind if I just drop you off? My mom is working the clinic tonight," she lied. She knew it was rude, but she didn't care. There was something off about the girl and Em wanted her out of the car. "I'm not in the mood to explain to her why I'm driving around in this weather."

"Sure," Meg said, smiling the same placid smile. "I totally understand. I think I can walk on it enough to get to the waiting room. Thank you so much. I'll remember this."

Em nodded as Meg got out of the car, limping a bit but able to move. "Good luck. Hope your leg is okay."

As she backed out of the spot, Em looked in the rearview mirror but didn't see Meg. *She must be able to move pretty quickly if she's already inside.*

With one hand on the steering wheel, Em quickly checked her phone. Chase hadn't called. Em tried him three times in a row; each time, his phone went straight to voice mail. Em's car fishtailed a little in the parking lot and she held her breath. No way she was having an accident tonight. Her car had *just* come out of the shop. She squinted at the blinding snow ahead of her. She had to just go home—clearly it was too dangerous to be out on the roads tonight. Hopefully Chase had realized the same thing and was lying low. She turned off her phone, not wanting any more distractions.

Before pulling out of the hospital driveway, Em looked out the window for Meg once more and noticed that she had left something behind—a red ribbon of some kind. She opened the door, hopped out, and picked it up. She gasped. A red ribbon . . . She let the ribbon fall back into the snow, where it lay like a thin stream of blood. Something about it made her heart stop. A red ribbon. It meant something, though she didn't know what.

Then it hit her: Gabby had said the girl who told her about Zach had been wearing one. *A red-ribbon-wearing fashion victim.*

How could she have forgotten that description? Em knew that there was more than one red ribbon in Maine, but she couldn't shake the feeling that Meg was somehow connected to this whole mess.

Even after Em was home and safely tucked into her bed that night, her thick white down comforter pulled up to her chin, she was still shaking.

She watched snow fall outside her window, praying not to see anyone's face reflected back at her. She couldn't stop thinking about what Chase had said—sometimes there are things you can't take back, no matter how much you wish you could. They snowball, picking up speed, tailspinning beyond your control. Unstoppable.

She thought of what else he had said, about karma. *Maybe it's true that people get what they deserve.*

Em shivered. She hoped not.

CHAPTER EIGHTEEN

Through tears, in a strangled, hysterical tone, Ty had asked Chase to meet her at the Piss Pass. He agreed instantly.

He already felt like a pushover.

Part of him wanted the strength to show up and tell her off—to call her a bitch and be done with her. She wouldn't be able to sweet talk her way out of this one. He would never forget how it felt to see himself on display for everyone to ridicule—a clammy sensation, like being touched by a hundred dirty hands all at once. It was nauseating.

But another part of him, the part influenced by the knifing sadness in his chest and the memories of how it felt to look into Ty's eyes, was terrified. Scared that if he did cut her out of his life—which he had *every* right to do, which he *should* do—he would lose not only her but a piece of himself. Through Ty,

Chase had seen glimpses of what it would be like to live beyond the confines of his normal everyday existence.

He had felt happy.

And then she'd wrenched that away from him. She'd tricked him into taking a chance, and it had backfired. Which was exactly why he usually took every precaution, planned things down to the details, studied his playbook obsessively. Because the minute you lost control—or worse, gave it up—you got hurt.

It was snowing as Chase drove to the Piss Pass, and it was almost as if the cold air were freezing his thoughts, making it even harder to focus. He worried he was going crazy. He took out his phone to call Em; he'd already told her that he wasn't going to meet her at the Football Feast, but he also hoped that hearing another person's voice would help calm him down. No answer. His thoughts were so all over the place tonight, he couldn't even remember what he'd said in his message.

He didn't know why Ty wanted to meet at the Piss Pass; he didn't know what he was going to say or how he'd explain that fundamentally she'd ruined his life. He just wanted to get this over with and to move on. Closure. That's what he needed. Closure.

Of course, the moment he laid eyes on her, he knew being angry and conveying the depth of her betrayal wouldn't be easy. Ty looked hauntingly beautiful in the snowy, moonlit night. It was like there were spotlights on her eyes and strands of gold woven into her flowing red hair; her white-blond streak looked almost like it was glowing. She was wearing a long, maroon dress that blew in the wind, and she was leaning against the guardrail, looking out over the traffic below. As he got out of his car, she turned to him gratefully.

"I'm so glad you came, Chase," she said in a low voice.

"Yeah, I came." Chase approached her slowly. There was really only one question he wanted answered. He cleared his throat, and then, with a force he wasn't expecting: "Why, Ty? Why did you post those things? I've been—I've been nice to you. I thought we *had* something. Why would you do that?"

"I'm a terrible person," she said. She was strangely calm, in the way only a hysterical person can be. She didn't blink. Her mouth was drawn in a thin line. "I am awful and totally undeserving of your love. I'm sorry."

"You're still not giving me a reason," he said, clenching his fist. "I'm asking you why? What did I do to deserve this?"

"I do wish things were different, Chase," she said in the same frighteningly even tone. "I wish we'd never met at all."

With that, she was climbing up the rungs of the rail. It took a moment for Chase to register what she was doing. He grabbed for her shoulder but touched only air.

"Ty, stop. Get down." Panic was winging through him. "What are you doing?"

She was on the other side of the railing now, gripping it and leaning back over the highway like she was on a trapeze. Just her toes were touching the bridge; her heels slanted down into the night air.

"This is all over, Chase." She smiled then. It was a strange smile that Chase had never seen before.

All he could think about, suddenly, was Sasha. Up on that ledge. There had been no one behind her, no one to beg her to come back to solid ground.

"Ty, please. You're really scaring me. Come back over here and we can talk about this. Come on." Chase reached for her, terrified. He didn't want to actually grab her; he worried he might push her over the edge. He tried to make his arms look as welcoming and sturdy as possible. She turned sideways, hanging on with just one hand and one foot. She was teetering slightly, as though the wind would be enough to knock her over. Chase heard a noise come out of his mouth that sounded more like a whimpering dog than a human.

"Ty," he said desperately. He was on the verge of tears. "I'm begging you, please. It doesn't matter what you did—I just want you to come back over here."

"Oh, but it does matter, Chase. All our actions matter. Can't you see that?"

In the snow and dark it was hard to see, let alone think. As Chase stood there, arms outstretched, Ty seemed to waver before him. He blinked, trying to regain focus. And when he reopened his eyes, it wasn't Ty hanging off the bridge. It was Sasha.

Like an old television set, the images of Sasha and Ty flickered back and forth. Chase was gripped by a fear deeper than anything he'd ever felt. *Sasha—Ty—Sasha—Ty . . .*

Oh god what have I done?

And then, as though he were watching a scratchy old horror film on that flashing TV, it all came flooding back.

He had kept secret tabs on her. He watched and waited, not knowing exactly what he was waiting for. Until the beginning of junior year, when the football team decided on a teamwide prank—try to get a naked picture of a chick from school, and post it to a private website, for team eyes only.

Chase picked Sasha Bowlder.

Somewhere in the back of his mind, he knew he'd never gotten over her or the feeling of being rejected, humiliated, by someone who had been his best friend.

He started wooing her online, with a fake screenname and password, hoping she'd send him what he wanted without too much trouble.

She was shy at first, but over time their online conversations grew more involved. Deeper. Sometimes I think about how I grew up, and whether that made me stronger, *she said one afternoon.* Doesn't it sometimes feel like everything is such a charade? *she asked another day.* Like, it's all laid out in front of you, just waiting to be snatched away.

After a week or so, most of the other guys had forgotten about the whole prank.

But Chase didn't forget. And he didn't stop. It went on for weeks, and then months. In a weird way, Chase liked talking to Sasha more than anyone else. She got *him. At certain points, he would forget it was supposed to be a joke—and that he still resented her for being such a bitch to him in seventh grade.*

She felt it, too, whatever was happening between them. She let him in. Told him about her fears. Her fantasies. And the days she felt a numbness creeping in, like a fog that would swallow her whole.

And then, with little explanation, she stopped it. She announced—a week before she jumped—that she wouldn't speak to him anymore. She said their relationship was too intense and she didn't know what to make of it. He never wanted to see her, and she couldn't handle the loneliness. He didn't understand her—no one did, not really. She was tired and sick of being played. And so, she rejected him.

Again.

Chase was furious. He was blind angry—the irrational kind, the kind that got into his fingers and toes, the kind that burned. He fumbled on the field—for the first time, maybe ever. Then he went out with Zach and the guys and they were being such assholes, as usual; when he got up to grab napkins at the burger joint, they laughed and called him their servant. Chase's anger swelled, a blackness.

He got home that night and all his bitterness swung back in Sasha's direction. I'm trash, huh? That's all I am?

He was sick, too, of getting kicked and crapped on and beaten on by everybody.

He decided to kick back.

There was a clear moment, as his hand hovered above the UPLOAD *button, when his mind screamed:* Wrong! Wrong!

But two wrongs don't make a right. He clicked, and Sasha's sexy messages and raw confessions all got posted to the Ascension High Facebook page.

By the time he woke up the next morning, the administration had already taken the photos down, but the damage was done. Anyone who hadn't seen them the night before had heard about them, had seen screenshots. When Sasha came to school the next morning, it was like she was an animal in a cage. Stared at, mimicked, mocked. It was her worst nightmare, and Chase knew it.

Because it was his worst nightmare too.

Standing on the Piss Pass, Chase retched. He couldn't believe what he'd done, how stupid he'd been. He hadn't understood what he was messing with.

How it would all come back around.

It was his fault. He knew it as deeply as he knew anything. He'd known it all along. Everyone had teased her. But *he* was the reason Sasha had leaped.

Now Ty leaned dangerously into the open air above the highway. He wouldn't lose her, too. He couldn't. He had no choice but to climb the railing himself, to meet her where she was and coax her back to solid ground. The snow made the metal slick. He felt whooshes of wind every time a car barreled past below them. He could barely keep his grip; his fingers were too cold. There was only about a foot between the railing and the end of the ledge.

With the snow falling down around him, stinging his eyes and blinding him, Chase could barely see Ty. It was impossible to differentiate her face from Sasha's. His center of gravity seemed to be in his throat.

"Please, Sasha—Ty—I'm sorry. I don't know what's going on, and I don't care. Just come down to the ground with me, okay? We'll forget any of this ever happened."

Her voice sailed out into the wind. "I just want one kiss," Ty cried out.

"Wh—what?" Chase was shuffling toward her, closer, along the narrow ledge. The wind vibrated through his body. Below them, a truck thundered through the pass.

Ty turned to him. He thought he saw tears streaming down her face. "Please kiss me," she said.

"If I do, will you stop this?" His legs were shaking. His fingers were so cold he could hardly feel the railing.

"It will stop," she said, and now her eyes were dark pools. "I promise."

They were just a few inches apart. He leaned forward, and then they were kissing. It was more intense than their first kiss.

He felt waves of electricity pulsing through his body, hot and cold alternately rolling through him. He stopped thinking. He took one hand off the railing and reached out to grab the back of her neck, pulling her closer. She resisted for just a second, pulling away.

"I'm so sorry," he breathed.

As he inhaled again, he felt something in his mouth. Like when he woke up from the dream with a tickle on his tongue, except this was like a mouthful of feathers, not a single plume. He coughed, and the convulsive action made him almost lose his footing. He gagged again, spitting. And out of his mouth, into his palm, came a red orchid.

At that moment, with the most clarity he'd ever felt in his life, Chase realized two things.

The first was that Ty was not standing on ground. Not even her toes were touching the cold concrete of the overpass. She was hovering before him, in midair.

The second thing, this one even more shocking than the first: Ty was not beautiful at all. Her body was transparent—gray, papery—and he could practically see through it. Her hair looked singed. Her lips looked black; her eyes were twin holes.

"Sometimes sorry isn't enough," she whispered. Her face was calm again. Like a black sea at night—with everything lurking beneath.

He gasped. He tried to shift away from her, but he didn't

know where to put his feet, the ledge was so narrow. He stumbled and his shin bashed against the bottom of the railing.

He tried to croak out a question—*who are you, what are you?*—but nothing came from his mouth as he moved it.

Then she blew him a kiss—it was the smallest, softest puff. But it was enough to send him reeling backward.

It was then that Chase had his third and final crystalline realization: He was no longer holding on to the railing. He was plummeting toward the highway below.

He thought one last word.

Sasha.

ACT THREE

Penitence, or The Wrath of the Furies

CHAPTER NINETEEN

There was a very small memorial service, one that felt cursory and fake, like people were avoiding talking about what really happened and what really mattered. Em left early. Everything about Chase's death and its aftermath felt wrong. She skipped the school assembly that had been called at the last minute to talk about students' emotional reactions to Chase's fatal fall and Sasha's suicide attempt. Grief counselors were available through the guidance office to help students process their feelings.

Em knew they were all trying to do the right thing, but she couldn't help feeling like all these adults were just as confused as the kids. She wondered if she should tell someone about Ty, about Chase's infatuation with her, about the mysterious girl who had appeared in Ascension just before everything started to snowball into chaos. She didn't know who to tell.

Less than a week into the new year, there was a buzz in the air, and it was a drone of death.

She blamed herself, in part. She knew he'd sounded desperate. She'd known, and she hadn't done everything she could to find him. And now . . . he was gone. She couldn't stop thinking about that night. What had he been thinking? Since his death, she had replayed his voice mail several times, until hearing his voice started to freak her out and she deleted it impulsively. *Something came up,* he had said.

But what?

Since Chase's death, she had been having nightmares, most of them plotless, full of dark, swirling shapes. But last night, the nightmare had taken form. She was driving on the snowy road, the same one on which she'd encountered Meg, the girl with the scarlet ribbon. She was headed for the Piss Pass, and past it, Chase's home. She could see him in the distance, at the end of a tunnel of snow and light and tree branches. He was shouting and waving his arms, and she couldn't understand him. All she knew was that something was desperately wrong, and she needed to fix it. But just as she got close to him, almost close enough to understand, Meg appeared in front of the car, and she had to slam on the brakes. She skidded to a halt, but the brakes locked, and she went sailing into blackness.

She woke up choking back a scream.

Everyone was saying Chase's death was a suicide—her parents, teachers, everyone at school. And it seemed like that, sure. But something about that night—Meg's presence in it, specifically—was haunting Em.

Em sat now at her kitchen table, absentmindedly stirring some lumpy oatmeal. She definitely wasn't hungry, but her mom had left her a note on the kitchen table: *Please eat something, Em. We love you.*

And as she lifted a spoonful of oatmeal toward her mouth, it hit her. She knew what felt wrong about that night. As Meg's name kept drumming in her head, she remembered the last time she'd heard the name: When Chase was talking about his new crush object. She had two cousins, he'd said—Meg was one of them, Em remembered. And what was the other one's name . . . it was at the tip of her tongue . . .

Her spoon clattered to the table as it flashed into her mind. Ali. The other girl's name was Ali. She'd met them both: Meg in the snow, and Ali on the train. It wasn't a coincidence. She was sure of it.

In the cafeteria, at lunchtime, Em sat with a thin turkey sandwich at the table nearest to the garbage bins. The first couple of days back at school, she'd eaten in the library, hiding from Gabby's hurt stares and trying to focus on her homework. Today, the library was reserved for Mr. Landon's senior American literature class. He'd stolen her sanctuary. So Em had decided to give the cafeteria a try.

Bad idea. Gabby sat at their usual table, right in the middle of things, conferring with Lauren about a new "suicide-awareness club" she wanted to start. Gabby didn't even look in Em's direction, and neither did Fiona or Lauren or anyone else in their friend circle; Gabby had made it clear Em was Out. Zach hadn't come to school in days, but Em realized, with a bit of surprise, that while she wondered how he was coping with the death of his best friend, she didn't really miss seeing *him.* The way he'd acted at the Feast didn't inspire heartbreak. She wondered, though, if he'd show up to the basketball team's pep rally, which was coming up in two days. He was one of Ascension's best players—he had to be there.

Was this what the rest of her high school career was going to be like? No friends, no boyfriend, no idea how to explain anything that happened to her or to the people around her. If only she and JD had the same lunch period. He was in Honors Chem right now.

"I think Singer was gay," someone said a little too loudly.

Em snapped to attention when she heard Chase's name. She looked for its source. Two tables over, a bunch of soccer players were hunched toward one another. They had their lunches—trays full of french fries and meatball subs—spread sloppily in front of them, and they took big bites as they talked, spewing crumbs with abandon. Like everyone else at Ascension, they were trading theories on Chase.

"What, you think he was scared to come out?" This, from a sophomore whose name, Em thought, was Charlie.

"Yeah, must be. I mean, those pictures of him—the paint and shit? And those poems? Total *Brokeback Mountain*." That was stupid Sean Wagner talking. Emily felt her stomach twist in disgust. Why did he even exist? He contributed nothing to the world.

"Shut the hell up, man," said Nick. "He's *dead*. Don't talk about him that way."

Em put down her sandwich.

Another one spoke. "Did you hear that he was holding some weird flower when he jumped?"

Em's blood went to ice.

"Christ." The boys all leaned away from one another slightly, as if even talking about flowers made them targets for ridicule.

"Really?"

"Yeah. A crazy red flower. It just goes to show, you don't know anyone. Chase *Singer*, man. Who knows what that kid was up to? He had everything going for him . . . and now he's dead."

A red flower. A red flower. A red flower. Em fumbled to get the sticky Saran wrap back around her sandwich, trying to tamp down the crazy beating of her heart. The mayo smeared her fingers. She tried to tell herself, frantically, that the flower could mean anything—it could be coincidence; it could be a crazy rumor.

But deep down, she *knew*. A red flower. Just like the one she'd had pinned to her purse—the one that had appeared out of nowhere in her car the first time she hooked up with Zach; the one that had reappeared even after she'd tossed it onto the train tracks. As with the ribbon, she knew that there must be many red flowers sold throughout Maine. But these were more than just coincidences. She felt it. She needed to figure out what was going on. She stood up unsteadily. She had to get out of here.

Bang. Turning around, she slammed right into someone's tray. Coca-Cola soaked through her shirt. She looked down at the stain and kept right on walking, fast. Freaked.

She practically ran down the hall, away from the cafeteria and then out of the building. In the parking lot, she wrapped her scarf more tightly around her neck, trying to figure out what to do. Where could she find answers? And then, as though someone had whispered the idea into her ear, she suddenly knew exactly where to start. She was skipping the rest of school and going to Chase's house.

No one answered when Em knocked on the door to Chase's trailer. Not that she expected anyone to be there. JD had told her—JD, who was suddenly more plugged into Ascension's social network than she was—that right after the small memorial service, Chase's mom had gone straight to her mother's house in Bangor, more than two hours away. She was staying there indefinitely.

But Em was easily able to shimmy open a windowpane, reach her gloved hand around toward the lock, and slide open the trailer's metal door. The door creaked as it swung open, revealing a dim interior.

Em took one step into the trailer, tentatively, calling out again. Just in case. No answer. She stepped inside, closing the door behind her. She uncoiled her scarf. It was surprisingly warm. She took off her gloves one finger at a time, trying to calm herself. The trailer was quiet—and in shambles. Chase's mom had clearly left in a hurry. There were dishes in the sink, and the food still stuck to them had attracted a small colony of roaches. Em looked away, tears filling her eyes. She was here; she didn't want to back out now. Paper was strewn on the coffee table next to a pile of crumpled tissues and a bottle of prescription pills. Mixed among the chaos were bouquets of sympathy flowers, and the air smelled heavy with stuffy sweetness. No bloodred mystery flower. But grief. Grief everywhere, practically pouring out of the walls and seeping into Em's skin.

She had been to Chase's house only once, on the day he fought with Zach, but it wasn't hard to guess that his bedroom must be down the hall. It wasn't exactly an expansive space. Em could see a full-sized bed with a floral comforter in the room at the end of the hallway, and next to it was the bathroom. There was only one other door.

In Chase's bedroom, Patriots posters were taped to the wall and a handful of fake-gold trophies were lined up according to height on the dresser. Neat as a pin—almost eerily so. The weights flush against the wall. The bed made. It was hard to imagine Chase even being able to *fit* in that twin-sized bed. Em's gaze fell onto Chase's playbook, sitting square in the middle of his desk; she was surprised to feel her breath catch, her eyes water again, as she brushed her fingers across its cover. She felt the gravity of death—of sadness—sinking into her bones.

She walked over to the dresser, ran her fingers over the trophies. She inched open the top drawer of the bureau, slamming it shut when it revealed only a pile of plaid boxers. She looked at Chase's small blue desk and raised her eyebrows when she saw a laptop sitting open on top of it, the screen dark, but the light in the corner blinking. Chase, too, must have left in a hurry. He hadn't even bothered to turn off his computer.

She was beginning to feel silly for coming here. She was no Nancy Drew, no mystery solver. She didn't even know what she was looking for. Maybe Chase *did* just jump off the Piss Pass, plain and simple.

A pile of papers sat next to the computer, and Em walked

over to leaf through them. A math test, a biology handout, an old pep-rally flyer. Nothing, nothing. As she glanced over each page, she set it off to the side, on top of the laptop keyboard.

Bing! She must have pressed a key hard enough to wake up Chase's computer from sleep mode. Em went to close the screen, but something caught her eye. Chase's email was open—but it wasn't the ChaseS@ascension.edu that Em was used to seeing on mass email lists among her friends. This account was registered to AscensionSecretAdmirer, and aside from a few spam messages and newsletter updates, there was only one email address in the "From" column: SashaB@ascension.edu. Sasha B.? There was only one Sasha B. at Ascension—Sasha Bowlder.

Em's eyebrows knitted together and she took a deep breath. She tugged her hair back into a ponytail and sat down gingerly, her finger hovering over the mouse. Then she opened the most recent email in the list.

I can't do this anymore, it read. *You can't give me what I want. I don't want to get my heart broken and I'm giving up.*

It was just one line, in response to a longer message from AscensionSecretAdmirer: *Hey sexy,* he'd written. *Where have u been? I haven't heard from you in a week. You have a new boyfriend or something? I thought things were cool between us.*

Em's heart sped into her throat as she clicked through the messages, her eyes blurring as she kept them on the glowing screen. She scrolled down to the bottom of the screen, reading from bottom to top. It was like she was climbing up through threads, picking apart the strands of a secret history.

He'd contacted her for the first time months ago. Said he had a crush on her but couldn't tell her who he was. She'd been eager—embarrassingly so, even—at first. Up for maintaining the mystery, the charade. The first few emails were light and flirtatious. She'd asked: *Do we have any classes together?* He'd responded with a wink. *That's for me to know and you to find out, cutie.* She'd gone as far as to send him a picture of herself wearing a mask—one of those masquerade-ball ones—and asking him to do the same. He resisted. They'd gravitated toward more serious topics after the first few exchanges. It was almost like they had more in common than Chase let on—to anyone. *You really understand me, Sasha,* he'd written. *Not like so many of these rich kids around here.*

I am one of those rich kids, she'd said. *But you see that there's more to me than that.* At the bottom of this email, there was a poem, and Emily recognized its words as one of the ones that had been posted to Ascension's Facebook page: *I know I'm not pretty, I know I'm plain, but you make me feel beautiful because we're the same.* She'd attached a photo to this email, too, an artsy, sepia-toned one of her staring into her computer's webcam. Her bare shoulders were showing. Emily shivered; Sasha looked so vulnerable.

She confessed how lonely she was, how she didn't understand why nobody—except Drea—liked her. *What scares me,* she said, *is that if the cool kids wanted to be my friends again, I don't know if I'd drop Drea.*

You would, Chase responded. *That's just how it works.*

After two months of this, the secrecy had started to chafe. Sasha wanted more. *I really want to know who you are. I need to see you. Can we meet?* Her tone got more desperate. She told him how she had started working out, hoping to be "hot for you when we finally get together." Chase had pushed back. *What's the fun of meeting? Then all the mystery will be gone.* The next time he'd emailed her, she'd sounded smaller somehow. *I'm beginning to wonder if this is all in my head,* she said. Then nothing, for a week, except for Chase's emails to her. *Hello? Hey, what happened to you? I'm starting to think you don't like me any more . . . ;)*

Then the final email from Sasha, breaking it off. Coldly.

And then her photos and emails had showed up on Facebook. It was Chase. Chase had made Sasha trust him and then violated that trust.

Exactly as Ty had done to him.

Oh my god. Chase had died exactly the way Sasha almost had. The realization tumbled through her brain, pounding and threatening. Her arms tingled and her breath sped up. Chase. Ty. Sasha. Their fates were *almost* mirror images. They'd both been exposed, although in different ways. What had Chase said that day in the old gym, the day he died? *I'm beginning to think that people really do get what they deserve.*

With tears pricking her eyes, Em backed out of Chase's room and down the hall. She couldn't get the image of the red flower out of her mind. If karma had come for Chase, she didn't want to think what it would mean for her.

Fifteen minutes later Em had pulled over on the side of the road, trying to catch her breath. Her palms were sweating. She was too scared for tears, too cold to shiver. Weird cousins. Death. Betrayals of trust. Vengeance that seemed perfectly planned. She didn't know what to think about any of it, but Sasha was the missing link, the first domino, the scream that started the avalanche. None of this freaky stuff had been happening before Sasha's suicide attempt. The key was with Sasha. Em was sure of it.

CHAPTER TWENTY

It was still daytime as Em drove to the hospital, but it could have been midnight. The sun had already gone down, and the roads were dark. At every turn she thought someone was going to stumble out into the street in front of her—that blond girl, Ali, from Boston, with those cold, empty eyes that always seemed to be laughing. Or Meg, the girl from the snow-covered road, coming back for her scarlet ribbon.

Em kept slamming on her brakes whenever she saw movement: the wind rustling the bare trees; a deer bounding off, white tail high, a warning signal. She realized she had barely slept in weeks. She blinked her eyes hard, trying to stay focused on the road.

The sound of her phone ringing jangled her nerves even more. She looked down at the screen. It was her mom. She realized it was nearly four p.m.—the school day had ended.

"Hi, Mom." Em tried to keep her voice on an upswing. She felt that she was on the verge of telling her mom everything, of pulling over, breaking down, and spilling it all.

"Hi, sweetie," her mom said, a note of concern in her voice. "I wanted to check in, see where you are."

Em imagined the words tumbling from her mouth: *I'm driving to the hospital to see Sasha Bowlder. Chase humiliated her, she hurt herself, and now he's dead. Someone's following me and I'm scared that they're going to hurt me too. . . .* Even in her inner monologue, the words sounded insane. No. She couldn't say anything yet. Once she saw Sasha, things might be clearer.

"I'm just out and about," Em said vaguely. "I'll be home in a few hours."

"You driving carefully? It's supposed to start snowing again."

Em squeezed the wheel, trying to focus on her mom's voice. "I'm being careful, Mom." Em's voice almost cracked. "I promise. I'll see you soon." If school had called about Em missing classes today, her mom was clearly letting her off the hook.

"Okay, Emily. I love you." The words felt heavy in Em's head. As she hung up, she couldn't help thinking of Chase's mother. She wondered what Mrs. Singer was doing right now. How empty that sad trailer would feel to come home to, when she ever came home. *If* she ever did. The thought made Em nauseous and she rolled down her window for some air, despite the chill outside.

The assisted-living condo facilities that surrounded the hospital glowed eerily as she finally approached. She pulled into the nearly empty visitors' lot. *Shit.* Visiting hours ended at four p.m. Her parents worked at a different hospital—one of the larger ones in Portland—but she wished she could tell them what was going on. Maybe one of them would know what to do.

She smoothed her hair, which was all staticky from the cold, and tugged at her wool sweater, suddenly very itchy, as she walked into the echoing reception area of the East Wing. It was a place for hopeless cases. This was where Em's grandmother had been for nearly two months before she died, after sustaining head trauma during a bad stroke. She recognized the nurse on duty, Carol, as one who had tended to her grandmom. Other staffers bustled around, but only one of them manned the desk near the doors Em needed to go through. Em shifted on her feet; hospitals made her anxious. She dawdled by the entrance.

As soon as she saw Carol push through the double doors on the other side of the desk with a stack of manila folders in her hand, Em took a quick look around and walked briskly toward the desk. In a single move, she pulled open a filing cabinet drawer, shoved it closed, and opened another. It was horrifyingly easy to find the patient files. B for Bowlder. Sasha. Room 17. She threw the file back into its spot in the drawer and headed for the swinging doors. She tried to look like she was supposed to be here. No one seemed to notice.

The sounds of the nurses' station faded as Em crept down the hall, which was freshly scrubbed and smelled both antiseptic and old. Like dried flowers. Like death. She looked for room 17, around one corner, then another. She hated how quiet the hallway was, and how loud her footsteps sounded, even in sneakers. She tried not to look into the rooms she passed—the glowing monitors like sinister creatures looming next to each bed. She scanned the numbered placards next to every door.

Then there it was. Number 17. This door, unlike most of the others, was closed.

Em paused and glanced behind her—no one there—before pushing the metal bar and stepping inside.

The hospital room was small and dark; the only lights came from the electronic monitors next to the room's sole bed. Those beeped, quietly, eerily, steadily.

Em felt hot and flushed. She fumbled to unbutton her coat, fingers shaking. She hadn't known what to expect—she'd never seen anyone in a coma before. Sasha lay there silent and unmoving.

Em took two shaking steps toward the bed. She pulled her sweater cuffs between her fingers and her palm and shoved her thumbs into holes in the loose knit. She grabbed her hair and shoved it into a bun. For a moment she considered backing out, but then she remembered the way Chase had rubbed her back as she'd sobbed in the gym that day. Zach's warm hands and stubbled face, Gabby's wide blue eyes, blinking at her trustingly—and then, just a week later, with hate. How quickly everything had fallen apart.

You can do this. Em tucked some remaining strands of hair behind her ears and moved closer to the bed.

She would fix things; she would make the horrible mistakes of the last few weeks disappear. She would sit down and bare her soul to the sad, sleeping Sasha, and she would be absolved of her sins. All of them. There had to be some way to escape her mistakes so that they wouldn't get her the way they'd gotten Chase. There had to be some way to stop whatever was happening.

Sasha, she'd say. *I'm sorry. I'm sorry for all your pain and I'm sorry for mine too, and Gabby's, and what I've caused.* Em bit her lip, thinking about mistakes, about disgusting impulses, about those shaky, exciting moments with Zach by the fire, in the car, on his bed. . . . About the way she'd felt possessed by her desires.

She gulped, tasting metal, fighting back the lump in her throat that was choking her.

And then Em heard something—a tiny rustling, a whisper. Her chest seized. There was someone else in here. She whirled around, but the room was empty. The robotic beeping continued.

But did it sound faster now?

Em's heartbeat quickened too. What if Sasha woke, right here, right now? What if she could respond to Em's confession and, like an angel, deliver her, forgive her? If Sasha woke up—if Sasha was *okay*—it would make everything else okay too. It would have to.

Em took two steps closer to Sasha, and then another two, her sneakers squeaking timidly on the linoleum floor.

"Sasha . . . ?" Em whispered. Nothing. She licked her lips. "Sasha? Can you hear me?" Em leaned over the body in the bed. Her index finger brushed Sasha's right hand. For a brief second she noticed the glinting snake charm on the dresser next to Sasha's bed. It was just like the one that Drea always wore. Its eyes appeared to be watching her. She leaned in a little closer.

Suddenly, Sasha Bowlder sprang up like a jack-in-the-box. A maniacal smile spread over her deathly pale face. A smile like Ali's: all-knowing. Wicked. Her eyes were inches from Em's—black, dead. A puppet's eyes.

Em let out a whimper; it caught in her throat and she choked on her own saliva. Coughing, struggling for breath, she tried to back away, but a cold force kept her rooted to the spot. She put her hands out, as if to shield herself from those black-hole eyes.

Em felt like she was nailed to the floor and at the same time like she was drowning, suffocating. She couldn't breathe.

And then Sasha's mouth opened, and a creaking whisper

came from that sick, smiling face. Em could smell her breath—like burnt ashes.

"Ready for your turn to pay, *Em*?" A trickle of deep-red blood spilled over from Sasha's bottom lip and down her chin.

And then it began, a shrill, high, piercing sound that penetrated Em's brain, cutting through the feeling of suffocation. It was the machines. They were screaming—or was that her? *Beep, beep-beep, beeeeeeeeeeeeeeeeeeeeeeeeeeeeeeeeeeep.*

Em stumbled backward, into the monitors, sending one of them clattering to the ground. Then she turned and bolted into the hallway. She ran, gasping, heart exploding, running to save her life.

Three nurses and a doctor headed past her in the opposite direction.

"Code! Code!" she heard them shout behind her.

And just before she went out of earshot, she heard this: "Code Black." She kept running, the cold slamming into her like a wall, but as she did, she heard the words again in her head.

Code Black. She knew what that meant.

Sasha Bowlder was dead.

CHAPTER TWENTY-ONE

"JD? JD, are you there?" Em shouted into her phone. She wasn't even sure if he'd picked up yet. That thing in the hospital . . . she couldn't get the image out of her head. *Ready for your turn to pay, Em?*

Terrified thoughts lashed like eels squirming in her head. Sasha was dead; so was Chase. He was dead because his actions had led to Sasha's death.

Now Em was going to pay. She was going to pay for something she'd done: an eye for an eye.

An eye for an eye makes the world go blind. She had heard that somewhere.

"Em? Hello?" She heard JD's voice faintly in her ear.

"JD!?"

"Em, are you okay?"

"Oh my god, JD." She was crying now. "I saw her."

"You saw who? Em, what's going on?"

"I can't . . . I can't explain. I'm going to pay—I don't know what it means." She was hysterical now, gasping and gulping.

"Em. Calm down. Just come over here and we'll talk." JD's voice was soothing, like cream applied to a burn.

"Okay. Okay. Okay." She repeated the word, trying to convince herself.

"Em, I've never heard you like this. Do you want me to come get you?"

"No. No. I'm fine. I'm coming." She turned on the car and eased it slowly into drive, thinking only about getting to JD's and collapsing into his arms.

She turned on the classical station, hoping the music would steady her racing thoughts. Em knew that there was only one thing she'd done recently that would be worth paying for. The only transgression for which revenge made sense: Zach. What she'd done with her best friend's boyfriend. How she'd felt about him. How little control she'd had over her own emotions—how little control she'd wanted to have. Those were sins, definitely. She swallowed back the feeling that she was going to be sick.

Thou shall not covet thy best friend's boyfriend.

As she mulled it over, biting on her lower lip, compulsively pushing her hair back from her forehead, she saw a car approaching behind her. It was surprising; she'd decided to take the usually deserted back road, the Peaks Road route, to her house. It was slightly quicker, if you knew how to hug the turns. You had to be careful at the downhill stretch, though. Especially in wintertime.

The car was coming faster than it should have been. And when it got just a couple of car lengths behind her, it started flashing its brights. It was like a disco ball in her rearview mirror, nearly blinding her in the dark.

What the hell? Em sped up slightly. No change, the blinking continued.

And then in the split second between the flashes, Em had her own moment of flashing terror: It was blond, scary, bloody Ali, who'd been stalking her for weeks.

The one who had first given her the flower, she now realized—the one who had probably left her that note inside her coat pocket.

As soon as the idea came to her, she *knew.* She was being hunted. And this time she would end up like Chase. She would be the one to pay.

Acting on sheer panic, Em took a quick left, down Old Mark's Lane. Then a right onto Pemaquid Road. The car was still behind her, even closer now. In a panic, Em pulled around Pemaquid's hairpin turn and then back onto Peaks. The car tailed her, coming closer even when Em thought there was no room between their bumpers. She was taking short little breaths now, eyes wide, shoulders hunched. And then, as the two cars approached the steep slope of Peaks Road's most dangerous stretch, the car slammed into her from behind at a slight angle. From the moment of impact, it was like slow motion, like watching a cue ball hit the eight ball at just the right spot. Em felt the car moving straight toward a low snowbank. And then, with a horrible jolt, it was embedded there.

There was no time for making sure that she was all in one piece. In a mad dash, she tumbled out of the car and into the night. She was desperate. Willing her feet to move even as they dragged heavily along the ground. Sobs racked her body. "Leave me alone! Stop! Stop!"

She got about twenty feet before she realized that whoever was following her was also shouting.

"It's okay," a girl's voice called out. "It's okay! It's Drea! From school!"

Em slowed down, but only a little. She turned around, but kept moving backward, stumbling over branches and rocks, the breath still rasping in her throat.

"It's me, Drea Feiffer. There's something wrong with your car." Drea stepped into the beam of her headlights, revealing herself fully. Standing there, her clothes the same color as the night, all black and gray and silver. She'd buzzed one side of her head, leaving black strands to fall asymmetrically over her left cheek. She was holding up her hands, as if to prove that she came in peace. "I was behind you on Peaks when I noticed something leaking from your car. I was worried it might be brake fluid."

Em was relieved and also, suddenly, furious. Was this chick for real? She'd run Em's car off the road because she thought it was leaking brake fluid?

"Really. My friend Crow taught me about cars. I saw you were going for the downhill part and I was worried that you wouldn't be able to stop. I had a weird sixth sense about it. So I bashed you. Gently. It was a gentle bash."

"You rear-ended me because you thought there *might* be something wrong with my car?" Em shook her head, trying to make sense of it. With a shudder she remembered where she was coming from. The hospital. Sasha's room. Sasha was dead, and Drea didn't know it yet. Em softened, unballing her fists and pushing her hair away from her face.

"Let's check it out. If I'm wrong, I'll have Crow fix your car, no charge."

"And just how are we going to check it out?" Em leaned over, putting her hands on her knees to catch her breath. The world was still spinning a bit.

"I have a toolbox in my car." Strangely, Drea stuck out her hand toward Em. "I'm really sorry I scared you. You look like you just saw a ghost."

Em turned her face away, stomach lurching. She didn't take Drea's hand. "Let's just get this over with, okay? It's freezing out here." She jogged a bit, partially because she was cold, partially as though to shake off the way Drea was looking at her searchingly.

Em hung back a few feet while Drea grabbed a flashlight and poked her head under the hood, muttering to herself. Em crossed her arms and hopped a little from one foot to the other, feeling the freezing air sear her lungs with every breath. The woods on the left side of Peaks Road were thick and deep, part of the Galvin Nature Preserve, where the boys played ice hoops. She squinted, trying to make out the pond, but she could barely see through one layer of brush.

Drea rattled and cursed under the hood and emerged looking shaken. Then, with an air of resignation, she lay down on the salty, slushy road and slid herself under Em's car.

"Do you, like, need a hand?" Em asked helplessly. But then Drea was shoving herself back up onto her knees and walking over to where Em was standing. She wiped her hands on her black jeans.

"It really was the brakes, Em. The line looks like it was cut clean."

"What does that even mean?"

"Um, that you would have died if you'd gone down the Peaks stretch," Drea said with a shudder. "You would have just kept picking up speed. Like a roller coaster without a way to stop." An owl or something hooted in the distance.

"But . . . but . . . how did it happen? I just got my car serviced and everything." Em's cheeks burned in the cold. She wasn't wearing a hat.

"I don't know how things happen. I just know how to fix them." Drea smiled grimly. "Jeez. I owe Crow a beer. And you owe *me*, like, an entire bottle of vodka, or your homecoming crown or whatever. I just *saved your life*, Winters." She got quiet suddenly. Em watched Drea's guard fall, just for a second, as she turned away, squinting into the dark. "Maybe my track record's getting better."

Em thought again of Sasha. "What did you say?"

"Nothing." Drea turned back to Em. The walls were back up. "I'm just kidding about the crown. It would clash with my snazzy movie-theater vest."

Em just stared, not really at Drea, not really at her car, just at the unfocused blackness in front of her. The brakes had been cut clean. Suddenly she felt hopeless, resigned. Something bad was going to happen. Something bad was *already* happening. There was no way to stop it.

Drea snapped her fingers closer to Em's face. "Earth to Em. Can I give you a ride home or something?"

"Sorry. Yes, thank you. I'll just be a minute, I need to grab my purse," Em mumbled as she bent into the car to retrieve her bag. It didn't even seem like Drea was listening anymore—too focused on packing up her metal tool kit—but as Em came back toward Drea's little Honda Civic, Drea froze.

Em looked behind her, half expecting to see a moose. But Drea wasn't looking past her. She was looking *at* her.

"That," Drea was saying, pointing at her bag. "Where did you get that?"

Em looked down and blood rushed to her head. Instinctively, her hand stretched out, as if to protect herself from the orchid's glow. She had kept the second one, which Ali had pressed on her in Harvard Square, afraid to throw it away again. Afraid Ali would come back. Drea was staring at it fixedly.

"This flower?" Em felt her breath getting shallow again. "I don't know. Some girl gave it to me. It's weird."

"Weird how?"

Em blew warm breath onto the tips of her freezing fingers. "Weird because I can't get rid of it. The first time I . . . I watched it get crushed under a train. And then this girl gave it back to me. I'm not even sure who she is . . ." She trailed off, wondering if this was when people got committed to the insane asylum.

But Drea didn't scoff, as Em expected her to. Instead, she wordlessly grabbed the orchid from Em's bag. With her other hand, she dug into her black jeans for a Zippo. And then she set the flower, with its many folds, on fire.

She threw it on the ground once its entire body was aflame. It smoldered there.

Drea looked back at Em, the tiny fire casting a candle-like glow on her face. Em had never noticed that Drea's eyelashes were so long and curled. That, combined with her strong nose, made her really pretty, in an unexpected way. Her prettiness certainly didn't go with her badass reputation. Em found herself wondering, randomly, whether or not Drea had ever been in love.

"What did you do?" Drea's voice was soft but forceful. Em realized that she had never before seen Drea Feiffer look scared, not even the time in fifth grade when Carey Wallace threatened to beat her up for being a freak.

"What?" Em swallowed back the sudden dryness in her throat.

"They won't just show up. What did you do? Why did you get a flower?"

Em was so surprised by the questions, she couldn't respond at first. She didn't like the way Drea was staring at her. Had Drea heard something around school? How could Drea Feiffer know anything about her life? "I—I didn't do anything."

Drea pursed her lips, cocked her head to one side, and studied Em. Then she shook her head as though she had come to a decision about something. "Pretending won't do any good, Em. When you're ready to talk, find me." Then she was in her glove compartment, rooting around. "In the meantime," Drea said, backing out of the car with something in her hand. "This might help."

She took Em's hand and closed her fist around a small gold snake charm—a miniature version of the one Em had seen Drea wearing for years. Then Drea jerked her head, motioning for Em to get in the car. Em looked at her, waiting for more explanation, but Drea was quiet. Other than the pulsing music coming from the car speakers, they drove home in silence.

"Thanks for the ride," Em said a bit sheepishly when they pulled into her driveway. She knew she wasn't going inside—it was way too dark in there to be alone, and she knew JD was waiting across the yard.

"No problem." Under the motion-sensor driveway light, Drea's eyes pierced hers. "Don't forget. Come see me when you want to talk. I might be able to help."

Em didn't answer as she got out of the car.

JD was frantic when he answered the door. His hair was sticking up at so many crazy angles, it looked like he had been electrocuted. "What happened to you? What took you so long? Are you okay?"

Em whispered fiercely in response: "Are your parents home?"

"Yeah, they're home. Seriously, Em. What's going on?"

"What are they doing?" She shouldered past him, dropping her voice to a whisper. She didn't feel like dealing with Mr. and Mrs. Fount tonight and their inevitable questions about school and SAT prep.

JD raised an eyebrow. "They're upstairs watching a documentary about blue whales," he mock whispered back. "Now will you tell me what's going on?" He tugged at his sweater and looked at her over the tops of his glasses. "You sounded crazy on the phone."

"I think I *am* going crazy," Em said, dragging him toward his basement door. She kept talking as they descended his stairs; down in the rec room, there was a ratty sofa that JD called his therapist couch. "My brakes are fucked up. Drea Feiffer rescued me. I think someone is stalking me. I think there's a ghost stalking me." The statements came out in rushed staccato, but she stopped rambling at the bottom of the staircase.

Her voice caught in her throat as she saw what JD had prepared: a plate of homemade nachos, two cupcakes, and a little pillow fort on "her side" of the couch.

"JD . . . this is so nice."

"Well, I'm telling you, I really thought you were going to be carted away. I was worried." He shrugged, running his hands through his hair. He ducked under a low beam and came over to the couch.

Em collapsed on the couch, breathing in its familiar scent and feeling its knobby pills against her forearms.

"This couch is so uncomfortable," she said, pulling at one of the little balls of wool.

"Do the ghosts think so too?" He looked at her with a quizzical smirk. "What were you saying?"

"JD, listen. Can I tell you something? Can I tell you everything?" She tried to take a bite of her cupcake but couldn't.

"Yes." He hadn't sat down yet. He was hovering.

"Something weird is going on," she said, biting her lip.

"Very informative, Em. A lot of weird stuff has been happening around here. Can you be a bit more precise?" he asked, stuffing his hands into his smoking jacket's pockets.

He was teasing, but she resented it. She fluttered her hands, like she did when she was looking for the right word. "I'm trying, JD. Give me a second."

"Okay, okay." He held up his hands, motioned for her to continue.

She put the cupcake back down and stared at him. "Someone has been following me." She pointed vaguely to the basement window, as though that would help clarify her story. "Remember that day in Boston? She was there then."

"*Who* was there?" JD sat down now, looking at her with concern.

"This girl. This girl named Ali who's been showing up

in windows. And on the T, in Boston that day. She's stalking me, I think, because of something I did . . ." Em trailed off when she saw the way he was looking at her. She'd seen him look at Melissa this way, when she was going on about how Tess Hoover and Brian Rinaldi had cut the line together at the seventh-grade trip to the amusement park and how that meant that they must be boyfriend and girlfriend. Indulgent. Amused. Like . . . *aren't these kids so cute?*

"You don't believe me, do you?" she said dully.

JD sighed. "Em, I know this is hard for you." The pity in his eyes had only gotten deeper. "I don't know what you're talking about with this stalker stuff, but I know you're upset about Chase. I know you'd been talking and hanging out a little bit, but you have to remember that none of it is your fault. You couldn't have changed anything." He put his hand on her leg and patted it. She jerked away, as though his touch were scalding.

"No. That's not what I'm talking about. That's not what this is about." Em shook her head violently.

"Look, people's imaginations go into overdrive after a tragedy, you know. I read that somewhere. So if you want to tell me your stories, I'll listen. I just don't want you to scare yourself like this."

"JD. I've spent a lot of time trying to blame this on my *overactive imagination*," she said, her voice tinged with anger now.

"It's not that. It's more than that. I mean, it does have to do with Chase, but . . ." She broke off, trying to collect her thoughts.

JD leaped in. "Exactly. This all just goes back to Chase. Dying. Probably even Sasha, too. It's been a fucked-up time. No wonder you're freaking out."

"No, JD. I'm *freaking out* because I keep seeing the same girl over and over and because she gave me a regenerative red flower that *happens to be* the same thing that was in Chase's hand when he died and because someone just cut my brake lines and apparently sorry's not enough and that's why I'm *freaking out.*" By the time she finished her diatribe she was halfway up the basement stairs, fighting back tears, struggling to put on her coat with dignity, which was difficult when her vision was so blurry she couldn't even see the arm holes.

JD looked blindsided. "Where are you going?"

"I'm going home," she spat out. "I'm going home. At least my pillows aren't condescending."

But those couldn't protect her, either; she knew that. She'd have to do that herself.

She heard JD running up the stairs behind her, and she whirled around at the front door.

"Em," he said. "What did I do?"

"You judged me, as usual." She glared at him. "Why don't you try having a life of your own before you make decisions about other people's?"

"I have a life," he said quietly, his face dark.

"Right. Driving me around everywhere and telling me what to do. Nice life," she said, feeling the cold air hit her face as his front door slammed behind her.

CHAPTER TWENTY-TWO

It was hard enough not knowing what the hell was going on, who to tell, how to stop it. But something about the fact that JD didn't understand made Em's heart hurt in a way she'd never felt before.

Forever and always, JD had been the one she trusted. When she was scared to jump off the dock at Galvin's Pond when they were ten, he did it with her—even though there was goopy pond grass floating nearby. When she told him stories, she never felt like she had to edit out the weird stuff—the strange places her brain went, the seemingly nonsensical connections she made between things. When she'd told him about Zach, even . . .

But now she felt like she was behind a wall. If JD didn't understand, who would?

His texts started up the moment she was back in her house.

Em. I'm sorry. Come back and talk to me.

Or I can come over there?

Hello? Emerly? Silent treatment?

She powered off her phone without responding. She felt humiliated; she'd exposed herself to him, and he had treated her like a child. She trudged upstairs, leaving the kitchen light on. She noticed her parents had left a note saying they'd gone out for dinner. They would be home in a few hours.

In her room, Em flipped open her laptop.

There he was again, trying to chat with her now.

Em? I can see you're online. Can we just talk?

I'm sorry if I was a jerk. I don't even know what I did.

What's going on???

She shut her laptop with a bang. She thought about turning on her iPod but there wasn't a single song she wanted to listen to. She pulled off her jeans and changed into her UMaine sweats. She shut off the light, then thought better of it and switched on her desk lamp.

She'd had enough of the dark.

Then she slumped into bed without even brushing her teeth. She lay there, listening to the clacking radiator, rolling from one side of the bed to the other. She couldn't get comfortable. In a fit of frustration, she dumped all her pillows onto the ground, keeping just one for her head. Finally, her eyes felt heavy. And just as she might have fallen asleep, Em heard frantic, furious knocking at the front door. She jolted awake.

It couldn't be her parents; even if they'd forgotten their keys, both sets, they would have dug around for the spare, hidden under a rock beneath the deck. It had to be JD, coming to apologize and talk in person.

For a second she debated just leaving him there in the cold. He'd have to give up eventually. But the knocks kept coming, echoing through the empty house.

With a sigh, she got up, slipped her bare feet into the puffy slippers next to her bed, and headed back downstairs. She told herself she was *not* going to forgive him. At least being mad gave her *something* concrete to focus on.

In the foyer, she steeled herself, cleared her throat, and flung open the door.

"JD—" But the words dried in her throat. Because there, on the Winters' rough granite stoop, stood the girl. Ali.

She was smiling brightly. In her hand was a gleaming red orchid. Beautiful, translucent, like something blown from glass. "Hi, again," the girl chirped. Her tiny nose quivered like a rodent's and her teeth gleamed white. "Santa never found out you were naughty. But we did."

The words crashed through Em's skull. *Santa never found out you were naughty.* It was almost exactly what Zach had said to her that night, the first night they'd kissed.

She slammed the door in Ali's face and for a moment stood frozen, heart pounding. There was a rasping sound coming from somewhere; it took Em a moment to realize it was the sound of her own breathing.

"Knock, knock," came Ali's singsong voice from the other side of the door.

Em unfroze. Terror coursed through her and she tore into the living room, then to the dining room, then to the kitchen, locking all the windows and pulling the drapes. She felt prickles along her shoulder blades, as though Ali were right behind her with every step.

She was being punished for what she had done with Zach. She was sure of it now—Ali had parroted Zach's words to her almost exactly. She would pay for her sins the same way Chase had paid for his. *Are you ready for your turn to pay, Em?*

She was crying now, whimpering. "Please leave me alone." She whirled around to scream at every skating shadow, yanking closed curtains and blinds. "I'm sorry. I'm sorry." She froze in the foyer, not daring to look outside, terrified of what she might see. "I didn't mean it. It just happened. It's not my fault. It wasn't even worth it."

In the hallway—as far from any windows as possible—she backed up against a wall and sank to the floor, trembling, drawing her knees to her chest. Barely breathing. She didn't hear anything. She pulled the sleeves of her sweatshirt down around her thumbs and bit them—a habit from childhood, from being freaked by scary movies and ghost stories.

That's what this was: a ghost story.

And then the knocking started again.

"No, please!" Her sobs rang out in the empty house. "Leave me alone! I said I was sorry. I'm trying to fix things. It—it was a mistake. Please just leave me alone!" She brought her knees to her chest, rocking, letting tears run into her mouth. "I didn't mean to let it happen." Her voice was rising hysterically. "It wasn't even fucking worth it!"

And then she heard Gabby's voice—sweet, familiar, beautiful.

"Em? Em, are you okay? Are you in there?"

Em raised her head, wiping her nose and face with the cuff of her sweatshirt.

"Em? It's Gabs. Please let me in. We need to talk."

Em stood up shakily, wiping her sweaty palms on her sweatpants. She took one tiny step forward, calling out tentatively, "Gabby?"

Gabby's face appeared, also tentative, also miserable, in one of the small rectangular windows next to Em's front door. She pointed to the doorknob.

"Em, please let me in."

Em opened the door and after a moment's hesitation, Gabby stepped into the foyer. Em scanned the lawn quickly. Nothing. Ali was gone. But after she closed the door, she made sure to double lock it.

Gabby was standing awkwardly in the dark foyer, wearing a puffy jacket Em didn't recognize and that was too big for her. "I tried calling," she said. "You didn't pick up." She was chewing on the inside of her cheek, and her face was streaked with tears and mascara.

"I was in bed." Em's voice was hoarse, and she swiped her eyes on the cuff of her sweatshirt when Gabby wasn't looking, hoping she wouldn't notice that Em, too, had been crying. "I turned my phone off."

"I drove by and saw your light was on . . ." Gabby fidgeted nervously with her zipper.

"I'm glad," Em said, wishing things didn't feel so awkward. For a moment they stood in silence.

"Oh, Em," Gabby gasped out suddenly. "I saw him. I had to go to Portland for a new pair of gloves and I saw him kissing some girl outside some restaurant. I almost crashed my car when I saw it. . . ." Gabby was blubbering. "He never takes me out to eat!"

Without thinking about it—without worrying about the fact that the last time they had seen each other, Gabby had pushed her into a coatrack—Em stepped forward and put her arms around Gabby, their mismatched frames fitting together as they always had. She could smell Gabby's signature vanilla body spray and breathed it in. They stood there for a while, hugging and sniffling.

Then Em pulled her into the living room and sat her on

the brushed-suede couch. The Winters didn't use their living room very often—most of their limited family time happened in the den, on old and comfy beige sofas, in front of the TV. Em associated this room with holidays, with reciting poems for her grandma.

"Wait here," she said, once Gabby was seated. She went into the kitchen, ripping into the cabinets for some Swiss Miss. The two minutes and thirty seconds that it took for the microwave to heat up the water felt like forever. "I'll be right in, Gabby," Em called, shifting her feet in front of the buzzing machine. She was so happy Gabby was here, in her living room, sitting on her couch, she felt like she could cry again. Part of her wanted to spill her guts about the fact that a freaky blond girl was skulking around in her yard, but she didn't know how to say it. And Gabby clearly needed her.

Em thought about what Drea had said: *When you're ready to talk, find me.* Oh, Em was ready. She was ready to find out what Drea knew, what the hell was going on, and how to stop it once and for all. But tomorrow was time enough to find Drea and figure out what the hell was going on. Tonight, it was Operation Win Gabby Back.

It had to be a good sign that she was here. If they could patch things up, maybe this would all be over.

On the way back into the living room, she checked to make sure the front door was still bolted. Then she settled onto the couch with Gabby, setting both mugs of hot cocoa onto the coffee table.

"I broke your Cabo mug," she said guiltily, as though Gabby would have noticed or cared that she was drinking from a plain white coffee cup.

Gabby didn't respond, but picked up one of the cocoas and blew at it, staring at the floor.

"I . . . I brought back these special licorice candies from Spain"—her voice wavered as she spoke—"and I couldn't share them with you," Gabby said.

Em nodded. She knew what she meant. Gabby and Em both had an obsession with all types of licorice. But they never ate it alone. They always shared.

There was a noise outside, a rustling. Em stilled, listening hard. But then everything was silent again, except Gabby's sniffing.

"Do you still have them?" Em asked.

"Yeah, there are some left. Zach doesn't even like licorice, you know—" Gabby broke off, crying again. Em saw a teardrop fall into the steaming hot chocolate. "I was wrong about him," Gabby said finally. "After I saw him with that—*whoever* she was—I went to his house and waited for him. When he showed up, I confronted him about it. Just blew up. And he told me—" Em could see, from the way Gabby couldn't meet her eyes, that she felt mortified.

"He told you what?" Em prodded.

"He told me that yeah, he's been with other girls. Who knows what else he's done. He's sorry. Bullshit. He said some stuff about not being able to choose. And then I threw my earrings at him—the ones he gave me for Christmas—and took off. And came here." Her tone made it clear that she'd done so because she felt it was her only option.

"Gabs, I'm glad you came." Em was.

"I don't even know who to trust anymore." Gabby put her head in her hands.

"You can trust me," Em said, feeling the ache throbbing in her chest, the ache of missing Gabby.

Gabby looked Em straight in the eyes. "Can I?"

Em leaned forward, willing Gabby to believe her. "Yeah, you can trust me. I know it's hard to believe right now, but you can. Gabs—"

Gabby interrupted: "I didn't want to come here, you know. But . . ." She shuddered. "God, Em, you're my best friend. Even after what happened. You're still my best friend. No one else understands." She quickly added, "But don't think I'm not still, like, completely furious with you. Completely."

Em's mouth was dry. She shook her head. "I know. I don't expect you to just forgive me out of the blue. But I want you to know my side. He screwed us both. I mean, not literally, of course," she rushed to add. "But he's an asshole. A manipulator.

He uses people, Gabs." Em shivered, remembering when JD had told her just that.

"That doesn't make it any better that you just *fell* for it. I know that you can, like, express this stuff so much better than I can, Em. You know what words to use. I don't. All I know is that I feel like total shit."

Em picked up her mug, then set it down again. "I know, Gabby. Believe me, I know." She sighed. "I'm so sorry."

Gabby drew the quilted throw blanket from the back of the couch down onto her lap. "How much of the other stuff did you know about?" Her voice had a tiny quiver in it. "The fact that Zach was . . . with other girls?"

Em told her everything. What Chase had said, how Zach's own best friend had described him. What Zach had revealed himself, the night she confronted him. She kept tucking her hair behind her ears, watching as Gabby sank deeper and deeper into the couch.

"I tried to tell you, Gabs. I wanted to talk to you so badly." Em cleared her throat. "He's so good at making people feel like they're special. Like what he feels for them is unique. That's what he did to me. I really felt . . ." She sighed and let it spill out. "I really felt like we had something that was different. And I knew I was doing something terrible but at the same time I couldn't fight it. It was like it was my only chance to have this earthshaking love that people talk about. That you had. That I thought you had. Your perfect life. Your perfect relationship. I just wanted . . ."

Gabby was staring at her stonily. Em pushed ahead: "But it wasn't earthshaking. It wasn't anything other than him seeing how far he could go, how much he could get away with. And you have to know that I'm so sorry. Sorrier than I've ever been about anything."

She meant it, too. She *was* sorry. In the back of her mind, as she spilled these secrets, she felt like she was putting her conscience through the car wash. If Gabby could understand, did that somehow wipe the slate clean?

"Oh my god." Gabby again dropped her head in her hands. "This is just so *embarrassing*. How am I supposed to show my face at Ascension ever again? And the *pep* rally is tomorrow. . . . We were supposed to go together. . . ."

"It's not about that, Gabs. This is bigger than that. *You* are bigger than that." Em touched her best friend's arm. "Gabby? Will you . . . will you ever forgive me?"

Gabby moved her arm away, but looked up at Em as she did. When she spoke, her voice was a whisper. "I don't know, Em. I just . . . I need you."

"I need you, too, Gabby." Em was crying again, softly. "My parents have been all on my case—'Where's Gabby? Did you two have a fight?'"

"Oh my god, mine too. It's almost easier to just be friends

again." Gabby sat up straighter. She smoothed her hair down around her temples. "Jesus. What a jerk. What a complete and total idiot. I hate him. And you know what? I hate him as much for what he did to you as for what he did to me."

That, Em realized, was why she loved Gabby so much. Because even as Gabby grappled with the crumbling of the perfect life she'd built, she still felt Em's pain too. Maybe Gabby thought about what other people felt more than she let on. She got it. From now on, Em would be strong for Gabby—she owed her that.

But would Em be strong enough to save herself?

CHAPTER TWENTY-THREE

Gabby ended up sleeping over. Em's parents came home around eleven o'clock, and even though it was a school night, they'd agreed (as Gabby's had, when she texted them) to let the girls sleep downstairs in the basement. Em thought they were happy to see Gabby around again. Though from the look on her dad's face, she'd have some explaining to do about why her car had to be towed—again.

They woke up in the morning and decided to stop at Gabby's, so she could grab her books and change. If she wore Em's jeans, she would have to pair them with stilts.

"Cool necklace," Gabby said as they walked out to Gabby's car, pointing to the serpent charm that dangled from Em's neck.

She'd put it on at the last minute. She'd try anything at this point.

After Gabby ran into her house for her bag and a quick change, Em asked, with some trepidation, if Gabby wanted to stop at Dunkin' Donuts.

"Um, of course!" Em could see that Gabby was in performance mode. Her makeup this morning was impeccable, and she'd woken up almost an hour before Em in order to take a long shower. She would come out on top of this Zach humiliation no matter what.

"You know what's terrible?" Gabby sipped her hot drink and looked out the window. Ascension looked gray and brittle. The steam from the coffee–hot cocoa mixture fogged up a tiny section of the glass.

"What?"

"I know that this is an awful thing to say, and I would obviously only say it to you, but . . . at least there's too much other awful stuff going on for people to even care about me and Zach. Like, petty gossip doesn't really matter much right now. People are *dying*."

"You're right." Em nodded. "Anyone who blabs about this must have some messed-up priorities."

They agreed then, tacitly, that this was the strategy: Information lockdown. The fewer words said about the Gabby Dove–Zach McCord breakup, the better.

Just before getting out of the car, Gabby swiveled in her seat. "You'll be at the pep rally tonight, right? I cannot deal with it by myself."

Em hesitated for just a second. The pep rally was the last place she wanted to go. But she wouldn't let Gabby down again. "Of course I'll be there," she said.

As they walked from the parking lot to their first-period classes, Em thought they must have looked like a formidable two-person army.

Em looked for Drea before the first bell rang, to no avail. Again as classes switched. Nothing. They didn't have any classes together, and Em had no idea where punked-out-Rainbow-Brite-goth types hung out during their off periods. Not near the theater, of course, and not down by the gym. Had she seen them loitering in the arts hallway in the past? She made a mental note: *Pay more attention to where different cliques hang out for next time you're being homicidally stalked by someone—some*thing*—that wants to punish you for your mistakes.*

Then, right before Em's lunch period, she caught sight of Drea's part-purple, part-black hair as it bobbed down the hallway toward the library.

"Drea!" she shouted, pushing her way through the throng of students pouring out of precalc. "Drea," she called again, getting close enough to grab her shoulder. She was out of breath. "We need to talk."

Drea, whose eyes were rimmed with purple eyeliner, didn't seem surprised that Em was chasing her down. "Oh, hi."

"Hey. I'm so glad I found you." Em fingered the snake charm at her sternum, hoping Drea would notice that she was wearing it. "How are you?" As she said it she realized that Drea must know by now that her best friend was dead. "I mean, really, how are you doing?" she repeated more earnestly. "Like, about Sasha."

"I don't want to talk to you about Sasha, thank you." Drea's tone was measured but not rude. Just firm. There were circles under her eyes. She shoved her hands into her jeans pockets.

"Oh. Okay. Sorry." Em licked her lips, nodding, trying to seem as approachable as possible.

"What did you want to talk to me about?" Drea stared at Em with something akin to boredom.

"Oh . . . well." Em felt ridiculous; until all the insanity had started, she had never had more than a two-minute conversation with Drea, usually limited to: jumbo popcorn, extra butter. But she had a feeling that Drea was her last hope. "You told me to come find you when I was ready to talk. About, you know. The flower and everything? The red orchid?"

"Shhh!" Drea's veil of boredom dropped in an instant, and she turned to look over her shoulder. "We can't talk about this here."

"Um. Okay."

Drea spoke under her breath. Unconsciously, she was touching the snake pin, which was affixed to her coat. "Can you meet me after school?"

Em hated the thought of waiting another three hours to get some answers, but apparently she had no choice. "Yes, sure, of course. Where?"

Drea hesitated, narrowing her eyes. Em had the uncomfortable feeling that Drea was evaluating her, or testing her in some way.

"My house," Drea finally said. "It's here." She fished a pen from her messenger bag and grabbed Em's hand. Her chipped gray nail polish was all Em could see as Drea scrawled an address on the inside of her palm. It tickled slightly and gave her goose bumps. Em nodded. Drea walked away without another word.

The next three hours were agony. Gabby texted her during lunch to say she'd gotten her mom to pick her up from school for an emergency therapy shopping trip. Classic Marty Dove. Em went back to eating in the library, alone. Then she sat through European history, unable to concentrate on a class discussion about fascism. All she could do was replay in her mind Ali's appearance on her doorstep. The heavy knocking. The shock-red orchid. Em's eyes pricked again with anxious tears and she jiggled her knees under her desk. Earth science was even worse. Zach was finally back at school—funny, Em thought, that he'd been too broken up about Chase to survive school, but not so broken up that he couldn't find time to cheat on Gabby—and the back of his head was the first thing Em saw as she walked into the classroom. She was glad he didn't turn around, not once through the whole period.

Her stuff was in her bag ten minutes before the final bell rang, and she was out the doors and headed for Drea's, before it had even finished sounding.

She knew her way *to* Drea's neighborhood, but she didn't know her way around it. Drea's street was close to the center of town, where there were older houses that must have existed even in the 1800s. This area stretched back into the woods, cutting a kind of ruralish strip through Ascension. The back of the neighborhood bordered the Behemoth, if Em had her directions right.

When Em pulled up to Drea's house, something about the sagging structure made her recoil slightly. There was nothing outwardly weird about it, but it looked very . . . lived in. As though in a few more years it might just collapse in on itself. Someone had started to shovel the walk, out from the front door, but the project had clearly been abandoned halfway through. Em walked to the front door, tramping over footsteps that were bigger than her own.

The doorbell was a jarring buzz. Em found herself looking over her shoulder as she waited for Drea. The fluttering feeling at her back returned, like there were moths there, leaving their dust all over her skin. She itched.

"Hi," Drea said as she swung open the door. Her long-sleeved, black waffle-knit shirt was open slightly at the neck to reveal a swath of silver chains, some with pendants and some without. Her hair—the half that wasn't shaved—was pinned back.

"I'm glad you came," Drea said, motioning for Em to follow her down the dim hallway. An obnoxious infomercial blared. As they passed the second room on the left, Drea reached in to close the door; before it shut completely, Em caught a glimpse of an older man—Drea's dad, she supposed—sitting in front of the television. Its blue light bounced off his glassy eyes. Em dimly remembered hearing something about Drea's dad having had a nervous breakdown. Drea kept walking, down the hall and then down a flight of stairs. Em followed hesitantly.

"Don't worry, I'm not going to, like, kill you or anything," Drea said sarcastically, observing Em's nervous expression with a smirk. "My study is down here."

Her study? Em's parents had studies. Sixteen-year-old girls did not. But sure enough, Drea led Em to the back of the basement, to a makeshift door composed of a sheet hung between two beams. Clipped to the sheet was an orange-and-black NO TRESPASSING sign. Drea pulled back the curtain.

Tugging on a string that hung from a single bulb in the ceiling, Drea illuminated her "study"—a paint-stained workbench piled with books, papers, folders, and newspaper clippings. Next to the workbench were two similarly stuffed bookshelves.

In front of all this was a ratty recliner that sat alongside a small desk and a floor lamp. The lamp was strung to the wall by an orange extension cord. Attached to that same cord was a plug that ran to a small dorm-room-type refrigerator. It was all enclosed by sheets. One of the sheets, the one closest to the wall, was decorated with cupcakes.

"Whoa," Em breathed.

"I know, it's kind of ghetto," Drea said, propping open a folding chair that she dug out from under the workbench. "But it serves its purpose. It's quiet down here. My dad never bugs me. And I have a system. I know where everything is."

"It's . . . it's awesome, Drea." Em was serious. "It's so . . . real."

"Yeah, it's *real*-ly dusty down here. Now let's get to work." Drea marched over to the fridge and opened it. "Tell me what's going on. Do you want a Coke?"

"Um, sure."

Drea pulled out two sodas and handed one to Em. Then she sat in the recliner, turned on the floor lamp, which cast a greenish glow on the whole space, and stared. Em shifted in her Bean boots, then started in.

"Well . . . I think that Chase—"

"We're not here to talk about Chase," Drea said sharply. "We're here to talk about you. Right?"

Em blushed. "Yeah. Sorry."

"So what's going on?"

Looking up at the ceiling as though it might offer a suggestion, Em asked, "Where should I start?"

"Well, what's freaking you out?" Drea took a slug of Coke, raising her eyebrows, and propped her feet up on the workbench in front of her. She was wearing steel-toed boots.

Em swallowed, and then said in a rush: "Okay, well, there's this girl—these girls—who are following me. I think. One of them keeps, like, appearing. In my windows and in Boston and everywhere. And I think there are two others like her. Chase Singer knew one of them, I think." Em looked at Drea, eyebrows raised, waiting for a laugh or a dismissal. But Drea was listening, face serious. "And I think they're part of the reason that he's dead. I think . . . I think they killed him because of what he did to Sasha."

There was a long silence then, between them. Drea looked like she'd been slapped. Em cursed herself for bringing up Sasha so indelicately. Drea probably didn't even know that Sasha and Chase had been involved; she certainly wouldn't know that Chase had been the one to circulate Sasha's pictures and messages. She hoped Drea wouldn't ask for more details.

But then Drea cleared her throat and leaned forward. "What did *you* do?"

"Me?"

"Yeah, you," Drea said, pointing right at the middle of Em's chest.

"I . . . well . . ." For some reason, Em couldn't force the words out, even though what she'd done was already pretty public knowledge. For all she knew, Drea might have already heard about it.

Drea just kept staring. "Em, did you come here to talk, or what?"

"Okay." Em tucked her hands up inside the cuffs of her shirt, closed her eyes, and blurted out: "So, over break I hooked up with Zach." There. She had said it. Em opened her eyes to check Drea for a reaction; there seemed to be none. "Zach McCord." Still nothing. Drea looked at her impassively, eyebrows slightly raised. "Gabby's boyfriend."

"Gabby . . . ?" Drea waved her hands around questioningly.

"Gabby Dove. My best friend." Em sat down heavily in the folding chair. If Drea didn't know anything, how was she going to help?

"Ohhhhhhhh. It all becomes clear," Drea said. "You hooked up with your best friend's boyfriend."

Em cringed. It sounded so trivial when it came out of Drea's mouth. "Yeah, I did. But it wasn't just, like, this terrible thing—"

Drea interrupted again. "Listen, Em. I don't want to sound mean. But I don't really care. I mean, I don't care about why you did it or anything. We're not here to become besties. I just want to know what happened so I can explain to you what's going on and maybe fix it."

"Okay." Em breathed a sigh of relief. She didn't feel like getting into the whole story again anyway. "Me too."

"So. All this stuff." With a sweep of her arm, Drea motioned to the literary debris that filled her nook. "It's all about the Furies."

"The who?" The word made an anxious feeling lash in Em's stomach.

"The Furies," Drea said again. The light caught her eyes, making them gleam golden. "Three girls. Three spirits. Three demons. Three witches. Whatever you want to call them. They're here, for sure. They're these three spirits who have been around forever." The way Drea said it, it was like spirits and demons were a common thing. Em was shocked to find herself listening closely, waiting for her to finish explaining. "They have other names too," she went on. "Sometimes they're called the Erinyes, which means 'the angry ones.' They're all over Greek mythology—I'm surprised you haven't heard of them. They'll haunt you if you've done something bad. They seek vengeance for wrongdoings. They basically wait for people to curse themselves and then decide what they think that person deserves. If they think you're guilty, they'll destroy you—regardless of the context, regardless of the circumstance, regardless of whether or not it makes the situation better."

"The Furies," Em repeated. She rubbed her fingers against her temples. "So . . . they're like ghosts?"

"Kind of. I think they take different forms in different places. I have a feeling that they've been appearing as humans in Ascension, though I haven't seen them."

"You actually believe this stuff?" Em scratched her neck uncomfortably.

"I don't believe it. I *know* it." Drea's face was dead serious.

"So the girl who's following me—you think she's a Fury?" Em's mind was clouded with questions and doubts. "Do you think that Sasha and Chase were connected to the Furies?"

Drea shrugged. "I don't know for sure, but I wouldn't be surprised. They've been around forever—there have always been stories about cruel, beautiful sisters in this town. And other towns around the world."

"How do you know all this?" Em asked. Her brain was reeling.

Drea ran her finger around the rim of her soda can. "Hobby," she said shortly.

"But why?" Em pressed. The basement wasn't cold, but she was trembling. "When did you first hear about them? Why did you start to . . . collect all of this stuff?"

Drea stood abruptly, chucking the empty can forcefully

into the garbage in the corner. "Look. This isn't about me, okay? This is about you, and what's happening, and what you're going to do about it."

"But it's crazy," Em said. If anyone knew she was sitting in Drea Feiffer's basement talking about ghosts . . . "Why—why should I believe you?"

As if she could read Em's thoughts, Drea asked, with a perfectly straight face, "Does anyone else believe *you*?"

Em shook her head.

"I didn't think so. That's why you're here. And that's why you should trust me. Because I believe you."

Em bit her lip. "So . . . let's say the Furies really exist," Em said. "Can they be stopped?"

"I'm not sure, but I'm going to find out." Em saw the determination in Drea's eyes. "I'm going to destroy them."

Em groped for words. "But shouldn't you, like, be on their side?" There was no way around it, she realized. She would have to tell Drea about Sasha and Chase. "Look, I'm pretty sure Chase was the one who made Sasha jump off the bridge. Now he's dead. Isn't that kind of what you wanted?"

Drea looked at Em through sad eyes. For the first time in her life, Em felt truly small.

"Really?" Drea squeaked out. "Really? That's how you think the world should work? That's why you think Sasha jumped off the Piss Pass? Because of Chase fucking Singer? No.

She jumped off the Piss Pass because she was sad and lonely and deeply depressed. And I didn't know." Drea's voice got higher and higher; she was talking so fast Em could barely make out her words. "I didn't know," she repeated. Em could see she was determined not to cry.

"I'm sure you—"

"You don't know anything, Emily Winters. All you know is your own little world and your own little life. But listen. The Furies aren't doing anything good. I don't *want* them to do anything other than disappear. Because what happens when *I* make a mistake? Who decides my fate? Me. Or at least the people around me. Not some otherworldly demon-goddess chicks hell-bent on destruction. They can't feel remorse, do you know that?"

"But what about—what about when they make a mistake?" Em realized she was gripping her Coke can like a vise.

Drea let out a dry laugh that sounded almost like a cough. "They've been around for centuries—and yet I'm sure they don't think they've made a single mistake." The greenish light played across her face.

"But how do they choose?" Em persisted. "And how do they know when someone's done something bad? What *counts*?" She wanted to say: *What I did wasn't nearly as bad as what Chase did*, but she bit back the words.

Drea shrugged. "Don't know."

"You don't know?" Em squeaked.

Drea leaned over and grabbed a book from under the bench. She handed it to Em. "Look, there's a lot I don't know. Here's what I do know. The Furies are after you. The red orchid is like their marker. It says so in there." She pointed to the ancient-looking book in Em's hand.

"And they can look like people." Em said it more as a statement than a question.

"They can assume human form, yes," Drea said. "When they're exacting revenge. When they're stalking someone."

"Like me," Em said.

"Like you," Drea echoed matter-of-factly.

Em gulped down the rest of the soda. "So what should I do?"

"Take these," Drea said, reaching over and placing a pile of newsprint onto Em's lap. "And start your reading. These are stories from all over the world that I think have some connection to the Furies."

Em threw her head against the back of the padded chair. "How is reading going to help me go to sleep without one eye open?"

"You can't fight something if you don't understand it." Drea gave Em another withering look. "Jeez. I thought you were supposed to be smart."

Em blushed. "Sorry that I'm not some junior-wizard-Hermione-on-crack."

This was enough to make them both smile, even slightly.

"Just read up, Winters." Winters. It made her think of Chase. Em took the books and printouts silently and tucked them carefully into her bag.

She didn't even wait until she was off Drea's street before pulling over, digging the biggest book out of her bag, and opening it up. Her head was spinning. Furies. Revenge-seeking spirits? This was crazy. Even if they did exist, she didn't think the biggest book in the world could explain why they'd choose to appear in Ascension, Maine—when the world was full of terrible people doing terrible things. Why would they choose to punish a bunch of high school kids? She flipped to the index and scanned it: *Alcohol . . . Alecto . . . Animal embodiments . . . Daemons . . . Erinyes . . . Familiars . . . Greek origins . . . Megaera . . . Seeds . . . Serpents . . . Tisiphone . . .* She didn't even know what half of these words meant. The text swam in front of her and her head started to throb.

She slammed the book shut. It would have to wait until she got home.

"Lots of homework!" Em called to her mom as soon as she walked in the door. Her mom, who worked half days on Thursdays, seemed to be looking at her strangely—like she knew something Em didn't know—but Em brushed it off as paranoia until she climbed the stairs to her room. Sitting on the floor just outside her bedroom door was a bouquet of daisies and a huge bar of dark chocolate.

"JD dropped those off for you," Em's mom said from halfway up the stairs. Em turned. Her mom was looking at her with a half smile.

"Mom, it's nothing," Em said. But she couldn't hide her own grin, either. She took the flowers and chocolate into her room and slammed the door, giving the bouquet a closer look as soon as she was alone. There was a note taped to the chocolate.

I should have been a better listener, the note read. *I just want to make you happy. Always. JD.*

Em's stomach was fluttering now, but not out of fear. She ran to her window and opened it, letting in a cold blast of air that felt nice against her blazing cheeks. She shook the string that ran between hers and JD's windows; there were bells attached to both sides, an ancient method of communication that they'd devised in third grade. She was relieved to see the string, which had been used only rarely since they'd entered high school (and gotten cell phones), was still intact.

JD's silhouette passed in front of his window, and she watched him lift his blind and then his window.

"Want to go to the pep rally with me later?" she shouted into the cold evening, her breath getting caught in the wind between their houses.

"You'll be seen with this guy in public?" JD pointed to himself, eyebrows askew. He was wearing a sweatshirt with a picture of a deer emblazoned across the chest and the word MAINE right above it.

"I would love to be seen with that guy in public!" Em yelled back. "I love deer. Bring your fedora."

"I'll bring you one too," JD said. *"À bientôt, escargot!"*

Em laughed. She loved that JD had picked up the expression from her. *"À bientôt, escargot!"*

JD was smiling like a kid as he closed his window, and Em just knew.

She knew, suddenly and without question, that JD loved her. In that way. In the way that her dad loved her mom. In a way that was real. She felt weightless. Despite all these disasters—the Zach-Gabby lust triangle, Sasha and Chase, the Furies—she knew she could count on JD, that he would accept her for who she was. That he would listen. That he saw her. She recalled that night on the couch at his house, and the moments on the bridge on New Year's Eve. Right now she wanted nothing more than to be close to him.

Always. JD. He was exactly right. It had always been him. Like the string between their windows, their connection was unbreakable.

Em was in love with JD.

CHAPTER TWENTY-FOUR

Every nerve in Em's body buzzed as she prepped for the pep rally. Despite all the horrible things happening around her, she felt electrified—so much so that she seriously thought if she touched a TV, it might turn on, or short-circuit.

Her thoughts were a flip book, bouncing back and forth between the Furies and JD. She was getting ready for a date with the boy she'd known since they were in diapers. That's what it was, right? A date? The thought made her breath come faster. Would they kiss tonight? By the bonfire, faces lit by shifting flames?

But alongside that image came a more disturbing one: Ali's monstrous eyes and face, shining ghoulishly the way people did when they held flashlights up to their chins to tell campfire ghost stories. Em shuddered and flipped on the bright orange reading lamp by her bed, even though the overhead was already on, as well as the vanity bulbs around her mirror. She'd had enough of dark corners.

When she opened her closet, she did so with a bang, as if to rustle out any lurkers. She batted at the hanging dresses, willing Ali—or one of her equally creepy cousins—to emerge. All was quiet. The closet smelled, as usual, like a combination of cedar and laundry detergent. Em breathed a sigh of relief, but it was marred by the realization that not seeing Ali in her closet only meant she'd see her somewhere else.

Pushing the thought from her mind, she pulled out her favorite pair of well-worn, dark-blue Levis and a white, long-sleeved shirt. She paired it with a nubby gray sweater, which she loved because of its enormous pockets. She ran a brush through her hair and arranged it into a low, messy bun. She didn't want to look like she was trying too hard. Not for JD.

That was the whole point—JD didn't care what she wore, what she looked like, what she said. Or rather, he cared, but he saw past that stuff. She got the feeling that to JD, she was just *Em*.

She liked that.

Her phone rang shrilly. The musical tone pierced the air suddenly, causing Em to jump and let out a small shriek. She exhaled when she saw it was just Gabby. Jesus. She was on edge tonight.

"Hi," she said, catching her breath. "You scared me. I'm getting ready for the rally and—" Em broke off when she realized that Gabby was crying. Sobbing, actually.

"Gabs? What's wrong?" She looked out her window instinctively. But her yard was empty. The moon was low, casting silvery-dark shadows onto the lingering crust of snow.

"I can't—Em—come get me—he hit me—we had a fight—" Gabby was hysterical, speaking in fractured sentences punctuated by sobs.

"Wait, Gabs, what?" Suddenly, Em felt very alert. "Who hit you?"

"Zach . . ." As soon as Gabby spoke the name, another sob transformed her voice, making her words inaudible for a moment. Then she blubbered: "He wanted to talk. I know I shouldn't have gone, but—" Her words were swallowed by another sob. "We had a fight and he . . . I can't believe this is happening. I'm here alone." Gabby was wailing now, her pitch getting higher and higher.

Em's blood was pounding in her ears. *Zach hit Gabby—tiny, beautiful Gabby. Oh my god.*

I'm going to kill him.

She tried to sound calm. "Gabby. It's okay. Please just tell me where you are." As she spoke, Em clenched the phone between her shoulder and her ear, pulling on socks and searching frantically for her boots.

"I just can't believe this is happening," Gabby said again.

"I'm coming to get you, don't worry." Boots on, Em started another mad search for her keys. She'd been using her mom's Toyota since her car was in the shop *again*, getting its brake lines repaired.

"I just jumped out of his car. I started walking . . . I'm at—I'm at the new mall. I needed to get inside." Another sob. "I'm so cold."

"Okay, Gabby? Listen to me. Just stay there." Keys, keys, keys. Where the fuck had she put them? "I'll be there in fifteen minutes. Just stay put, okay?"

"Okay." *Sniffle.* "Okay."

"I'm coming, Gabby." Em hung up and at last located her missing keys, which were on the windowsill, where she'd left them after talking to JD. Oh god. JD. She dialed his number.

"Yes, madame?" JD's voice had an excited lilt that made her heart soar.

"Hey. Hi. I'm so sorry, but . . ." She trailed off. Suddenly, she felt like she would cry.

"What's up? Sorry about what?"

"It's just . . . Gabby's having a crisis. A real one. I have to go meet her." Em hoped she didn't sound as frantic as she felt.

"Oh. Okay." JD sounded crestfallen.

"I'm not just, like, being weird," Em said, stumbling over her words, not sure how much Gabby would want her to tell.

"I want to go with you tonight. And hopefully we'll be there in time for the bonfire. I just have to go get her. She's . . . she's not even at home. She's at the Behemoth."

"The Behemoth? Why? Is she okay? Do you want me to go with you?" JD offered immediately. She did want him to come, but she didn't know how Gabby would react to his presence.

"No. I mean, yes, but no. I think I should just go alone and make sure she's okay. But thank you so much for offering."

"Sure. And you think you'll still come to the bonfire part?" His hopefulness made Em want to use the string as a tightrope and walk right into his room and his arms.

"Yes. I will. Promise. See you later, okay?"

"See you later. Call or text if you need anything."

With that, she was careening down the stairs, grabbing her coat from the hook in the hallway, and calling to whichever parent was home and watching the news in the den: "I'm going to get Gabby and then to the pep rally! Home later!" She tried to make her tone sound as un-freaked-out as possible.

"Okay, hon," her mom called back. "See you tonight." And then, just as Em was pushing out the front door: "And be careful!"

The new mall was glowing with construction lights when Em drove up. She'd heard that lots of the work was being done at night—overtime based on the project's lagging progress. It put her at ease. At least Gabby hadn't been here all alone for the past twenty minutes. She squinted into the floodlights, looking for Gabby's blond curls, but saw nothing but glinting steel beams and orange cones. The air was full of a noisy, mechanized whine, the chugging sound of concrete mixers and cranes. The workers didn't appear to notice her arrival.

She reached into her pocket for her phone to call Gabby, and as she did so, she remembered that she'd forgotten to put her snake-charm necklace back on after she changed. *Oh no.* Though she'd only had it for two days, the idea of leaving home without it made her heart beat to a panicked rhythm. She made a mental note to grab it on their way to the bonfire.

Great. Her old flip phone didn't have service, no matter how high she held it out the window, even when she pulled farther into the gravel lot. Gabby's Droid must have had better luck. Em was going to have to look for Gabby. Silently, she cursed her best friend. *Next time you're dealing with an emotional disaster, please make sure to wait close to the exit, Gabs.* Then she thought about who was really to blame—Zach—and she felt her breath hitch in her throat. She finally understood what people meant when they said they were blind with rage. Next time she saw him (like, in half an hour at the bonfire, if he dared to show up—which she knew he would), she would have to restrain herself from spitting on him, or worse. But this wasn't the time to think about revenge.

She got out of the car and called Gabby's name, but her words got swallowed by the noise and the space. Across the site, there was a portion of the complex that was nearly complete. Maybe Gabby was waiting in there to keep warm. That made sense. Em set off across the icy gravel, looking behind her every few steps, making sure to keep her car in view. She wished JD had come after all.

In the most complete wing of the mall, snow had piled in high drifts, where eventually big glass doors would be installed. Next to this building was a more skeletal lattice of beams. Here, men were working, pouring concrete into the ground, sealing off section by section. Em watched, mesmerized for a moment, as they dropped in long pieces of pipe, then covered the ground with heavy, wet concrete that looked like gray pancake batter. One of the men looked up. She stepped quickly into a gaping doorway before anyone could ask what she was doing there.

Em peeked around a corner, seeing nothing but store shells and concrete stairwells. She called out to Gabby. Her words echoed back to her in the enormous space, tinny and metallic. No response. Em's heart was beating faster now. What was going on? She paced around the entrance to the building.

"*Gabby?*" she yelled now, top volume. "Gabby, where are you?"

She grabbed for her cell phone again, knowing it was futile—why would there be service here if there wasn't any closer to the road? She was about to turn and run back to her car, back to the road, where she would call Gabby and find out her exact location, when she heard it: a tiny sound. Crying. It seemed to be coming from the right—the area closest to where the current construction activity was happening.

She took a step inside. "Gabs?" And another. "I'm here, Gabby. Just shout and I'll find you." The quiet crying continued, but no one spoke.

The farther she got from the entrance, the darker it was. Em held out her phone, using it as a makeshift flashlight. Her breath was coming in short spurts, clouding in front of her in the dark, frigid air.

She walked slowly down a long, empty hall. Big, rectangular holes—where huge display windows would go—revealed yawning black spaces, like open mouths.

Out of the darkness, Em thought that she heard her name, like a whisper, down a corridor that reached to the left.

"You shouldn't have gone so far in. I can't see a thing. I'm coming." She spoke too loudly, too harshly, but she didn't care; she spoke more to drown out her thoughts than anything else.

And then, miracle of miracles, her phone vibrated in her hand and gave a little *bing!* She must have entered a pocket of service. She stopped short and looked at her screen. But the message wasn't from Gabby. It was from JD.

At the pep rally, it read. *Gabby is here???*

Em's blood turned to ice and her vision went bright, like she was staring into a camera flash. Her arms went stiff at her sides and she froze.

Gabby's voice came again: "Poor little Emily . . ." And at that exact moment, the soft sound of crying turned into a cackle.

It was as though the curtain of black parted: There, right in front of her, stood the Furies. She knew now that Drea was right—that's what they were. Ali, whose bright red lipstick reminded Em too much of human blood. Meg, the pixie girl from the side of the road. She seemed to have found a new choker: Another shiny scarlet ribbon was tied tightly around her neck, knotted in a bow just under her right ear. It made Em think of that ghost story about the girl who always wore a green ribbon—how if she ever untied it, her head would roll off. And then there was the third girl. Em recognized her fire-red hair, striped with a white streak, and model-like features: She'd been standing at the side of the road after Ian Minster's party. All three of them had. This must be Ty, the one who'd seduced Chase. *Oh god.* Chase.

It was Em's turn to pay. Now. The realization came to her on a wave of fresh terror. It hadn't been Gabby on the phone. It was them, impersonating Gabby, luring her here.

"Leave me alone," she said, but it came out as a whimpered plea.

They were looking at her. No, they were looking *into* her.

And while their features were superficially beautiful, they were somehow horrible to look at. Their faces were masks. She had to get away.

One step back, then another, then she turned and sprinted. Her bun came undone and her hair flew behind her. *Run—don't stop running.* She didn't look back but she could feel them there. They trailed like smoke. She panted as she ran but they made no sounds. The hallway felt much longer than it had before.

She went the wrong way. She felt it, suddenly. She was running in the wrong direction. *Turn around.* The thought seemed to take forever to travel from her brain to her legs. She was moving in slow motion. Faster. She needed to move faster. Get outside. To the car. Leave.

Em. They were calling to her. *You can't escape. There's no way out. Don't you understand?*

There had to be another way out. This was a mall. There had to be another gaping nondoor somewhere. So she kept going, keeping her phone out in front of her for the weak light it emitted.

They followed her still. They weren't speaking aloud, but she heard them in her head. *Em. Em. Em.* An entryway appeared in front of her. She went through it. No. This was wrong. It wasn't another hallway—it was a big, empty room. She was trapped. *Shit. Shit.* There was a tendril-like touch on her neck. She screamed and threw herself across a low concrete sill, back into the hallway. Running, running.

She rounded a corner. No idea now which way she was going. It was like taking off the blindfold after being spun in Pin the Tail on the Donkey. She tripped over something—a pile of paneling, or some other thin strips of wood—and almost fell to the ground, catching herself right before she hit the floor. She cried out: "No!" *Keep going. Run. Faster.*

She steadied herself. And as she did, she saw it—a window- or door-shaped hole in the wall about fifty feet ahead. The construction lights, or the moonlight, she didn't know which, shone through it. She could see that it connected with the area where the workers were laying foundation—the banging of the pipes and the churning of the concrete mixer filtered faintly through the air. Finally. She could make it. *You're almost there.* If she could get outside, she could get the attention of one of the men. She could get in her car and drive. She could get away.

But then a crystalline voice seeped into her, less through her ears than through her pores.

"You can't get away from us." Em watched as Ty simply appeared in front of her, between Em and the exit. "Don't even try."

Not fair. The words pummeled Em's brain. She was so close. She wanted to reach out and tear Ty's head off. Em dragged a piece of hair out of her mouth, where it had become lodged during the near fall. "Get out of my way," she spat. She moved to the left. Ty blocked her. She tried to cut to the right, but Ty was there, too.

"This way," Ty said, motioning for Em to follow her down a narrow hall that led away from the open space. Strangely, it seemed as if Ty was trying to help her; but Em knew better than to trust it.

"Get *away* from me." Em tried to cut away again, down the hall, but Ty grabbed her arm. It was like being caught in a spiderweb—the feeling was almost nonexistent, but Em couldn't shake it. This must have been how Ty had tricked Chase. Teasing, mesmerizing, killing. Ty was wavering in and out of Em's vision. It made her feel dizzy, as though she were staring at a disco ball.

"You can't get away," Ty said calmly. "But there may be another way to fix things." For a moment Em got lost in Ty's green eyes. She looked Ty up and down, taken for a moment by her floor-length, Grecian-style white dress, with twisted straps that had gold strands woven into them. Her red hair seemed to slither at her shoulders. And she was flickering. "Follow me now. Or stay—let them have their way with you. Who knows what will happen then."

Em felt cold all over. She could hardly breathe. It felt like there was a fist squeezing her lungs. She backed up, but she felt like she was backing into something, someone. She screamed. "Help me! Please! Someone!"

"No one can hear you," Ty confirmed calmly, as though she were talking to a toddler. "Last chance. Follow me if you want to live."

Tears stung Em's eyes and her mind was reeling. Why would Ty all of a sudden want to help her? It didn't make sense! And yet, she had no choice; nowhere to go, no one to help her. Her lips were coated with salt and dirt. "Fine," she choked out. Her throat was spasming. "Fine."

Ty swept down the dark hallway that looked like a dead end. She was racing in front and Em had to run to keep up with her; Ty's white-gold dress was like a beacon up ahead. As she went she snuck one peek over her shoulder. She was sure she saw two figures flicker past the door they'd just gone through. Ali and Meg. They were off her track, at least momentarily. Maybe Ty really did want to help her.

Suddenly they had reached a truncated flight of stairs. Ty raced ahead, leaving an almost tangible mist behind her. And then Em was outside, on some type of second-floor terrace, sobbing with relief into the freezing night air. Ty was nowhere to be seen. Off to the left, stairs led down to the gravel and the construction site. As she sprinted down them, she saw a crane dropping three heavy pipes into the last section left to be covered in concrete.

And she realized that the pipes had dropped into the exact place where she would have been if Ty hadn't diverted her path.

Then she heard the screams. Someone calling her name. *Em. Em. Em.* She didn't know if it was real or just carried through the wind.

Ali and Meg. They'd been hit by the pipes; they'd be buried in concrete.

Trapped. They're trapped. Was that even possible?

She kept running toward her car. *Run home. Run to JD. Keep running.* Would she always be on the run? She was shivering uncontrollably, tears freezing on her cheeks. Not even looking for Ty, to thank her, not knowing how. Or why. *Why did she help me?*

She wiped her nose with her sleeve and ran her fingers through her hair anxiously. But still her face broke into a grin, and for a few breaths, relief swept over her, a feeling like stepping into a warm bath. They were gone. They'd been trapped, and she had escaped.

And then, just as quickly as the feeling came, it left. Because there they were. She stopped running. The breath left her body instantly, as though she'd been socked in the stomach. Ali and Meg. Leaning against her car like they'd been waiting for hours. They looked so nonchalant. Ali was running a hand through her blond hair; Meg was examining the fingernails on her left hand. Ty was picking her way across the lot toward them, holding the train of her white dress delicately in one hand, as though at a formal party.

"No!" The fear came rolling back. It was like being at the ocean, being knocked over by a wave and standing up only to have another one, a darker, more swollen one, smash her back into the sand. Em collapsed to the ground. She screamed, ripping her voice raw. "Fine. You got me. I'm here, all right? Take your revenge. Do whatever you're going to do. *Did you hear me*? *I said you can kill me*."

Ali looked at her, puzzled. She smoothed her hair over one shoulder. "But we don't want to *kill* you," she said, her mouth still blood bright. "Besides, we already took our revenge." She looked pointedly behind her.

That's when Em saw it. There was an empty car sitting right behind hers, parked askew as if it had been driven recklessly and then abandoned in a hurry.

She recognized it instantly. It was a beat-up blue Volvo. It belonged to JD.

She swiveled between Ali, Meg, and Ty—sputtering, reeling.

"What's going on? You—you tricked me," Em said to Ty, pointing her finger and watching as it shook in front of her face.

"You followed me because you wanted to live," Ty said simply. "That was your choice." She allowed her lips to curl back into a sneer. "You should have learned about choices by now."

"Poor Emily," Meg said in a singsong. "Apparently you're not as smart as they say."

Ali spoke up cheerfully. "It's much better this way, Em dear. It's perfect, really. The punishment has to *fit* the crime, you know."

And suddenly, all became clear. The screaming she'd heard. The pipes falling. The revenge they were after. *Oh god.*

JD.

CHAPTER TWENTY-FIVE

Em's fear was ice, stilling her heart. JD was about to be smothered in thick cement. Suffocated. Trapped.

She took off, tearing across the debris-strewn expanse, heading toward the machines. She saw the mixer churning. Soon it would be raised, tipped over, emptied. She yelled, "*Stop! Stop!*" waving her hands frantically, but she might as well have been invisible. The worker was too high off the ground. The wind rushed around her, whooshing in her ears, mingling with the laughter of the three ethereal girls. At the edge of the foundation, she dropped to her knees, peering into the underground chamber.

There he was. JD. She could see his hair and a plaid shirt. He was on the ground, about five feet down, lying prone. His left leg was crushed beneath a metal pipe. His eyes were open but unfocused. Em couldn't tell if he could see her.

"JD. JD." She choked out his name. She needed him to answer her. Now. "Please, JD. I'm here. Oh god, JD. Please."

He didn't answer. He just lay there. The mixer churned above her.

It came to her, crystal clear, the purest thought she'd had all night. Her punishment wasn't death. It was heartache. Loss. She was going to lose the one she loved.

The Furies were going to break her heart.

A sob racked Em's throat and she felt dizzy. She couldn't see through her tears, through her rage.

No. No, this wasn't her fate. Her thoughts came in staccato. She was not a victim. She would not let the Furies win. Possessed by an unfamiliar and powerful adrenaline, Em crouched to the ground and leaped into the depression between pipes, feeling a shock travel up through her feet and legs as she landed. She sprinted over to where JD lay, and with a heft and a grunt, she shoved at the pipe. Threw her whole weight against it. Her thoughts were singular now and running in a loop. Marching to a heavy drum. Move the pipe. Get JD out. Move it. Get him. Save him.

JD groaned faintly. "Em?"

"Hi. Hi, JD. I'm here. I'm going to get you out of here." He didn't respond.

She saw a red welt on his forehead, leaking blood—the pipe must have struck his head before crushing his leg. He must have come to rescue her—or the Furies had led him here. She cursed them and whatever power they came from. Her vision flashed as bitter anger flowed through her, taking over her thoughts. Hate. Hate. She hated them for what they were doing to her. She despised them for dragging JD here. This wasn't justice. This was cruelty.

She had no idea if the Furies would still be waiting for her when she emerged, but all she could focus on now was JD. She was getting him free. Her muscles burned, but she didn't let up. She pushed harder.

"Just hold on," she said, as much to herself as to him. "Just hold on, JD."

And then, with a final heave, the pipe slipped off JD's leg. Em's back and arms burned from the effort. Blood soaked through JD's jeans. She looked up at the mixer. One end of it was ascending into the sky. They were about to be buried alive.

She rolled JD over onto his side, and he winced painfully. "Okay, we're gonna move. JD, I'm going to move you, all right?" His eyelids were fluttering, but she thought she saw the vaguest of nods.

She grabbed his right arm and threw it around her shoulders. Unsteadily, she got to one knee, and then, with both feet on the ground, she lifted from her thighs, standing up with JD's full weight on her left side. She was gripping his wrist in front of her chest, holding him tight. She felt his heart beating through both their bodies. She felt the blood from his thigh soaking into her jeans. She took one awkward step forward, and then another. Every cell in her body throbbed with urgency. He was so tall that his feet were dragging behind them. She breathed and stepped. Breathed and stepped. He was groaning again, into her shoulder blade. The alien distribution of weight made her feel like she was walking on the deck of a storm-thrown ship. Then they were at the wall.

She couldn't climb a wall with JD on her back. She scanned the facade for a solution. It was so loud. And so dark. And he was bleeding, this boy who had always protected her.

There was a pile of rubble in the corner; it reached almost halfway up the wall. It took her four more arduous steps to reach it. JD was fading in and out now. Barely responsive. Em's lungs were burning with the strain. She wondered if the Furies were watching her, amused—if this was just added entertainment on top of their master plan. But she pushed the thought from her mind. She had to focus.

"I need you to help me, JD," she huffed. "I need you to stay right like this." And she maneuvered him to the top of the pile, sitting upright like a broken doll. His head lolled to the side. She held his face tenderly and wiped a streak of blood from his temple. For the first time, she took in what he was wearing—

dark jeans and a long-sleeved lumberjack-plaid shirt. No hat. No weird jacket. No deer sweatshirt. This is what he'd worn to the pep rally. He'd gone out of his way to look average for her. The realization was a stake stabbing into her heart.

"JD, listen to me. Just hold on."

She reached her hands to the top of the wall. Then she pulled with her arms and pushed off with her legs, vaulting herself up. She landed with the edge of the wall digging into her stomach; she felt her left elbow rip through the sleeve of her sweater.

One leg up, like a frog. Onto her knees, scraping them through holes that had suddenly appeared in her jeans. Then turning around, facing the pit again, getting back onto her stomach, now reaching her arms down toward him. Shouting, shouting, not even recognizing her own voice.

"JD! JD! If you can hear me, lift up your arms." She felt desperate. "JD—we're going to do this together and then we're going to eat barbecue pizza and play board games and go swimming together all summer long. I'm going to kiss you so many times. In the moonlight and in the water and against the oak tree that your dad thinks is on your property but that my dad insists is on his. Just please, JD, make this happen." She was babbling, blubbering, tugging at the collar of his shirt, as far as she could reach.

Somehow, with strength she didn't even know she had, she was able to raise the right side of his body enough to get her hand under his arm. She yanked it until she could do the same on his left side. And then, with her hands, and then her elbows, tugging at his torso, she was able to get him fully upright. *I love you.* Pull. *I love you.* Pull. *I love you.* Sweat beaded along her hairline; her nose ran and dripped onto her lips.

There was a loud mechanical screeching as the concrete mixer began unloading its contents. The viscous gray glop sank into the foundation, around the pipes, slowly filling in every crevice. She pulled harder, coming around onto her knees again to gain more leverage. *Please,* she prayed. *Please let me do this.* And then, with a final pull, just as the concrete started to cover JD's Converse sneakers, she heaved him aboveground, on the far side of the hole. She leaned over him, blanketing his body with hers, sobbing with relief.

"JD," she said, shaking his shoulders. "JD, thank god. Thank god. It's going to be okay. I'm going to get help."

She put her ear to his mouth. His breathing was shallow. She felt for his pulse. It was weak.

She whirled around, wild with grief.

"Where are you?" she shouted into the night. "Where did you go?" She was frantic and furious. "Ali! Meg! Ty! Come here! Tell me! What now?"

There they were, off to the side, in the shadows. All three of them appeared to be flickering now. And Em knew, somehow, that they were about to vanish. And once they left, Em knew JD would be gone too.

"Wait. Stop." She stood up, stumbling with weakness, dirty and crying and bleeding from her knees. "This is wrong. You know it. You must know it. This is not justice. This is not karma. This isn't *helping* anything. You're not *teaching* anything."

Ali and Meg were barely visible. They were practically translucent. But Ty was still hovering nearby. Em could make out the whites of her eyes, the white in her hair. It was entirely creepy—like they'd only ever appeared for this moment. Em moved toward the Furies and grabbed for Ty's arm.

"Ty. Please. What you did to Chase—what you're doing to me. It doesn't make any sense. It's not right. This isn't how the world should *work*."

The words seemed to vibrate between them, taking on a shape of their own. And finally, with an expression in her eyes that looked almost human, Ty stepped forward, away from her sisters.

She held out her hand and opened her palm to reveal five gleaming red beads. They looked like berries, or round pills. Like the orchids, they had a crystalline quality.

"If you swallow these," Ty said to Em, "you can save JD. But I'm warning you—there are rules, and there are consequences."

Em looked at Ty, at the seeds in her palm, and then back

at JD, whose breath was now coming in desperate rasps. She hesitated. Was this a trap? Would these five tiny pills just poison her, kill her along with JD?

She thought of the promises she had made to him. The things they would do together. *I'm going to kiss you so many times.*

"What kind of rules? What kind of consequences?" Em demanded, her heart in her throat.

"They will bind you to us forever," Ty said simply, her smile shimmering as she wavered in and out of Em's vision. "And you can't tell a single soul about them, or about us, or about tonight. JD will be in danger all over again—worse danger—if you tell him what happened."

"So what will he think?" Em was filled with a sense of desperate hopelessness. "What will he remember?"

"That's not for you to know," Ty said. "Are you going to take them, or not?"

The decision was easy. She would save JD—or try as best she could.

The seeds felt smooth and cold as Ty passed them to her. Like tiny stones. Em put all of them in her mouth at once.

"Swallow," Ty said. "Whole."

Em did, feeling the beads against her tongue, sliding down her throat, which was raw from screaming. They tasted bitter. She could almost feel them settle inside of her, sending a hot sting through her chest and stomach.

And then she heard a rustle behind her. JD shifted. His eyes fluttered open. He opened his mouth, coughed slightly, and whispered, "Em?" She watched, jaw agape, as he propped himself up on his elbows. His breathing was normal again. He blinked and looked around. He was coming to.

"Oh my god." Em turned around in amazement, about to ask Ty what had just happened. But they were gone. All three of them had disappeared.

Em didn't have time to think about it, because just then JD moaned again. She went over to kneel beside him. He struggled to sit up, then collapsed backward onto the ground.

"It's okay," she said, leaning over him, one hand on his chest, the other in his hair. "I'm here."

And yet she had the strangest sensation of somehow being *elsewhere*, too. The air around her was heavier than usual—rusty and burnt.

Then JD's hand was on hers, and he was asking her what had happened. Em was looking at him, weeping, begging for his forgiveness.

"It's all over now," she whispered. "I'm so sorry, JD. I'm so, so sorry."

CHAPTER TWENTY-SIX

Two weeks later

Gabby's mom was forecasting a mild, snowless spring. Winter had come so fast and furious that year: *It was like there was something else in the air,* Marty Dove was fond of saying. It's not that the month of January wasn't supposed to be cold—it was—but . . . it was like this cold had no *point.* It was freezing, without any beautiful, snowcapped reward.

Days came and went. Mostly, Em and Gabby went straight home, doing deep-conditioning treatments, watching crappy rom-coms, and scouring the Urban Outfitters catalog for new wardrobe splurges. They didn't speak of Zach, who had transferred last week, courtesy of his stepdad's string-pulling, to the New Hampshire boarding school he used to attend himself. Better stepping-stone to Yale, he had told the football team. Em knew it had more to do with his failing math grade than anything else. But mostly, she was relieved to realize she didn't care anymore what the real reason was for anything Zach did.

Em spent a few afternoons hanging out with Drea, and she was reading as many of her books as she could get her hands on.

Em's dreams were filled with dark spaces, cavernous gaps between reality and nightmares that threatened to swallow her whole. In the dreams, she was constantly on the verge of stepping into an angry abyss, one that was reaching inside her even as she teetered above it. Sometimes Chase was there, sometimes JD. Sometimes Ali and Ty and Meg. Sometimes Zach. She woke up some nights with a scream swelling in her throat.

When she couldn't sleep, she went to her window and looked outside. She saw shapes—no, she didn't *see* them as much as feel them, sense them. The Furies, like the ice, wouldn't melt. Patches of them were frozen in her memory.

And JD . . . well, that view was just as cold. His blinds had been closed since the night she'd called 911 at the Behemoth. The morning after she saved his life, she woke up to see that the string between their windows had snapped—weighed down, probably, by heavy icicles. He left for school before she even woke up—math-team practice, his mom told hers—and their routes never converged in the hallways. She texted him, sent him chats; his responses, when they came at all, were perfunctory.

Em was trying to understand it. She knew the Furies must have somehow made him believe something that wasn't true . . . but she didn't know what. And she couldn't tell him what had really happened, of course; she'd vowed to keep it all inside. She could tell he was mad at her—it was the Furies' fault, she had no doubt. But how could she defend herself? How could she begin to explain? How could she risk putting him in danger again?

Everything in her ached, as she slowly realized that even though she'd gotten him from dying, it didn't mean she got the old JD back. It was like she'd chosen, by swallowing those pills, to sever their connection. It was unbearable. It was insurmountable. The few times she caught his gaze, his eyes looked kind but flat. Not full of the feeling they used to hold.

Em knew that the Furies had gotten exactly what they came for after all. She had not defeated them—in fact, she had somehow bound herself to them for life. She didn't even know how, or what that meant. And in the meantime they'd broken her heart.

But at least JD was alive. And as long as he was living and breathing, he might someday love her again. In this way, it was like Em and the Furies were engaged in an invisible tug-of-war. At least Em still had a piece of the rope.

Some mornings, as she watched the sun rise, filling in the sky from behind stark branches, she thought about how she could make amends. Tell him what happened—that night and all the nights leading up to it—how she'd felt, knowing finally that she loved him. She could tell him what Drea had told her. Make him understand. And then . . .

And then what? Her thoughts always shredded apart here, full of longing and hope and uncertainty. Sometimes the frustration was so great that she wondered which was better—to live with love always just out of her grasp, or to know that it was gone forever?

Ty's words reverberated in her head, as they frequently did: *I'm warning you—they will bind you to us forever.* She didn't know by what chains she was bound. But she would escape them.

She was going to teach the Furies a lesson about getting what you deserved.

At an elite boarding school in New Hampshire, a boy with sandy hair and a perfect smile walks out of the gym after basketball practice. He furrows his brow with concentration as he composes his text message.

Gotta study tonight, baby. Can't wait to see you tomorrow.

But he doesn't put his phone into his gym bag. Instead, he

types out another text to a different number: *Hey cutie,* it reads. *Want to meet up tonight? I've got some free time.*

"What does a girl have to do to get her number in there?" A silvery voice cuts through the evening air.

He looks up. There's a girl in front of him, a girl who definitely does not go to his school. He would have noticed her. He would have been all over it weeks ago.

She's beautiful. Tall. Beach-blond hair, a perky nose, and rosebud lips highlighted by bright red lipstick.

"I'm Zach," he says, holding out his hand. "Sorry I'm so sweaty—just got out of basketball practice."

"I know who you are," the girl responds with a laugh that sounds like coins falling into a fountain. "I brought this for you." She extends her hand with a flirtatious smile. She is holding a deep red orchid—delicate yet dramatic.

The boy takes it, surprised by its weight. "A beautiful girl and a beautiful flower? What did I do to deserve this?" He winks.

The girl's smile broadens slowly as she says, "I think you know."

ACKNOWLEDGMENTS

Thank you . . .

First and foremost, to Lexa Hillyer and Lauren Oliver for giving me this opportunity and offering brilliant guidance along the way. Lexa, your intelligence and positive attitude are inspirational; Lauren, your vision and drive are unique.

To everyone at Simon Pulse, especially Jennifer Klonsky and Emilia Rhodes, for pouring so much energy and editorial smarts into *Fury*. To Stephen Barbara and Foundry Literary + Media for representing me and Paper Lantern Lit with style.

To Jeff Inglis, Peter Kadzis, and Phoenicians past and present for trusting and supporting me through this and many projects.

To my friends in Portland, especially Maggie Carey (and Keith), Christopher Gray, Keagan McDonough, Nicholas

Schroeder, Sonya Tomlinson (and Jay), and all you theater people, for boundless warmth and creativity. To Will, who knows why. To Dafna Garber for ten years (and counting) of unexpected best-friendship. To Laura Smith, Laura Schechter, and Jacqueline Novak for letting me write through Fourth of July 2010—my favorite holiday because I spend it with you, my oldest and dearest loves.

To my extended family, all aunts and uncles and cousins and little cousins, for being top-notch cheerleaders. To the memories of John and Marjorie Fulton, John and Eva Mayer, and Rob Vrana. And to my parents, Evelyn and Donald Fulton, for always championing my brain and loving me in your own generous ways.

ABOUT THE AUTHOR

ELIZABETH MILES lives in Portland, Maine, and writes for an alternative newsweekly. *Fury* is her first novel. Visit her online at ElizabethMilesBooks.com, find her on Facebook (facebook.com/elizabethmileswrites), and follow her on Twitter (twitter.com/milesbooks).

DRUMROLL, PLEASE . . .
MEET THE FABULOUS ELIZABETH MILES, UP-AND-COMING NOVELIST AND MY BFF!

By Lauren Oliver

1. You're publishing your first novel. What can you tell us about it?

I'm thrilled to be publishing FURY, which is the first book of a paranormal horror trilogy that takes place in New England. It's sexy and scary! Simon & Schuster are publishing it simultaneously in the UK, US and Australia – it's exciting!

2. How does it feel to have written your first book? What was the most challenging part? What about the most gratifying?

It feels amazing, truly. The biggest hurdle was carving out time to write regularly. It came so much easier when I did. The most gratifying part was when the words just came spilling out, and I knew in my fingertips and my brain that they were good. I've also really enjoyed observing and participating in the editing process. This was a new experience for me and I learned so much.

3. You're a journalist. How does writing fiction differ from journalism, in your view?

Gosh, they are such different animals, fiction and journalism. For one thing, when I was working on FURY I didn't have to constantly worry about "getting something wrong" – stuff that I make up can never be factually inaccurate! I also had to learn to linger. When I write news stories and analysis, the goal is to be as straightforward and concise as possible. Certainly I don't strive for abstruseness when writing fiction, but there is room to wander, to provide back story, to describe details that might not immediately push forward the plot, but that help create mood and atmosphere. It's more lyrical.

4. So – you live in Portland, Maine, huh? Tell me three of your favourite things about Portland (and "when Lauren comes to visit" does not have to be one of them, as it goes without saying!).

a) Being so close to the water, and the woods.

b) Portland is a small city full of creative, exciting people who also know how to relax, enjoy good food, and create the lives they want to live. Everyone knows everyone, after a while. I feel like I'm part of a community.

c) When I moved here, I caught an acting bug that had been dormant since high school. On a whim, I tried out for a community theatre production of "Oklahoma!" and got cast as Ado Annie – one of my all-time favourite female roles ("I'm just a girl who can't say no / kissing's my favorite food" – ahem . . .). I've been performing pretty much non-stop ever since, and the opportunities just keep getting better and better. I love the people I've met through theatre, and I love the chance I get to inhabit different characters and behave in ways I'd never be able to off-stage.

5. What about your three least favourite things about living in Maine?

a) Being six hours away from my best friends and my family (not just trying to earn points here).

b) See "everyone knows everyone" in "b", above.

c) The cold can get rather oppressive, after about five months. But it just makes summer that much more delicious . . .

6. You have two cats. Describe, discuss.

Wow, I can't believe you're giving me a separate platform to discuss the cats. Their names are Ender and Bean (named after two characters in a great sci-fi book called *Ender's Game*). I got them as kittens when I moved to Maine. They are brothers, with orange fur and terrifically sweet dispositions. When I moved to Maine I was going through a bit of a rough patch, emotionally, and they really helped brighten my spirits. Bean is slightly aloof and has outstanding jumping abilities. Ender, who prefers being held, often sits with his legs splayed – very crass. I love them so much. Thank you for asking.

7. What are three things readers would be surprised to know about you?

a) I'm actually a big scaredy cat. I can't watch scary movies without covering my eyes and I am a little afraid of the dark. In this way, it's rather strange that I'm writing a book that's meant to send shivers up people's spines.

b) I'm an only child.

c) I love frogs and toads.

8. What are some of your favourite books? Music?

Before I Fall, obviously. Also: *The End of the Affair* (Graham Greene), anything by David Foster Wallace, *Middlemarch* (George Eliot), *Anna Karenina* (Tolstoy), the *Anne of Green Gables* series, *The True Confessions of Charlotte Doyle* (Avi), anything by Anne Carson, *The Witch of Blackbird Pond* (Elizabeth George Speare), *My Side of the Mountain* (Jean Craighead George), *The Sun Also Rises* (Hemingway), *The Mists of Avalon* (Marion Zimmer Bradley), *Very Far Away from Anywhere Else* (Ursula K. LeGuin) . . . I could go on, but I won't. I really love books, you know?

As for music: I love show tunes, of course, plus classic rock like Dylan and Van Morrison, pop heroines like Britney and Beyonce, and indie-rock girl stuff like Rilo Kiley, Joanna Newsom, and Neko Case. I've been listening to The National a lot recently.

9. If you could eat one thing RIGHT NOW, what would it be?

My grandmother used to make this steak-and-potatoes dish that had a virtually unpronounceable German name (phonetically, it's something like "Gedinska steak and kertuffletushspice"). The steak was simmered in a tomato-based sauce, and the potatoes were cubed and cooked with sour cream and paprika. She made a lot of delicious things, but that was my favourite, and I'd kill for some right now, and always.

10. Will you corroborate the fact that you and I used to be part of a cheese club in high school? What about the same a cappella group? Do you remember any of your solos?

Will I corroborate it??? It has a permanent spot on my resume. And of course our shared experience in the Quaker Notes was formative. My solos, duh: Silver Thunderbird, Right Here Waiting (sniff sniff), O L'amour, Soul to Soul, Because the Night. I also remember that you sang Better Man, among others, and that a few of those a cappella parties reached levels of crazy I haven't seen since.